MELODY ANNE

D0032516

Her Hometown Hero

WITHDRAWN

Pocket Books

New York   London   Toronto   Sydney   New Delhi

Pocket Books
An Imprint of Simon & Schuster, Inc.
1230 Avenue of the Americas
New York, NY 10020

First Pocket Books paperback edition July 2015

POCKET and colophon are registered trademarks of Simon & Schuster, Inc.

For information about special discounts for bulk purchases, please contact Simon & Schuster Special Sales at 1-866-506-1949 or business@simonandschuster.com.

The Simon & Schuster Speakers Bureau can bring authors to your live event. For more information or to book an event, contact the Simon & Schuster Speakers Bureau at 1-866-248-3049 or visit our website at www.simonspeakers.com.

Interior design by Yvonne Chan

Manufactured in the United States of America

10 9 8 7 6 5 4 3 2 1

ISBN 978-1-4767-7858-7
ISBN 978-1-4767-7861-7 (ebook)

New York Times bestselling author Melody Anne

HER HOMETOWN HERO

"As I said, you *won't* be driving home."

"Look, Dr. Whitman, just because I don't have some fancy-schmancy truck doesn't mean I'm a menace to the highways. I'll take it slow." Sage scooped up a large mass of snow and began forming a ball.

He took a cautious step backward. "Now, Dr. Banks, I would just put that down slowly if I were you."

But the snowball in her hand and his arrogant smile were just too much to resist. She let the ball fly. The snow exploded against the side of his head.

"I can't believe you actually threw that."

She was already regretting her impulsive decision. "That was my pager," she said, and she immediately turned and began running toward the side doors.

Suddenly, strong arms wrapped around her waist, and then she and Spence were launching into the air. His back landed with a splash in the snow while she bounced against his chest—his delectably hard chest.

"Let me go," she said, but a giggle burst free.

"Not until I get my payback," he said, and she found herself on her back, the snow making a crater around her body. She closed her eyes and waited for impact. When nothing happened, she cracked her eyes open and looked up. With the fire that was burning in his gaze, she was amazed there was any snow at all left around them. The moment his lips touched hers, she was lost in a pool of heat and desire so strong she didn't recognize the feelings. This was a first kiss to end all kisses.

Also available from Melody Anne and Pocket Books

Baby, It's Cold Outside
(with Jennifer Probst, Emma Chase,
Kristen Proby, and Kate Meader)

Her Unexpected Hero

Who I Am with You

This book is dedicated to my dirty girls,
Stephanie Gerard and Nicole Sanders.
For twenty-plus years,
we have been through thick and thin.
And I pray that we never grow up,
never stop dancing,
and definitely never stop dreaming.
Without dreams, wishes would never come true.
I love you girls!

ACKNOWLEDGMENTS

As I continue this journey in this magical land of writing, I have so much to be thankful for that a single page or two in a book could never possibly express how happy I am and how grateful I am to the people who make my world a better place. There are times I don't see anyone for days or weeks while I finish up a story, but you all hold your arms wide open when I return and that means more to me than you could ever imagine.

I have friends and family, some of whom I have had my entire life and some whom I've been blessed with in the later years, and each and every one of you makes my life complete.

I live in a small town, which is why I write so much about family, because that's what living in a small town is: it's having a huge extended family, where people wave when you drive or walk by and where if someone asks if there's anything they can do for you, they mean it. I love that and never want to change it. Thank you to my community for inspiring me and supporting me. I am so glad to have raised my kids in a safe and beautiful place.

Thank you to my family at Pocket Books who

make me feel like a rock star and who support me, encourage me, and make me feel like I have a place in this world where I'm allowed to let my imagination come to life on paper.

Thank you to my team at home who work long hours, keep me sane, and remind me to live a little. Without you, I couldn't do what I love!

Thank you to my family, my beautiful daughter and son, my husband, and my four dogs. Home is my safety net. It's my favorite place to be, and nothing brings me greater pleasure than to have it filled with all the people I love.

Thank you to my fans! You have been with me from the beginning and your encouraging words inspire me, motivate me, and often bring me to tears. There are so many who mean the world to me, and I've been lucky enough to meet several of you. You inspire me more than anything else. Cynthia Pak, I still think of you each time I brush my teeth after our crazy time in New Orleans. I love you all so much. Thank you, thank you, thank you.

"Hi, sweetheart, how are you doing?" Bethel asked in a frail voice, crossing her fingers that her acting abilities would carry her through this phone call.

"I'm fine, Grandma," Sage said unsurely. "But you sound a little unlike yourself. What's the matter?"

The girl's voice was full of worry. *Check*, Bethel thought.

"Oh, I don't want to bother you, dear. I know how busy you are." Bethel couldn't help adding a long-suffering sigh. "I was just wondering how the residency applications have been going. Have you had any offers?" If Sage had even the slightest clue about the amount of meddling her grandmother was planning, Bethel would be toast—very *burned* toast.

Of course, she couldn't have done any meddling at all without the help of her friends Judge Martin Whitman, Eileen Gagnon, Maggie Winchester, and the ultimate meddler, Joseph Anderson—but her lips were forever sealed, for all their sakes.

"It's great, Grandma. I have six interviews scheduled over the next two weeks. I'm really hoping to get in at Johns Hopkins. It would do wonders for my career."

"That's wonderful to hear," Bethel said, and immediately began coughing.

"Grandma? Are you okay?"

Bethel felt a mountain load of guilt as she faked an illness she was far from feeling. "Just . . . a . . . minute . . ." she gasped, then put the phone on mute so Sage couldn't hear her.

"Are you sure we should do this to Sage?" she asked her best friend, Eileen.

"It's up to you. I'm feeling pretty guilty," Eileen replied.

"I just worry so much about her," Bethel said. "I want her home."

"Grandma! Are you there? Do I need to call emergency services?"

Bethel quickly unmuted the phone.

"I'm all right, darling. Don't you worry about me," Bethel said weakly. "What about the hospital near home? Did you apply?"

"I struggled with whether to do that or not, but in the end I did. It would be great to get to see you more often, but it just feels like I'm giving up if I come home. People usually grow up and move away, not run back home the first chance they get," Sage told her.

"Honey, it's not giving up to come home. Sterling may be tiny, but the hospital has an incredible program. We have excellent doctors acting as mentors, and you'd also be here where you belong." At least that was true—it *was* a prestigious hospital, thanks to its generous endowment from the Whitmans and the Winchesters.

"Yeah, I know all of that. There are several people in my class who are hoping to get in there. I just didn't want to ever move back home unless it was for a terrific job. Then I could feel proud of myself—like I'd really accomplished something while out in the big, bad world."

"You *have* accomplished something—something huge. How many of your fellow college students went on to medical school and were always at the very top of their class? How many kids from your own high school even went to college?"

"Not many, but that's not the point."

"Of course it's the point. You *are* a success no matter what you do from this point forward. You've done so well, darling, and you set your sights admirably high. So be proud of that, but don't miss out on interviewing here. Or are you afraid to try? It's possible the hospital wouldn't even offer you a residency." Bethel knew pigs would fly before that happened—Sage was guaranteed an offer. But the girl's grandmother was proud of her sly use of psychology. Suggest that Sage might not get something, and she'd jump to prove she could.

Sage didn't take the bait. "That wouldn't be the end of the world, I have to say. If I came home, I'd just be dealing with ranchers all the time instead of city trauma. It's not exactly the most exciting place to continue my medical education."

"Now, Sage, you shouldn't speak so badly about the hospital here. It's saved my life more than once. You remember when I had that stroke a couple of years ago? Well, they fixed me up real nice. Eileen says no one would have any idea that I almost died!"

"You didn't almost die, Grandma. It was a minor stroke, though you scared me to pieces."

"I don't like frightening you, child," Bethel said before forcing herself to cough pathetically again. It was a good thing they weren't on a video call, because she couldn't wipe the smile off her face. She wasn't one to brag, but surely she'd have made a big splash in Hollywood.

"Well then, don't say you came close to dying," Sage told her. "You know it would destroy me."

"Okay, dear. I'm afraid I can't visit too long—I'm just not feeling all that well, but I'm sure it's nothing serious," Bethel said in a quavering voice. "Besides, I don't want to bother you . . ."

"You know you're never a bother, Grandma. Please talk to me. I'm starting to really worry."

"Well . . . The doctor did say he's worried about my blood pressure. I just can't seem to get around as well these days . . ." Bethel trailed off as if too weak to continue speaking.

"You should have called me right away! I didn't

know anything was wrong. How long have you been feeling ill?" Sage had begun to scold her grandma, but she immediately backed down, her voice lowering as quickly as it had risen.

"I'm sorry, sweetheart. I didn't think it was that big of a deal. I'm going to have to get off the phone, though. I'm really tired now. Just keep me updated on your choice for your residency." Before Sage could say anything more, Bethel hung up, then grinned at her friend.

"You know, we are horrible, horrible people," Eileen said with a wicked grin, enhancing the slight wrinkles on her face.

"How else was I supposed to get her home?" Bethel asked. "She's so dang stubborn and thinks she can make it all on her own in some big city. It's time for her to come home and settle down. Besides, I *am* a frail old woman." The twinkle in her eye and the weekly dancing lessons she took belied her words. She did a mean cha-cha.

"Frail, my foot," Eileen scoffed. The two women had been friends for over fifty years, and neither of them could get anything past the other. "Still, I don't know about all of this. If Sage finds out—gets even an inkling of what we have planned . . ."

"It's worth the risk, my dearest friend," Bethel said. She called Martin and Maggie so the foursome could put Joseph Anderson on speakerphone and they could all go over the plans again. If Sage had known what was brewing, she wouldn't be happy with any of them.

But a bit of matchmaking is what kept the five friends young at heart. They suppressed their feelings of guilt as best they could. It was painful, but what else could they do? They had a new mission—and it was a doozy.

01

The Montana road was familiar, but Sage Banks was tense as she drove for endless miles without passing a single vehicle. In the spring, summer, and fall, the area was usually spectacular and welcoming, with the wheat blowing in the wind, birds singing their magical melodies, and farmers smiling with a polite nod as you passed by.

It was night, however, and she was caught in the middle of a summer storm, making visibility basically zilch. The rain slashed across her window and the wind pushed her car around like a toy.

The blacktop looked treacherous. Thick puddles of water from the unexpected June storm formed small lakes on the asphalt. Sage kept her foot light on the gas pedal and her fingers clutched the steering wheel like a vise.

"Perfect. Just perfect," she muttered as the car hydroplaned for a heart-stopping second before straightening out again.

She hated driving in this kind of weather, hated that it reminded her every single time of the loss of her parents and her grandfather, who had lost their lives too soon when their vehicle had slid off the road into the river.

She couldn't think about that right now, couldn't focus on something that would make her tear up, make her visibility even worse than it was. No. It was better to think about the fact that she was driving here in the first place.

She hadn't wanted to accept what in her book counted as failure—to come back to the place she'd worked hard to move away from. She'd won a big scholarship, worked her tail off, and made it through medical school. Residency was her time to shine, but it was really hard to shine at a place where everyone had known you since you were a little girl.

Her boss, Dr. Thompson, was going to be the man who'd bandaged her knee when she took a tumble down Rice Hill, stitched her up when she fell off her bike, bruising her ego far more than her body, and seen her when, embarrassment of embarrassments, she needed her first "young woman" appointment. He had to be a hundred years old by now.

It just wasn't fair.

Even to herself she sounded like a petulant child, but . . . She shook her head to change her focus. This topic wasn't any better to think about. First she had to pay more attention to the road. And then she had to accentuate the positive. She'd get to spend more time with her grandmother, and she loved Grandma Bethel more than any other person on this planet. Bethel had always told her that when life handed you lemons, you got to make lemonade.

"I guess I'll be making a lot of lemonade over the next several years," she muttered with a strained laugh. It was time she accepted her fate with a smile.

But since her grandfather had died in the same wreck that had taken Sage's parents, she had an unbreakable bond with her grandmother. They needed each other, and it had been just the two of them since she was ten years old.

Plus, it wasn't like her to throw tantrums or to dwell on her "misfortunes." She knew a number of good students who hadn't received *any* offers of residencies, and she'd been offered several. She also knew that a lot of residents would never become full-fledged doctors. If she didn't pull herself together, and fast, she could end up throwing everything she'd worked so hard for right into the garbage can.

She had chosen to accept this position. The thought of being two thousand miles away when her grandma needed her had been thoroughly unappealing. So, as much as she hadn't wanted to come back home, it had been the right decision. She refused to regret it.

As Sage topped a rise in the road and neared the picturesque town of Sterling, she thought of the people she'd met in Stanford and LA—where she'd gone for her undergraduate and graduate programs—

who would never consider being stuck in a town like Sterling, Montana.

Maybe they were right. But it *was* still home, and whether she liked it or not, she was back for at least three years. *This won't be so bad*, she told herself with a determined glint in her eyes. *Call it a midyear resolution.*

As Sage came down the other side of the hill, another car turned a corner, and its lights temporarily blinded her. She focused on the wet pavement and the barely visible lines on the side of the road, but she turned the steering wheel too far to the left as she tried to regain her bearings.

A horn blared, and before she could stop the car, she felt her tires slipping on the water and loose gravel on the shoulder of the road. The ditch was quickly coming up to meet her, and it wasn't looking too friendly.

"Perfect!"

That was the only word that made it past her lips before the car skidded down into the hard earth and her head slammed against the steering wheel. Her fear vanished as everything went black.

THAT HAD BEEN too close. His heart in his throat, Spence Whitman pulled over to the side of the road, turned on his emergency flashers, and leapt from his car, leaving his door swinging in the strong wind as he dashed into the ditch. There wasn't any smoke right now, but that didn't mean it wasn't coming. He needed to assess the condition of the driver and do it fast.

Pulling his phone from his coat pocket as he scrambled down the bank, he dialed emergency services, connecting just as he reached the car.

"Nine-one-one. What's your emergency?"

Spence had yanked open the door to find a red-haired woman pressed against the steering wheel, a slight line of blood dripping down her cheek. "It looks like a twenty- to thirty-year-old female. Unconscious. Her car slammed hard into the ditch between milepost seventeen and eighteen. She has a visible contusion on her right cheek and a rapidly forming contusion on her forehead."

"Are you a doctor, sir?"

"Yes. This is Dr. Spence Whitman."

"Emergency vehicles are on their way."

"Thank you." Spence hung up the phone as he began checking her vital signs. "Ma'am, are you okay?"

It was stupid to ask that question, or any question, when she was clearly knocked out. He knew this, but he couldn't help it, not when it was so ingrained in him from his training. Lifting his hand to her neck, he was relieved to find her pulse strong. Though she was out cold, at least she was breathing steadily, and the bleeding from the cut on her cheek was already slowing.

He ran his hand carefully along her body and was

happy that he didn't discover any obvious signs of serious injury. That didn't mean there wasn't internal damage, but as smoke began rising from the hood of her car, he didn't want to take any chances by hanging around. He needed to move her.

Just then, she moaned and her eyelids fluttered open. She blinked up at him with confused emerald-green eyes.

"You've been in an accident," he informed her in his most businesslike manner. "Can you tell me if anything hurts?"

She stared blankly at him while she tried to get a handle on his words.

"My name is Spence Whitman and I'm a doctor. I need to move you from the vehicle. Can you tell me if your neck or back hurts?"

"No, they don't," she murmured after a brief pause.

"That's really good. Could you please lift your arm for me and wiggle your fingers?" After another pause, she did as he asked. "Great," he said. "Now I'm pulling off your shoe. If you could just wiggle your toes for me . . . Great. That's a very good sign." He kept his voice professional, calm, reassuring. It was what he did and he was on autopilot.

"Okay, we're going to get you out of this car now." He didn't grab her right then, but waited for her to answer. It was difficult for him to move so slowly, but he didn't want her frightened, and because she'd hit her head, there was a chance she wasn't fully processing what he was saying.

"Okay," she said, her voice weak.

"We're going to be nice and careful about this," he said as he slid his hands beneath her and began shifting her weight against his chest. Dark gray smoke began to billow from the hood of the car, making it more apparent that their time was running out.

She groaned when he stood, cradling her close before he began moving cautiously away from the car in the heavy rain. He knew this had to be hurting her more than she'd expected—it was difficult to know how much you'd been hurt in a car accident until you moved. Finally, sirens blared in the distance, filling Spence with relief.

"Spence?"

Spence stopped as he looked down at the woman in the quickly fading light. She'd said his name like she knew him.

"Yes, I'm right here."

In this town everyone knew everybody. He must have run into her at some point. But after high school, Spence had gone straight to college and then medical school, and he'd lost touch with some of the people here in the years he'd been gone. He'd become something of a city boy over the years. He loved living in Seattle, loved the hustle and bustle, and he was quickly becoming a highly regarded trauma surgeon. A good life, with a lot more privacy. Still, he made enough trips back to Sterling that it bothered him not to remember who this was.

Even as those thoughts played in the back of his brain, Spence remained focused on the injured woman in his arms and the help that would soon arrive. As he watched her pulse and her breathing, he heard the ambulance pull up. *Thank heavens.* He was soaked through and wanted to get them both out of this monstrous rainstorm.

He reached the road just as the back doors to the ambulance opened, and he waited for the paramedics to unload the gurney. The patient was soon placed safely on it and carted into the back of the vehicle.

"Patient was able to move fingers and toes; coming in and out of consciousness. I'm concerned about internal injuries, but I had to move her from the vehicle. Have a full body scan done as soon as you reach the hospital," Spence told the paramedics.

"Are you going to follow, Dr. Whitman?"

He occasionally helped out at the local hospital, so he knew these people. "Yeah, I'll see you there."

Spence got into his car and scrubbed a hand across his face, trying to clear the rain from his vision. He was exhausted after working all day at the hospital, but a new trauma case had him fully alert and ready for round two. He could leave her in the care of the other doctors, but he'd been the one to find her, and he would see it through.

As he pulled up to the hospital, he watched the paramedics wheel the woman inside. He followed with a confident gait, already in emergency surgeon mode. He was the king of his domain, and he didn't hesitate as he went through the emergency room doors. It didn't matter which hospital he was in. They were all different and all the same. And one thing was for sure—this was where he'd always belonged. That had been true from the moment he'd rescued a young boy from drowning in the local lake. That simple act had changed his entire future.

He'd known from that moment on that he would become a doctor. Maybe he hadn't admitted it to himself at that point; he'd probably thought he'd never be good enough to wear a stethoscope. But he'd worked harder than everyone else he knew so he could be worthy.

The journey he'd had to take had been well worth all its trials. He felt that way just as much today as he had ten, even fifteen years ago.

02

"Ouch!"

Sage glared at the nurse sticking a needle into her arm. The woman must work for the KGB.

"I'm sorry, Ms. Banks."

I just bet you are, Sage thought savagely. Okay, that was a bit petty, but Sage's arm was throbbing where the ten-foot-long needle had been plunged.

She'd been poked and prodded for the past hour and she was done with it. But besides a headache, and now a throbbing arm, she felt fine. It was just a little accident. Why were these people getting so worked up?

She knew precautions had to be taken, but her scans had all come back in the clear, with no concussion and no broken bones. She was beginning to worry that this wasn't going to be the ideal place for her to do her residency—not if the staff was secretly a bunch of bloodsucking vampires intent on destroying the human population of Sterling, Montana, one needle poke at a time.

"I'm fine. I just want to go home," Sage said for what felt like the tenth time, though she knew the doctor had to sign her out. She was just sore and grumpy and taking it out on the staff. Perfect. She'd feel bad about that tomorrow, too.

"We're waiting for your final test results, and then the doctor will be in to speak with you. If there's anything wrong, this is the best place for you. He's the only one who can sign the discharge papers," the nurse repeated.

"How much longer until he gets here?" This waiting game was getting old.

"I'm right here."

Sage froze as she looked at the man blocking her doorway. No way! There was no possible way the man standing in her doorway was whom she believed it to be. Fate couldn't be that cruel.

"Here are the charts, Dr. Whitman."

Sage's stomach heaved when the nurse said Spence's name as she flitted over to him. Yes, *flitted*. There was no other word for it. It seemed that Spence Whitman still had the same effect he'd always had on the ladies. Both young and old.

It also seemed that she hadn't been dreaming when she woke up after the accident. Here was the man—in the very sexy flesh.

She immediately remembered when she was sixteen and she'd worked up the courage to ask him out on a date. She'd thrown herself at him, just one of many young women who had been in love with him.

After she had professed her undying love to him, he had simply kissed her on the cheek, told her she would one day be a heartbreaker, and then walked away, devastating her. Sure, she'd been too young for him to do anything more, but from that moment on, she'd avoided him. Embarrassment had eaten her alive.

"How are you feeling, Ms. Banks?"

The professional tone, the standard, distant smile that said he was interested in her only as a patient . . . the cluelessness in his eyes. Sage's humiliation was complete. The boy she'd been in love with since she was ten years old had zero idea who she was. That was how unimportant she'd ever been to him. Not that it should have come as a shock. But still, though she was now old enough to know better, and wise enough not to care, she had to admit—to herself only, of course—that it did hurt. In the mood she was in now, she didn't even try to be nice, sending Spence a look that could frost the caverns of the South Pole.

His false smile vanished, and he contemplated her briefly with baffled surprise. Sage was sure he wasn't used to anything but a simpering twit when he walked into a female patient's room. Well, her days of simpering were long gone.

She'd really hoped she wouldn't be crossing paths with Spence when she'd accepted her residency. The last she'd heard, he was some hotshot doctor in Seattle. It was just her luck that he happened to be in town, most likely visiting his family, at the same time she was rolling home.

"I'd be feeling much better if everyone would quit poking and prodding me and would just let me go home."

"Has her family been notified?" Spence asked the nurse, obviously not finding it very appealing to speak directly to Sage.

Only someone with an extremely small brain could have missed her obvious hostility. So he had *some* intelligence going for him if he could read her disdain. Since he was her treating physician, she was relieved to know he knew something, unlike everyone else around the place.

But wait. *Why* was he treating her? He shouldn't be working here. He worked in Seattle. Maybe they were permitting him to treat her since he'd been the first person on the scene. She really, *really* hoped that was the case.

The alternative would mean . . . No. If she refused to even think the thought, then there would be no possible way it could be true. She wouldn't ask, either. As all her other options had gone down the drain the minute she'd accepted the offer to be in this program, she had to stay at this hospital and she didn't want to work with Spence Whitman, her childhood crush.

When the man himself turned and gave her a megawatt smile that, despite her anger, had her knees shaking just a bit beneath her warm blanket, she strengthened her resolve. Locking her knees into place, she sent another glare his way—this one not cold, but guaranteed to melt steel—and felt a smidgen of satisfaction as his movie-star smile faltered again and he stood there looking unsure what to do next.

"Yes, Dr. Whitman. Her grandmother has been called."

"I'll go ahead and release you, Ms. Banks, but I need you to get plenty of rest over the next few days. Make an appointment with your general practitioner as soon as possible."

He spoke while scribbling on his pad, clearly avoiding her eyes. Of course, she could look away from him, too. But she was trying to prove something to herself—that he didn't affect her.

"I'll send a prescription to the pharmacy in case the pain is too much in a few hours." With that, he walked from the room.

"Good riddance," she muttered, causing the nurse to turn and look at her as if she'd sprouted three heads. "Oh come on, he's not that great," Sage snapped, and the woman turned and left, probably chasing down Spence to tell him their patient clearly had brain damage.

"Sage!"

Sage turned to find her grandmother in the doorway, sporting red cheeks and tears in her eyes. "Hi, Grandma . . ."

"Oh, sweetheart, I've been so worried." Bethel

rushed to the bed and sank down in the chair next to it, grasping Sage's hand.

"I'm fine, Grandma. It was only a little accident. They were just being thorough, that's all."

"I don't think we should take you home. What if something terrible is wrong and we don't find out until it's too late?"

"I promise you that I'm virtually unscathed despite all the drama. And nothing could possibly make me feel better than some of your special hot chocolate and a full night's rest." Sage was desperate to get out of this bed and out of this hospital. She'd be here plenty beginning next week, when her residency began. At least due to this experience she'd be more understanding when her patients began feeling restless. Maybe all medical staff should have to be patients before treating anyone.

"Of course, darling, if you really think you're safe to leave, then I'll take good care of you. Eileen, Maggie, and I can take shifts so you aren't alone for a single minute."

Still, Bethel didn't look reassured. Sage would have to try really hard not to wince as she was leaving. The thought of her grandma, Maggie, *and* Eileen hovering over her nonstop was enough to send her blood pressure shooting through the roof. Hardly the best way to get some rest.

The aches were starting to set in and she suspected that she'd have a rough few days of it. But it wasn't as if she hadn't been sore before. She'd just have to grit her teeth and bear it.

"Could you go ask the nurse about my clothes while I use the bathroom?"

"Certainly, sweetie. I'll be right back."

Bethel left the room and Sage climbed slowly from the bed. To her surprise, she had to stand there gripping the bar on the side. Her head had begun spinning, and the resulting nausea forced her to take several deep breaths to avoid passing out. When the nausea went away and she took her first steps, pain sliced down her spine. Nope. The next few days weren't going to be fun. At least her residency didn't start for a week.

That would give her plenty of time to study up on her specialty, emergency medicine, while she was recuperating. She was actually looking forward to it. When it came to books, Sage was a pro. She had an incredible memory, which in medical school, at least, was an advantage. In love, not so much.

But there was no time to dwell on romance, or in her case, lack of romance. She'd signed up for years of school and continuing education when she'd decided to be a doctor. She didn't regret that decision. It was just that seeing her old crush after all these years was messing with her head.

No. It couldn't be that. Her head must still be foggy from the wreck. Yes, that was it, she assured herself. Her grandmother returned promptly and handed her the clothes, then gave her privacy as she put them on very, very slowly.

Home, hot chocolate, and bed. That was all she needed. *Sure it was,* her mind said mockingly, but Sage quickly shut off that traitorous thought and then sat and waited for her grandmother's return. In a few days she'd be right as rain . . .

"I can't believe you've been in town for two days already and you haven't called me. I thought I was your best friend."

The ridiculously beautiful Grace Sinclair glared at Sage from the doorway of the small bedroom at her grandmother's house.

Rest just wasn't going to happen, not with what felt like everyone she'd ever met since moving here at the age of four showing up and wishing her well. If one more person held her hand and told her how sorry they were, she'd give them a reason to be sorry. All right, she could admit how petty and unappreciative that sounded, and she was thankful that she'd never said such a thing aloud.

"It's so great to see you, Grace. I can't believe it's been almost a year," Sage said, guilt consuming her that she'd let so much time go by without even a phone call to her dearest friend. "I guess the only excuse I can come up with is the last year of medical school was grueling and I barely found time to breathe, much less speak to anyone outside of the classroom."

"I don't care about any of that. I've just missed

you like crazy, darling. I can't believe, number one, that you were moving back home and didn't bother telling me, and then, number two, that you get in a near-fatal car crash and still don't feel I'm worth a phone call." Grace's long fingers sat stiffly on her shapely hips, and her dark brown eyes shot fire.

"I was planning on calling you soon, but last I heard, you were still in New York," Sage said, hoping she looked apologetic enough to appease her friend.

"I moved home a couple of months ago," Grace told her, her shoulders slumping as she entered the room and plopped down on the mattress, just as she'd always done when they were girls.

"What? Why? I thought you loved it there. Whenever we talked, you said New York was a place people came to and never left, and that's where you were determined to stay."

"Yeah, that's what I thought, too, but you know, life just happens, whether we want it to or not," Grace said with a sadness in her eyes that Sage couldn't recall seeing before.

"It looks like we should have talked a long time ago." Sage reached out and took her hand—Grace seemed to be the one who really needed comfort.

"Yes, we should have—not because my life went to hell, but because we're best friends and we should never forget it. I love you, Sage, more than any other person in the world, and I've missed you so much." Grace pushed her long, dark hair behind her ear.

"I've really missed you, too. Does this mean that we're actually living in the same place again for the first time in eight years? We're going to get to see each other for longer than three days?"

"Yes, that's exactly what it means. I know this is probably the last place in the United States that you wanted to do your residency, but I'm so glad you're here," Grace said, then pushed Sage farther over to make space for herself on the bed.

Sage hardly noticed the aching in her body. It was just so nice to be with her best friend again. What idiots they'd been to let so much time pass!

"I didn't want to come back, but now that I know you're here, Grace, I'm feeling a lot better about the decision. Okay, enough moaning and groaning. Tell me everything you've been up to. If I recall, the last time we talked, you were dating some hot Italian guy, and you already had your future children's names picked out."

"Ah yes, Vincenzo," she said a little dreamily. "That boy was incredible, and I mean with a capital *I*," she added with a giggle.

"Why do I hear a *but* coming in?"

"But . . ." Grace said with a wicked smile. "He was only incredible in one area, if you catch my drift." She gasped to see Sage's cheeks turn scarlet. "Oh my gosh, Sage. Are you seriously still a virgin?"

Was it written on her forehead? She didn't want to admit it to her gorgeous, successful, charming best friend. Guys fell all over themselves simply to be in Grace's presence. It wasn't like that with her. They'd run into her, literally, before they even knew she was standing there. It was mortifying.

"That's it! I'm taking you to Vegas, dressing you in my shortest, tightest outfit, and we're going clubbing. You'll star in a regular orgy before the night is over!"

Was she kidding? Frighteningly enough, Sage wasn't sure.

"Yes, I'm kidding, Sage. You can put away the deer-in-headlights eyes now. Seriously, have you looked in a mirror lately? You're an utter knockout with those green eyes, flaming red hair, and curves that could cause a pileup. Why don't you exploit your natural assets a little more? Some of us have to work a lot harder to look as beautiful as you."

"You have *got* to be kidding me, Grace. You've always been the most stunning woman in the room. How in the world can you say that? Now I *really* have to know what in the heck went on in New York."

Her own insecurity was forgotten as she looked at Grace with new eyes. Who was this woman? What had happened to her best friend? And more important, would Sage have to hunt down the Italian lover and spike his cocktail with arsenic? Wait! She was a doctor. She could dig up methods less easily traceable, and make it look like a natural death.

"I promise at some point to tell you all about New York . . . I do—I swear," Grace added when Sage looked at her doubtfully. "But right now, only happy thoughts are allowed. Please tell me you aren't still guarding the V card."

Yep, that was the Grace she knew, not pulling any punches, coming right to the point. "There hasn't been anyone worth giving it to, Grace."

"Oh, honey, at some point, you just have to get it over with. If you have these high expectations, and I know you do, you could be lonely forever. Sometimes it's okay to have a little fun. As long as you don't act like Heidi Benson and give it to the whole world."

"You know how busy medical school can be."

"Those are just excuses, doll. We can all make excuses until the cows come home, but you do realize that it's perfectly okay to let loose and enjoy yourself once in a while, don't you?"

"I know it's okay to have fun. I just happen to think that learning medicine is a lot of fun." When Grace looked like she'd just swallowed and chewed an entire lemon, Sage repeated herself more emphatically. "It *is* fun."

"Yeah, for smart kids like you. Even high school was a struggle for me. Add to that the fact that my best friend is freaking Albert Einstein's reincarnation, and it was never fun. I wouldn't have made it if I hadn't cheated off you so much."

"That's not true, Grace. You did just fine in college without me. I think you just can't stand sitting down for six hours straight. There's nothing wrong with that."

"That's true. I hated having to sit there while the teachers went on and on and on. Who cares who the twentieth president was?" She stopped to send a vicious glare Sage's way. "I swear, if you utter his name, I will smack you right here and now."

Sage closed her mouth. Grace knew her well—yes, she'd been about to blurt out James A. Garfield. But today her head was feeling better, and Sage wanted to keep it that way. She remembered the time Grace slammed Bobby Tetter's head into a locker just for correcting her grammar when she had said *seen* instead of *saw*, or vice versa. Bobby was always correcting people. The guy was sure to be a teacher. And man, did Grace have a mean right hook.

"I wasn't going to say it," Sage lied.

"Good. But still, I'd rather be smart and have all the answers. I really wish I'd taken my education more seriously. I guess I always just thought I was going to grow up, get married, and have a dozen kids. I didn't think I'd ever need to use a degree. But I've learned that what a person expects doesn't matter. You could get your dream, live just the way you imagined, but you should always have a backup plan. Otherwise . . . well, otherwise, you might find yourself in a tight spot."

The sadness in Grace's eyes ripped Sage apart. Why wasn't her friend telling her what had happened? Surely it couldn't be so bad that the two of them couldn't fix it. "We've always handled everything together, Grace. I know I can help if you'll just let me in."

"I will. I pinkie swear, best friends forever," Grace said, holding up her hand.

It was the code. Sage took her pinkie with her own and shook, then kept her mouth shut. It was hard to do, but she'd respect Grace's wishes, and right now Grace wasn't ready to share. But it wouldn't take her long.

"You know you have to move in with me, right?" Grace said. "I'm sure it's been heaven living at home again, having Grandma serve you and wash your clothes and treat you like the princess you are, but I demand that we become roomies. After all, that was the plan after high school. If I'd paid more attention during school and could have gotten into Stanford with you, that might have happened. But at least we're both still single and in the same place now, so we can carry out our plans. I can start packing you up right away."

Sage's eyes brimmed with tears. "I'd be more than happy to move in with you." Heck, she wanted to leave this very minute.

"Why do I hear a *but* coming?" Grace asked.

"No. That's not it. Let me wait a few days before

I break the news to Grandma. A week at most. She's missed me a lot since I left and I know my return and our time together have been special to her. If I move out while I'm still supposed to be resting, it will break her heart. I don't know why she likes babying me, but she really does. And it *is* kind of nice, though I would like to have five solid minutes of awake time without being asked if I'm okay."

"I get that. We've waited this long, I can stand to wait another week. Maybe I'll just sleep here on the couch so Grandma can take care of me, too."

"Did you say you need someone to look after you, Grace?"

The two looked over at the door as Bethel walked through with a tray containing her patented lemonade, special homemade granola, and two thick sandwiches.

"Always, Grandma. What's that?" Grace asked, instantly sitting up, yanking one of Sage's pillows from beneath her head so she could prop herself up against the headboard.

"Don't worry about permanent brain damage," Sage griped at her, and sat up much more slowly than she normally would have.

"I thought you girls might be hungry," Bethel said, not hearing Sage.

But Grace had heard, if the smirk on her face was any indication. She ignored Sage's grumbling.

"You didn't have to do that," Grace said, but she

took the tray eagerly, grabbed one of the sandwiches, and bit in.

Sage was always amazed at the amount of food her best friend could put away without ever gaining a pound. No wonder so many girls in high school had despised her.

"I love to take care of my girls," Bethel said. "Besides, you've always done so much for me."

"That's because I adore you," Grace said when she'd finished swallowing.

"If you need a place to stay, dear," Bethel said, and Grace had to turn away for a second to hide her emotions.

"I was just kidding, Grandma, but it means the world to me to know I always have a place if I need it," Grace said, giving Bethel a radiant smile.

"Well then, I won't keep you girls. I'm sure you have a lot of catching up to do." And Bethel left.

"We're going to break her heart when you move in with me. Maybe we should wait a month . . . or ten years," Grace said, only half kidding.

"A week, Grace. One week at most." Sure, if Bethel became too upset, Sage would wait a while longer, but she really hoped her grandmother wouldn't mind. Sage *had* missed Grace terribly.

"All right," Grace said. "If need be, we just won't tell her. You're going to be working a lot of hours. You could always come in the front door and then sneak out your window like you used to do when we were kids."

"That will have to be our plan B."

The two young women laughed heartily as they continued catching up. But Sage's medicine soon kicked in, and though she fought hard to stay awake, sleep overtook her.

04

Driving her grandmother's old Chrysler slowly through the center of town a few days later, since her own car had been totaled in the wreck, Sage smiled when a couple of kids on their bicycles turned and waved.

Sterling had a population of only three thousand people spread out over many miles, and despite those miles, if you wanted privacy, you weren't going to get it. The nearest large city was about thirty miles away, but Sterling had everything you could possibly need, though maybe not exactly what you'd want.

For a teenager, it could get a little boring, and the local teens had been known to tip a few cows on a Friday night, or party in some of the farmers' barns, but nothing too terrible ever seemed to happen in the close-knit community. The biggest industries were oil and ranching, as was the case for a lot of Montana towns. There wasn't much else to do with the miles and miles of open land.

She drove through the one-stop-sign "metropolis" and reached her grandmother's house in a few minutes. She'd been too afraid to tell her grandma that she was planning to move—hopefully tomorrow.

Pulling the car into the small driveway, she paused to look fondly at the planters sitting on the large front porch. Sage thought there must be a city ordinance requiring every house to have an inviting wooden front porch with colorful flowers adorning it.

She finally climbed from the car, feeling much better after almost a full week of total rest and relaxation—too much rest, if anyone cared to ask her humble opinion. Before she was able to take two steps, she heard the familiar creaking of the wooden screen door as her grandma stepped outside.

"I've been so worried," Bethel said as Sage came up the front path. "You were gone too long."

"You shouldn't be worrying about me, Grandma. And you shouldn't be out here in the heat." Sage climbed up the steps and threw her arms around Bethel. The familiar scent of butterscotch and flour drifting off her grandmother's clothes would always be a reminder of home and happiness.

"I just hate knowing that you're out there driving all by yourself after that terrible wreck, sweetie. You've only been feeling better for a day. I could have driven you."

"I told you I'd be fine, and see?" Sage spun around in a circle. "I'm all safe and sound. And for the millionth time, it was a minor wreck, though my car might disagree. Now let's get you back inside where it's cool."

"Don't you be fussing over me, young lady. I may have a few years on you, but I can handle myself just fine. A bit of heat won't slow these bones down. Now be a good girl and come inside. I've made you muffins and there's fresh lemonade chilling in the fridge."

"That is *just* what the doctor ordered," Sage said with a grin.

"You will make a terrific doctor, darling. It makes me feel so safe having you back home again." Bethel scooted over to the fridge and filled a glass with icy-cold liquid.

Bethel's reference to home sent a pang through her. How in the world was she supposed to tell her grandma she wanted to live with Grace? What if the woman was really crushed and thought Sage didn't love her enough to stay?

"I met up with Grace down at the diner for lunch," Sage said as she sat back. "I've missed her so much. I can't believe how long it's been since the two of us have gotten to hang out. Did you know that Kelly Purly is going to have another baby?" Kelly had gone to school with Grace and Sage. It was strange to think that she was a mother now.

"Yes, it seems that everyone is having babies," Bethel grumbled. "It sure would be nice if I got to be a great-grandma before the good Lord decides to pull me from this world."

"Grandma, you look tired. Why don't you go lie down?"

Bethel let the change of subject pass, much to her granddaughter's relief. The last thing Sage wanted to do was have another discussion about eligible men and to field questions about whether she was ever going to have a family. She was only twenty-six, not on the verge of retirement.

"You're right, dear. A nap would do wonders for this old body," Bethel said, then she took her time leaving the room.

Sage watched her go with a worried frown. She needed to discuss her plans with her grandma, but she didn't have the energy for it right now. Or that's what she told herself. In reality, she was just too chicken. Maybe over dinner . . .

Suddenly, the afternoon caught up to her, and she felt completely drained, so she decided to lie down for a few minutes. Famous last words—sleep claimed her instantly.

"TIME TO GET up, sweetheart," her grandmother said, shaking her awake. "We have a party to go to."

"What? What party?"

"Oh, sorry. I forgot to mention that Martin Whitman is having a giant gathering at his place this evening. We can't miss it." Bethel was the picture of excitement.

"Are you up for it, Grandma?"

"Listen, girlie, I was dancing long into the night when you were still in diapers, so don't try mothering me. I feel just fine and I deserve to go to this party."

"I'm sorry, Grandma, but I'm a little tired." So tired, in fact, that she didn't notice that her grandma sounded awfully hearty for someone supposedly under the weather. "Would you mind going with Eileen so I can stay home and rest?" She really didn't want to go to the Whitman Ranch, not now that she knew Spence was in town. He was sure to be there.

Just the name Whitman had her on edge again. But that was ridiculous. If Spence was going to be in town often, she'd have to get over it. Besides, her reaction was so over the top. Maybe if she'd taken Grace's advice and had a few solid flings while away at college—no time in med school!—she wouldn't be harboring these feelings for her childhood obsession.

"I suppose I could go with Eileen, but her eyes aren't so good these days. We were kind of hoping you would drive us, but I understand if you aren't up for it."

Sage couldn't stand to disappoint her grandma—plus she really didn't want the two women to be out driving the winding country roads, especially after dark.

"I'm sorry, Grandma. I'll just take a quick shower and drink a strong cup of coffee, and then I'll feel much better. I'll take you."

Sage climbed out of bed, kissed her grandma on

the cheek, and rushed into the bathroom. When Spence hadn't even known who she was last week, her childhood embarrassment had been renewed. She'd compared all men to him through the years, and he hadn't even thought of her once. How mortifying was that? To be around him now just wasn't something she could handle. It was best to move forward with her life, focus on who and what she wanted to be, and let go of her childhood crush.

Easier said than done.

After showering and dressing quickly, Sage put on mascara and lip gloss. She couldn't decide what to do with her long red hair, so she threw it up in a ponytail and called it good, if boring. She looked at herself in the mirror with a tentative smile.

There had been men who'd told her she was beautiful, but she always had a hard time believing it. She was considered short at only five foot four—that was average height, dammit!—and even if she had been acceptably tall, she wasn't model material. She just didn't have the exotic look that Grace did. Her curves certainly stood out, but who needed curves when they weren't being used?

She wanted to tell herself that if she stopped comparing herself to other people, maybe she'd appreciate what she did have. Didn't quite work. But she wasn't without good points, and she knew it. She examined her deep emerald eyes critically. She'd always wanted to have blue eyes that shone like the sun reflecting on a lake, but she could live with green. In fact, a friend had once told her that her eyes were her best asset. Sage had laughed at the time and glanced pointedly at her chest. Men seemed unable to look past her cup size long enough to notice anything about her eyes, and she'd always been irritated by that. She refused to date a guy who couldn't pick her face out of a lineup. Hmmm, was that why she'd hardly ever dated?

She ran a finger over her full lips and smiled once again. At least her lifelong diligence in wearing sunscreen had spared her from a superabundance of freckles, but she'd have killed for the ability to tan. Darn Celtic blood.

"We have to leave, Sage," Bethel called out from the kitchen.

"Coming." Sage turned her back to the mirror, squared her shoulders, and walked out of the bathroom.

"You look beautiful, dear," Bethel said as she surveyed Sage's outfit. Her granddaughter wasn't dressing up, dang it, but then again, no one really did at these country parties. The evening had cooled as soon as the sun had set, so Sage wore her favorite pair of jeans and a thick sweater over a modest blouse.

"You look great, too, Grandma. Do you have a hot date tonight or something?" Sage had been teasing, and was shocked when her grandma turned a shade of pink. *Wow.* The young woman's eyes grew wide as she realized the woman who'd raised her might actually be sweet on someone. "Uh . . . are you . . . dating someone, Grandma?"

"No, no, nothing like that," Bethel replied hastily, then rushed over to grab her purse and jacket.

Sage wanted to fire questions at her, but she could see she'd flustered the poor woman, so she let the subject drop. She'd be keeping an eye on her grandma tonight, though. She wanted to know who had her acting like a teenager going to her first boy-girl dance.

The idea of sharing her grandmother with some-one else sparked a smidgen of jealousy in her, but Sage pushed it back. She wasn't always around, and if Bethel could have someone to love her, she more than deserved it. Plus, this meant her grandma might not be so opposed to Sage's plan of moving in with Grace.

Her grandfather had been gone for sixteen years. It was long past time for Bethel to move forward with her life.

"You deserve whatever happiness you can find," Sage said, embracing her beloved grandmother.

"Now you quit fussing over me and worry about yourself," Bethel grumbled, but the pink still hadn't left her cheeks. "We need to get going. We're running so late that I'm sure Eileen is wearing a hole in her living room carpet."

Sage wrapped an arm around her grandma's shoulders and led her to the car. She could do this—she could attend the party even with Spence there. Tons of people always showed up for these country blowouts. She probably wouldn't even see him.

Of course, when had fate ever been that kind to her? She shut the front door, resigned to whatever the night held.

05

"Come on, Michael. Are you going to put some oomph in that or ride like a girl all day?" Spence yelled at his little brother as they raced across the wide-open pastures.

"I have no trouble keeping up with you, old man," Michael yelled back, then leaned down over his horse's neck, pushed his knees in, and shot forward to take the lead. They rode fast and hard over the flat land, exchanging front position every few minutes. After they made a tight loop, they raced back toward the stables, crossed into the yard in a photo finish, and looked toward Camden, who was laughing at them.

"Who won?" Michael asked as he jumped down from his horse. Spence followed speedily behind him and stared expectantly at Camden.

"Haven't you guys outgrown your competitiveness?"

"Not at all," Spence said impatiently. "Now who won?"

"It was a tie. Dad's waiting in the barn." Camden rolled his eyes and shook his head in mock annoyance while he walked inside.

"Damn. I was sure I had you that time," Michael said with a grin that took any sting out of his statement.

"Someday, little brother." Spence threw his arm around Michael's shoulders and they led their horses inside to start brushing them down. The animals had received a hard workout, so the two brothers spent added time brushing them and spoiled them with a few extra treats.

"Boys, I need some help," Martin called. Spence immediately headed to his father's office, with Michael on his heels.

"What do you need, Dad?" they asked in unison, then smiled at each other. Yes, they always thought and said almost the same thing. They'd been inseparable for twenty years, from the second they'd come home from the hospital on that fateful day their lives were forever changed.

Jackson entered the room, and Spence looked around at the three men who weren't his brothers by blood, but for whom he'd die without hesitation. For those two decades, it had been the four of them through it all, and even after becoming adults, they still couldn't go long without getting together.

Michael was Martin's only biological child, but from the moment Martin had brought Spence, Camden, and Jackson home on a cold winter morning, the day they'd rescued Michael from drowning in the lake, he'd never treated any of them any differently than he did his own son. He'd loved them and had raised them to become the men they now were. His guidance had shaped them in ways nothing else could. Spence would do anything for Martin and their patchwork family.

Martin had come up with that expression. He said they were all pieces of a quilt, and a quilt did no good to anyone with each piece on its own. Each square was certainly beautiful, but once put together, it served a purpose—to provide warmth and security. And as a family unit, they were one powerful force.

"Sorry, Dad, my mind was wandering. What did you need?" Spence said with a sheepish smile.

"Now, boy, you're thirty-four," Martin said. "A bit too old to be ignoring me. If you slowed down once in a while and just focused on the here and now instead of always being three steps ahead, you'd enjoy life a little more."

"It will never happen again," Spence told him with a wink. They both knew he was full of it. Of all the brothers, Spence was most often found lost in his thoughts and calculations. His ability to think ahead and focus with such intensity made him a great doctor.

He'd worked at some of the most prestigious hospitals and research facilities in the country, but he still managed to come back home once in a while and work where his family was, to be close to the place where his life had changed for the better.

Luckily, all four boys had more money in their bank accounts than they could ever spend, thanks to their father's generous trust fund and to very wise investments on their parts, so each of them could do what they loved, and be where they loved to be. It was a freedom few people had.

"I don't want you boys to forget about the party tonight," Martin said. "It's for my dear friend Raymond Smithers. Also, the third leg of our tripod, Joseph Anderson, has made the trip all the way from Seattle to attend, so don't even try to get out of this."

"I'll cancel my plans," Camden replied promptly. He stepped away and lifted his phone to his ear.

"I spoke to Austin Anderson earlier and he told me he was coming, too. I'm looking forward to spending time with him. We've both been busy, so it's been a while," Spence said. He'd met Austin while at Harvard, and they'd been fast friends ever since.

"Yes, I'm looking forward to seeing your friend again," Martin said. "Joseph said he'd be flying in later with his family and some of his brothers' families, too."

"It's still so strange that Austin is married with kids now. It makes me feel old," Spence said with a laugh.

"Well, you *have* been letting the grass grow underneath your feet when it comes to settling down," Martin groused.

Spence turned in surprise. It wasn't like his father to make such a comment. This had to be because Joseph was visiting. Austin had told Spence about his suspicions that his father, George, had been engaging in serious matchmaking with his brother, Joseph Anderson, trying to marry all their kids off. If so, it had worked, as all of the kids were now married with kids of their own. Spence would certainly have to make sure this longtime friend wasn't putting ideas into his own father's head.

Trust still didn't come easily for Spence, not after so many years in the foster-care system, and not after the hell his college "sweetheart" had put him through. He had decided that he was far better off keeping his relationships about one thing, and one thing only.

Sex. And plenty of it.

When the silence stretched on, Spence shook off his thoughts and turned toward his father. "Where do you need me?"

The boys spent the next several hours setting up tables, chairs, and a dance floor in the huge barn. When they were finally finished, they had time only to shower and dress before the masses descended. After all the hard work, it was a good thing the four of them kept extra clothes at their dad's colossal house.

One of the perks of living in Sterling was knowing the neighbors, plus the fact that crime was low. Of course, when they were kids, that had been a disadvantage. They hadn't been able to get away with anything because people were always watching—and talking.

Now it was nice. He was a better doctor when visiting here because he knew his patients well. As he wandered back toward the house, for some reason the woman he'd met earlier in the week popped into his head again. He should know who she was, that was for sure, but maybe she'd recently moved to town. That would explain not knowing her.

But her attitude didn't make sense. She'd been crabby—downright rude, actually—so why was he even thinking about her? There were plenty of women who were more than willing to give him their attention, so why in the world would he think twice about the car crash victim? Maybe because she was a mystery?

There was just something about her . . .

Before he could dwell on it any further, Camden bumped into him. "What are you so dreamy about?" his brother asked with a sly smile.

"I'm not dreamy," Spence said, feeling like an idiot for getting caught zoning out.

"I think it's about a girl. It's always about a girl."

"You're partially right. I was thinking you look

like a girl," Spence said before punching his brother in the arm and heading downstairs.

"Yeah, right back at ya," Camden yelled, but Spence had taken the lead.

It was time to greet the guests and, of course, to mingle—his father's favorite pastime.

06

The music was blaring as Sage opened her car door and stepped out. "Hold on, Grandma. Let me come around and help you and Eileen."

"Quit your fussing," Bethel snapped. "Someone might hear you and think we're nothing but a couple of frail old women. You do realize I'm only sixty-five? It's not like I have a foot in the grave already."

A petite woman, Sage's grandmother didn't look a day over fifty, especially with her pink hair. It had originally been a dye job gone terribly wrong, but Bethel had loved it so much that for the past five years her hair had looked like it belonged on a Barbie doll.

Sage had grown so used to it she didn't even blink anymore. When Eileen decided to join her best friend with her own pink-colored hair, she and Bethel had been nicknamed the Pink Ladies, a nod to one of their favorite movies, *Grease*.

It was fitting. The two were usually full of life and laughter and always seemed to be getting into trouble. And that worried Sage on occasion. It was probably a very good thing Sage had come home when she did. She'd have to find sneaky ways to get her grandmother to rest, especially since the woman's health wasn't the best right now.

But as Sage really thought about it, something just wasn't quite adding up. Just last year, she had been horrified when the police chief had called her. He'd been left with no choice but to arrest both Eileen and Bethel and their third accomplice, Maggie Winchester, after the three of them thought it would be amusing to go skinny-dipping in the local pool after hours. The poor night guard who knew the women well had heard the commotion and called the cops, then had turned beet red when he'd discovered who was trespassing.

That certainly didn't sound like a woman who wasn't feeling well. The women had told the sheriff they were simply looking for a thrill.

When the pool owner had found out who had been up to the mischief, all charges had been dropped. The three women had enjoyed themselves immensely and were trying to figure out what their next big antic would be. Sage really hoped they took so long to find a new way to get their kicks that they would eventually forget about doing it.

"I didn't think you ladies were ever going to show!"

Sage jumped at the boisterous voice of Judge Whitman as he joined them at the car.

"I would never miss one of your parties, Martin," Eileen said. "I'm ready for your special punch." The way Eileen fluttered her eyelashes was enough to make Sage grin.

"Well now, Eileen, you'd best only take one cup this time," Martin replied with a laugh. "You remember your impromptu table dance last time you had a couple of glasses."

"That would have been just fine had little Stevie Walker not had a camera," Eileen replied. "The brat posted it on that dangfangled contraption of his where all the world could see me acting like a fool. You remember when we were young—those blankety-blank computers were only for the space people."

Sage struggled not to laugh. "You mean NASA, Aunt Eileen?"

"Now don't you mock me, girlie. I may be old, but I have real good hearing, thanks to Doc Lamper's hearing aids." Eileen tapped her ear pointedly.

"I would never think of mocking you," Sage said, wrapping an arm around the woman. "I love you far too much."

Martin put his arm around Bethel as the four of them made their way inside the barn.

"It's chilly out here tonight," Bethel said with a shiver.

"It's plenty warm in the barn." The wink Martin sent Eileen's way had the woman blushing again. Sage really wanted to figure out when this flirtation had begun. She would be more than pleased for both of them if they became an item. There was no age limit on falling in love, and both Martin and Eileen deserved a second chance at forever happiness.

Sage found it amusing that Martin always chose to have his parties in the barn. His home was five times the size of a normal ranch house, with so many wings she'd gotten lost in it a few times as a child, but his man cave was in the barn, and he loved to have shindigs there.

Lights and music greeted them as Sage skimmed the room with her emerald eyes. She spotted Camden dancing with Grace, and her eyes immediately narrowed.

Grace had been in love with Camden for about as long as Sage had been in love with Spence. The problem was that something had happened after Camden had left for college that had changed Grace forever. She'd always been confident, but she was different. And though Sage strongly suspected that Grace still loved Camden, her best friend wouldn't even say his name anymore.

However, Sage wouldn't be surprised at all if Grace confessed that her affair with the Italian guy had ended because she'd wanted to come home to Camden. Sage really hoped that wasn't the case, because she didn't think Camden was capable of a real relationship. Heck, all of the Whitman brothers seemed biologically defective when it came to staying with a woman longer than it took for the bedsheets to cool down.

Not that she knew from personal experience, of course; but the Sterling rumor mill never tired of the Whitmans. She tried to deny that she kept one ear out for the slightest news on Spence, insisting to herself that she was just curious—nothing more.

Sure, you're over Spence. Sheesh, her mind was mocking her again.

"I *am*," Sage muttered aloud, causing Bethel to glance at her with concern. "I'm gonna get a drink, Grandma. You're in good hands." She dashed off, intent on hiding in the corner for a while until Grace was free.

If she could just avoid spotting Spence, her night would be perfect. It was a very large barn, and if she stuck to the shadows, she had a chance of getting her wish.

07

"Sage Banks is looking good tonight, wouldn't you say, Spence?"

Spence turned to see his patient from earlier moving off into a corner, a drink in her hand. The name had been bugging him all week, but he couldn't place it. Now, as his friend Hawk Winchester made the comment, his memory came rushing back—the pretty redheaded sophomore who'd told him one summer how much she loved him.

Hell, she couldn't have been more than sixteen and he'd just finished his second year of med school. He'd given her a kiss on the cheek, thanked her, and then forgotten all about her. What a strange incident to remember.

Sage Banks was no longer a sixteen-year-old child—that was for damn sure. She'd filled out in all the right places, and though he was a doctor and had pretty much seen it all, he wouldn't mind seeing a hell of a lot more of Sage. Could she be mad that he hadn't remembered her? It had been a long time ago. But women didn't like to be forgotten . . .

"Oh . . ."

"Spill now. That's a guilty *oh*." Spence's best

friend, Austin, had spoken up as the three men looked at the woman in question, who was clearly trying to blend in with the decorations.

"I blame it on a lack of sleep," Spence muttered, not knowing why he felt guilty. He had nothing to feel guilty about.

"Seriously, are you going to talk in riddles all night?" Austin asked as he took a pull of his beer.

"Sage was in a car accident earlier in the week and I was first on the scene. It's been so long since I'd seen her last—heck, I think about ten years—that I didn't recognize her. That hardly makes me the devil. But from the looks she was shooting at me— they would have killed a regular man—you'd think I'd done something a lot more horrible than forgetting who she was."

Hawk and Austin laughed. "A regular man?" Austin finally said when he was finished choking on the swallow of beer he'd just inhaled.

"You know what I mean," Spence said, grinning.

"Yeah, that you're an all-powerful immortal who makes women swoon." Austin gave his friend's back a slap that would have knocked down a mere mortal.

"Have your fun," Spence said. "Still, I don't see what all the attitude was about."

Hawk looked at Spence as if the guy were a dense little boy. "Probably because she's been in love with you forever and you didn't even know who in the hell she was."

"What?"

"Come on, man. Don't act so surprised. It's pretty damn obvious that she's always carried a megawatt torch for you. We may be older than she is, but the love-struck looks she always sent your way were pretty damn obvious."

"You've got to be kidding me." Yes, she'd told him that she loved him, but that had just been a crazy moment. They'd been too far apart in years for her to ever have had serious feelings for him. "She didn't go to school with me. She was too young to have a serious crush."

"Yeah, she is a lot younger," Austin said, as he tried remembering the old days. "I recall when I came home from college with you for a visit. She must have just been entering high school, because from what I remember, her idea of flirting was bad—really, really bad."

Spence tuned his friends out as his eyes raked over Sage's delectable form. Whatever she'd been like in high school, Sage Banks was very much grown up now. Even though she was swathed in a thick sweater, he could see she'd developed into an attractive woman. Hmm. Possibilities were popping into his head. That he'd held that body in his arms—albeit to move her from her wrecked car—wasn't helping tame his imagination any, either. Now that he knew he was allowed to think of her sexually, his fantasies were coming to life in rapid succession.

"I don't think she has a crush on me anymore," he finally said, not realizing how much time had passed as he'd gazed at her with a brand-new hunger. Then he turned back to Austin and Hawk and smiled. "But I do think I could reignite some old flames."

"I would so love to see you knocked down—just once. If this girl was shooting daggers at you because you had no clue who she was, there's no way she's going to just roll over, forgive, and forget. I bet you twenty that she turns you down flat."

"I want in on that," Hawk said, reaching for his wallet.

Spence had never been able to turn down a dare. "Make it fifty each," he said to both of them. The sound of the men's laughter followed him as he made his way across the barn to Sage's quiet corner.

Lucky for him. Maybe he could up the ante and get a little kiss, too. He'd have her eating out of his hand within five minutes.

Stopping at the punch bowl, he grabbed a cup of Martin's special brew—he'd seen that she was gulping hers down mighty fast. Pasting on his most charming smile, he approached her chair with his back to the crowd, placing the two of them in a semi-private bubble.

"How are you feeling, Sage?"

Her head whipped up and her eyes went left to right as if searching for an escape route. Not the reaction he'd been hoping for, but he'd soon have her changing her tune.

"Um . . . fine," she replied, refusing to meet his eyes. "I need to find my grandma." She stood, which put her only inches away from him. He could have backed up a bit to give her room, but he chose not to.

"I'm glad to hear you aren't suffering after the wreck," he said, just in case she'd somehow forgotten he'd been the one to save her. He was a hero—she should give him a break for not immediately remembering her. After all, he'd seen a lot of faces over the years. He stretched a hand out and ran it along her cheek, where only the barest trace of a bruise remained. She jerked away from him as if he'd just hit her.

"I need to go."

"Let's sit and chat. Your grandmother is in good hands. I just saw her heading to the dance floor with Dr. Thompson."

"I don't want to sit and chat." She spoke between gritted teeth.

"I'm sorry I didn't recognize you after the wreck, Sage. It's been a long time," he said as his eyes caressed her body. "And you've certainly changed." There. That should clear everything right up. After all, he'd apologized. That was gold in his book, because he didn't say he was sorry very often.

She stared at him incredulously, further surprising him. Look, he was letting her know that he liked what he was looking at. He had no doubt that any other woman he gave his patented look to would be fluttering her eyelashes about now.

Not Sage.

"Seriously, Spence? Does that look really work on women? You just bat your pretty green eyes and they fall right in line with whatever you want?" The words came out like honey, but he was searching for the angry bees that were about to sting him.

"What has got you so pissed off? Just because I didn't recognize you? Sorry about that, but it's been a while. I'm just trying to . . . reconnect." He was beginning to feel irritation to match hers—her behavior was incredibly rude. This was his home—well, his dad's house—and she was a guest. She should be a little more polite.

"You are unbelievable. You walk over here, expecting *what* exactly I don't know, and then get offended that I'm not charmed by you. I haven't fallen for your charm since I was a pathetic kid, so you're wasting your time. Why don't you go dance with Cindy? It looks to me like her claws have come out and she's ready to sink them into some unsuspecting man—or in your case, a suspecting one. The two of you seem to be searching for the same thing tonight."

She tried to push past him, but his free hand shot out and he grabbed her arm.

"How about a dance?"

"Do you never give up? Is this because your ego

is bruised? Sorry, but I don't want to hang out. Find some simpering female who wants your company."

"Did I personally offend you, or are you just one of those man-hating women?"

She stared at him with an open jaw for a moment and then closed her eyes for the briefest second before opening them again and locking their gazes. "I once had a crush on you. It's long past. I don't associate with men who think dating and bedding a woman are the same thing. I also don't date men who engage in adding notches to their bedpost as a competitive sport. So tell me, Spence. Where do you expect this flirtation to go?"

"Whoa, slow down," he said with a laugh. "I'm just trying to get to know you." He was charming, dammit. Why wasn't she taking the bait?

"Oh, I'm sorry. I thought maybe you were just hoping to get me into your bed," she said with a knowing look.

"Well, if we hit it off . . ." He quickly found out that wasn't a wise thing to say.

"We won't. Trust me," she said, her expression pure ice, before she pushed him out of her way and sauntered off, mesmerizing him with the sway of her hips. Little Sage had her own claws, claws much deadlier than those wielded by the woman she'd spoken about so dismissively. Sure, Ms. Banks was hot, but she obviously had mental issues. Maybe he should just let this one go.

"Ouch! That looked painful," Austin said with laughter when he and Hawk came up.

"Standing nearby the whole time?"

"I'm just bummed I couldn't take video," Austin said with a shake of his head.

"I can't guarantee that I didn't," Hawk said.

"You both suck. I think my pride may be bruised," Spence said, though they all knew he was far from a puppy who needed to lick his wounds.

"I guess you owe me fifty bucks," Austin said.

"And me," Hawk added.

"How about triple or nothing? This might take a little time, though."

"Game on!" Austin and Hawk exclaimed.

"Oh yeah. Game on." Spence wore a confident smile. This could be fun.

08

FIVE MONTHS LATER

"Code silver to ER room six, code silver to ER room six."

Dammit, Spence thought. It was the first time all afternoon he'd had a chance to sit down with a cup of coffee and a bunch of charts. He was six patients behind and needed to catch up. To make matters worse, he'd just spilled his coffee. "Oh well . . . there's more where that came from." Rising quickly from his chair, he began moving down the familiar halls of the hospital he loved so much.

Walking to the code, he hoped this wasn't going to be a waste of his time—codes of this type often turned out to be nothing. Not much surprised him anymore. He'd seen it all . . . or so he thought. Turning the corner, he found a crowd was growing outside one of the ER rooms. When he pushed past the people, he discovered why.

Maureen—"Mo" as she was known in the emergency department—was a tough veteran nurse. She had a reputation for eating doctors and nurses alive, especially if they weren't doing the right thing for her patient. She was either loved and respected or rightfully feared. Spence had heard rumors that more than one new doctor ended in near tears telling them how Mo had kicked them out of the room for being "chronically stupid." Spence had liked her immediately from the very first shift he'd worked at Sterling Grace Medical.

This, however, was not a situation Spence was used to seeing. A "frequent flyer" psychiatric patient had Mo in a headlock while still in his hospital bed, and he was holding a knife to her rib cage with his other hand.

Looking more pissed off than scared, Mo kept him talking as calmly as she could, her voice lower than Spence had ever heard it.

"You don't want to do this, Mr. Ashton. I'm trying to help you."

"No, you're not. You're a part of them. The government sent you—I know it!" the man screamed, his shaky hand bringing the knife's blade up to the crucial vein in Mo's throat.

As Spence took a step closer to assess the situation, to figure out how to save Mo, he noticed all eyes were on Sage Banks. She slowly walked up to the patient, talking low and saying soothing things.

"Mr. Ashton, you need to be careful. Mo's husband, Vec, is a paralytic and she supports him."

Mo was eyeing Sage with a questioning look on her face as were the rest of the staffers, including

Spence. When a lightbulb of understanding lit in the nurse's eyes, Spence tried to clue in to what was happening.

All of them knew Mo was a widow. As he watched the scene unfold before him, he noticed Sage holding a small vial and syringe close to her leg. He could just make out the word *vecuronium* on the vial, and Spence knew instantly that Sage intended to paralyze the patient.

Sage was smart and could clearly think under pressure—this was the perfect solution to a potentially deadly situation. The paralytic drug would render the patient helpless but wouldn't cause any long-term damage.

Sage inched closer to the patient, talking softly, without losing eye contact, then picked up his IV tubing and injected the medication without his noticing. Within seconds the patient's arms went limp, and Mo was freed from his grip.

Spence ran forward, grabbing the nurse and pulling her from the room while the rest of the trauma team took care of Mr. Ashton.

"Are you okay, Mo? Wow that was a first," Spence said with a smile of disbelief on his lips.

"Are you kidding me? This was the second time that's happened to me today," Mo said, trying to hide the fact that she'd been shaken up. She wasn't about to show any weakness, especially in front of a mere man.

Her sarcastic remark left Spence with a grin on his face, grateful that this had ended so smoothly. "I have no doubt you were in control the entire time," he told her.

She eyed him for a minute before grumbling something and then turning to leave. She swiveled back and looked him in the eye. "Just so you know, that girl in there is a good one. Keep an eye on her."

Spence had no doubt she was talking about Sage. There was a long pause before his lips tilted up in a full-fledged smile. "Don't you worry, I fully intend to."

"If anyone wants me, I'll be on a cigarette break. On second thought, if anyone wants me, they can just wait until I feel like coming back into this loony bin."

With that, Mo was gone, leaving Spence to admire the woman's courage and bluntness. Then he turned back and looked in on Sage.

He could see that shock over the events was beginning to set in, but she was still working hard to ensure that the patient would be okay. In high-stress situations, there wasn't time to hesitate or process all of what was going on. A person just had to move and move fast.

When she turned and smiled weakly at the patient in the next bed over, Spence was impressed again by her composure. She just shook off her nerves and checked on him, too.

"Are you okay?" she asked.

"I seem to be doing better than you or that other guy," the man tried to joke.

Sage gave him a big smile before responding. "You're lucky I didn't give that medicine to you instead—you look a little shady yourself."

The man paused for a second before a glimmer lit his eye and he smiled at her. With one joke, all the tension in the room evaporated.

"If I was forty years younger, you could have given me anything you wanted and I would have been okay with it." Picking up her hand, he smiled and kissed her wrist, making Sage laugh.

"Flattery will get you everywhere in this hospital," she said before pulling up his blankets and then turning and leaving the room.

"Everywhere? Hmmm, interesting," Spence said in a deep drawl.

Spence watched as the tension immediately returned to her shoulders.

"Really, Dr. Whitman? Is it polite to eavesdrop on conversations that have nothing to do with you?" Sage asked, obviously not in the mood to banter with *him*.

And as much as he'd have liked to flirt with her, they needed to have a professional talk. "Follow me," he told her, and he could read her eyes. She was thinking, *Who the hell does this guy think he is to give me an order like that?*

Her words didn't quite match her thoughts, of course. "I need a break. Maybe later," she said as she turned to leave.

"I don't think so, Dr. Banks. This is important." He turned, knowing she would follow. She had a backbone, but when he put on the white jacket, he was in charge, and she knew it. She'd learned that in the five months she'd been a resident. He wasn't often at her hospital, but when he was, he was very much in charge.

She'd fought him the first couple of times they'd worked together. Then she had learned that he had a lot to teach, and she was an eager student.

"Fine," she said.

He didn't think she was going to be too happy about the news he had to tell her, but he also knew she'd get over it. That's one thing he appreciated about Sage. She adapted well, and she was going to make a hell of a fine doctor. He was grateful to know he'd be a big part of her training.

It was time to introduce himself as her new boss.

09

What was he doing here?

Sage was quite proud that she'd managed to avoid Spence most of the time. He spent only a few days a month at her hospital, and she hadn't been alone with him once while he was there. She hated to admit it, but he was a hell of a teacher, and she would normally be eager to learn from a man of his skills.

But since she couldn't think of him in a nonsexual way, she figured she was better off learning from anyone else. It seemed that lately, though, exhaustion was always muddling her brain, and she couldn't figure out what she wanted or needed anymore.

Might as well get this over with. Of course, it was just her luck that she was on the clock and couldn't be rude to Spence. She could at least *think* unladylike thoughts about him, though. There was nothing he could do about that.

"You did well in there, Sage."

"I'd prefer you call me Dr. Banks." Well, that might have been a tad rude, but he could suck it up.

"Why so formal? It's not as if we don't know each other," he replied, not acting in the least offended by her tone and demand.

"Dr. Whitman, I've had a long day, and I have a much longer night ahead of me. Could you just tell me whatever it is that you have to say so I can try to grab a ten-minute break before the next disaster?"

There, that was straightforward and professional. Okay, maybe a bit catty, but his ego was large enough that he wouldn't be offended. Plus, she was sure there were plenty of nurses present who'd gladly bandage any injuries she inflicted upon him. Hell, they'd kiss all his wounds and make them better.

And yet her words seemed to trigger some sort of response from him. The corners of his mouth lifted and a gleam shined in his eyes. He was enjoying this dance they seemed to be in. Truth be told, so was she, though she was fighting against it like crazy.

"Yes, your night is just beginning, isn't it? Don't fret, I'll be alongside you the rest of the evening," he said as he took a step closer, causing her to retreat automatically.

"What are you talking about?"

"Hasn't anyone told you?"

"Told me what?" She was thoroughly confused, and with an already muddled brain, she wasn't finding this guessing game at all enjoyable. She was used to being the smartest person in the room. But she was now surrounded by experienced medical staff and was just one of many highly intelligent people.

"I've just taken over as the head of the ER." Spence waited for her reaction.

But Sage knew he wanted to see emotion in her face, could tell by the way he'd delivered the message, dragging out the drama. Well, he would be disappointed.

"Fine. I need caffeine" was all she said as she turned on her heel and strode toward the doctors' lounge. Thankfully, they'd recently installed a beautiful espresso machine and she would never have to worry about caffeine withdrawal again while at work.

During her college years, she'd gone days and days on nothing but mocha lattes. Yes, she was a doctor, and yes, she knew she had a very poor diet, but didn't everyone have vices of one sort or another? It wasn't as if she smoked, did drugs, or drank much alcohol. If she wanted sugar to be her poison of choice, she dared anyone to question it. It looked like mochas would be her staple for as long as she was a doctor. Hey, there were a lot of calories in a mocha, so she didn't have to worry about starvation—just the caffeine shakes.

Scratch that whole idea. Serious shakes weren't a good idea at all—not if she wanted to help people. So she decided on only a small mocha coffee, then sat down and waited impatiently while Spence, who'd followed her, got his own cup. Could he be lying to her about working here permanently?

"I thought you were some big-shot doctor in Seattle."

"I am," he replied.

She certainly didn't have to worry about hurting his ego. It seemed to be invulnerable. And she was getting tired of this game.

"Well, even you, Dr. Whitman, with all your superpowers, can't be in two places at once."

"I just accepted this job so I can be close to my dad. I will still fly to Seattle a few days of the month and do surgeries, so I'm working for both places. Like before, only switched."

"But . . . I . . . I interviewed with Dr. Thompson. He's my boss. He said he'd been here forever—and that he was part of the place, someone who was never going to leave." If she said it, then it had to be true. It had to be!

"Dr. Thompson is retiring next week, actually. It's been very hush-hush. He bought a condo in Mexico and is moving on."

"He's too young!"

"Just because you don't want him to go isn't going to change the situation, Sage. Deal with it," he said, sitting back and crossing a foot over his knee.

"It's just that . . . well, someone should have told me if there were plans on changing the supervising doctors. It might have made a difference on where I decided to do my residency."

She was trying to calm down, but the longer he sat there with his trademark smirk and sparkling green eyes, the more she wanted to throw her hot mocha in his face and make some phone calls. She'd beg for another hospital to take her away from here.

"Like I said, it's been very hush-hush. Only the board and I know he's leaving. I can trust you not to tell—correct? It will be announced tomorrow." He looked at her with eyebrows raised in question, implying that he might have made a big mistake in divulging the secret.

"I have no one other than Grandma and Grace to tell. It's not as if I've had a chance to make friends or catch up with anyone since moving home," she snapped. Not that she would run around town saying anything anyway.

Good ol' trustworthy Sage. It was every girl's dream to be that person. The person everyone ran to with their problems. She'd like to be the bad girl for once, the girl everyone ran to for a bit of fun. Of course, that was never going to happen, so it was useless to even think such thoughts.

"So, you're my boss, but that's just a title. I mean, it's not like you're going to be hanging around down here. You have much more important things to do. You'll just . . . um . . . come in once in a while to check on how things are going, right?"

She knew she sounded almost desperate, but there was no possible way she could be around this man every single day. It wasn't like she got much time off. Residents seemed to be working every waking hour, and she wasn't allowed much time for sleep—not if she wanted to get through this and be a full-fledged ER physician when her residency was finished.

"I take a very hands-on approach with my residents," he said, leaning forward and smiling with reassurance. He was playing—and he was doing it damn well.

"And how many residents are you in charge of?" *Please say twenty*, she added silently.

After an uncomfortably long pause, his lips parted. "Don't worry, Sage, I will take a hands-on approach with all of you."

She gulped as their eyes remained locked together. "I . . . uh . . . better get back to the ER."

"Sage?" he called out when she was just beginning to open the door.

"Yes, Dr. Whitman." *Keep it professional*, she told herself.

"I just want to give you fair warning," he said, making her turn to look at him with a raised eyebrow. "I will be taking you out. In the interest of not breaking hospital rules, I'll wait until you're off the clock."

She nearly gasped at his audacity before a cheeky grin flashed across her face. "Well, then, I have nothing to worry about. I'm never off the clock."

She left the room, letting the door swing shut behind her. It would have felt far more like a victory if the sound of his deep laughter weren't following her down the hallway. One thing she knew for sure—she needed to polish up her armor.

10

"How does it feel to be back home?"

Spence kicked back, sipped on his favorite cognac, and smiled. "It feels a lot better than I thought it would. When I was last here and Dad wasn't feeling so hot, I got worried. So when the position opened up, I knew I had to take it."

"I'm sure glad to have you here. Don't get me wrong. Doc Thompson is great and has served the hospital well, but if I need to go to surgery, I think I'd rather leave my life in your hands," Hawk said as he sipped his Pepsi. He was on the clock, and if the fire alarm sounded, he needed to be sober.

"Hell, Hawk, I think you could fix yourself," Spence said with a laugh.

"Well, we both know I'd make a damn fine surgeon if I had any desire to be a cocky bastard like you and go to med school."

"You're so full of crap. There's nothing you want to do that you won't," Spence said.

"Yeah, I guess that's true. By the way, don't think I haven't forgotten the one hundred and fifty you still owe me."

Spence looked at his friend with a question in his eyes before the night of the party flashed back to his mind.

"I haven't lost the bet yet. I'm back home now, around for more than just a few days here and there," Spence said, not even worried.

Sure, Sage hadn't given him the time of day over the last five months, but now he was going to be around a lot more.

"I want you to know that Sage is a good girl. If this is only a game to you, then maybe you should just take a loss on this one," Hawk said, suddenly serious.

"I'm not a complete ass," Spence said, taking another long swallow of his drink as he squirmed in his seat.

"Come on, man. You can't BS me. I used to be you before I met Natalie."

"Just because you stunned us all by getting yourself hitched to the hot little schoolteacher doesn't mean the rest of us need to follow in your footsteps down the matrimonial aisle," Spence said, almost in a panic.

"Well, your brother seems pretty dang happy with his bride," Hawk pointed out.

"Yeah, well, Alyssa is one of a kind, and after all the hell that Jackson went through, I'm really happy that he ended up finding her. And I can't complain about my niece. She is simply amazing," Spence said, getting slightly misty-eyed even thinking about her.

"Well, since you were the one who saved Angel's life, you think the sun pretty much rises and falls on her," Hawk said.

"Ah, Hawk, she was a fighter from the moment she was delivered. It didn't matter that I was the one to do surgery on her, she was—and still is—a champion, and she would have made it no matter what."

"How in the world can you be such a softie when it comes to your niece and also love your sister-in-law so much, but still not understand the female sex?" Hawk asked, sitting back with a confused look on his face.

"I do understand women. They are essential to our happiness. I just choose to stay with them until the times are no longer fun."

"Okay, I really want you to explain this one," Hawk said.

"All relationships start out in the honeymoon phase, where it's all love and roses, and then when the couple gets comfortable with each other, they start to bicker, and eventually, they can't stand to even be in the same room anymore," Spence said, though he didn't sound convincing.

"So, according to you, Natalie is going to grow

two heads and become a monster one of these days?" Hawk questioned.

"No. Won't happen to you, because you found one of the sane ones," Spence said.

"And your sister-in-law?"

"Nope. My brother also found one of the good ones." Spence was emphatic.

"So then, it sounds to me like you're just full of crap. There seem to be a lot of good ones," Hawk pointed out.

"Yeah, I think I just might be full of crap," Spence admitted with a lopsided smile.

"All righty then. If you can admit that, then are you admitting that Sage might just be someone special, too?"

Spence thought a few moments before answering his friend. Did he think Sage was special? Hell yes, he did. She was talented, smart, and funny, and quick on her toes. Did he think the two of them had a future together? It was way too soon to even think about that.

"All I know for sure is that since that moment in the hospital when she looked at me like I was Satan's love child, I've been infatuated with her. I want to get to know her. It's not a game," he told his friend.

"Well then, you'd better step it up. I like the girl, but I also like winning, so I won't have a problem colleting my hundred and fifty," Hawk said, lightening the mood, making Spence let out a relieved breath.

"Triple or nothing," Spence said with a wicked grin.

"Ah, it will feel good to take your money," Hawk said as he stuck out his hand and shook.

11

"Get this person intubated now!"

The surgical staff moved efficiently around her—completely resourceful, all of them knowing exactly which role they were there to play. Sage was a part of this drama, a part of the process of saving lives. She thrived on it—lived for it. She was where she belonged.

Almost without thought, Sage was tipping the patient's head back and feeding a tube down his throat. Her hands were steady, her pulse calm. She was performing a procedure she'd done a hundred, maybe even a thousand times—first on dummies, then on real patients.

She still felt a pinch of nerves each time she did such a tricky procedure. It would be very nice when that was no longer the case, when she was as confident as the doctors who had been doing this for years. She would get there—it was only a matter of time.

While the nurses stripped the patient down and threw a hospital gown over him, she focused on the job at hand. That's why this worked. They all knew their jobs and they moved together as one.

"He needs a unit of blood, stat. That gash on his leg is still bleeding. Let's get the blood loss stopped."

Orders. Lots of orders. Shouted orders. Everyone responding. It was awe-inspiring. They were going to save this man's life, and she was right there, right in the thick of it.

"Dr. Banks, what comes next?"

Sage's head snapped up as she looked into the eyes of Dr. Snyder, the surgeon who was on call that night. He was new, someone she didn't know and didn't feel comfortable with, which made her slightly nervous.

When she didn't answer, he shouted out his next order. "Finish cleaning that leg wound. I want him in surgery ten minutes ago!"

Sage moved to the patient's leg and didn't hesitate at the sight of the protruding bone. This she could handle—blood, bodily fluids, torn skin. From the time Sage was eleven years old, or so her grandma told her, she was meant to be a doctor. That was when she'd brought home a kitten that had been run over and had a nasty wound on its side.

Most kids would have panicked at the sight, but she'd wrapped up the kitten, slowed the loss of blood, and ended up saving its life because she made sure they got it to the vet in time. The vet had been so impressed that she'd let Sage watch through the window as she operated. After this swift trip down memory lane, Sage Banks, MD, pulled herself together again and focused on cleaning John Doe's wounds.

"This is Mike Smith. Forty-year-old male, was skateboarding with his son when a car slammed into him. He went flying about fifty yards, so we could have some major internal damage," the paramedic called out as he read the man's chart to them.

"Got it. Is the OR ready?"

"Yes, Dr. Snyder. Ready to go."

"Let's move."

Sage started to follow when Dr. Snyder turned. "Stay in the ER. There will be more incoming. It's Friday night." With that, he was gone.

Sage sagged against the wall and took her first deep breath since the trauma patient had come into the ER. This was an unusually busy night, but at least she wouldn't be bored.

SAGE'S FEET FELT as if they would just fall off as soon as she undid her laces and removed her shoes. And doing that would take more effort than she had right now. She'd certainly had some long nights when she was in medical school, and whole days without any sleep, but none of it compared to the way she was feeling at this moment.

Add to it all the fact that she was frozen solid— her car had refused to start for a full ten minutes, and once it had started, the blasted heater hadn't worked, so she had to leave her windows down to keep her windshield from fogging up. In short, she was a broken Popsicle.

Rushing inside the apartment she and Grace shared, Sage moaned loudly as a blast of warm air encircled her. If she even thought about another cup of coffee, she was going to heave. She needed a nice cup of hot chocolate, followed by a steaming hot bath, and topped off by about twenty-four hours of dreamless, blissful sleep. Of course, she wasn't going to get even six hours. This was the life she'd signed up for. And despite everything, she was still sure she'd made the right career choice.

Her grandmother hadn't been nearly as upset when Sage had moved in with Grace as Sage had thought she'd be. As a matter of fact, Bethel had practically pushed Sage out the door, making her think her grandmother might be up to something. It was so nice living with Grace, though, that she refused to worry about it. She wished her friend was home. It would be nice to tell her about her hellacious day, and Grace probably had her own stories to share.

Focusing on other people's problems sometimes helped Sage feel less like a loser. After walking into the small, spotless kitchen and turning on the tea-kettle, she sat down and rolled her shoulders. The pot finally whistled and she added cocoa mix to her cup, stirred in the hot water, and topped it off with a nice fat dollop of whipped cream. She grabbed a package of cookies to round out her meal, and she soon found herself stretched out on the sofa.

"Mmm, this is *exactly* what the doctor ordered," she said with a smile.

But the smile fled when she looked down at her feet. It was past time for the wretched shoes to come off, and Sage didn't know whether she could bend far enough to undo them.

"I'll never know if I don't try. Hey, maybe I should seek psychiatric help for talking to myself. I'd probably get a professional discount." Her words made her giggle. Maybe it was good Grace wasn't home.

Suddenly, the lyrics "rub my feet, gimme something good to eat" were running through her head. If she had even an ounce of energy left, she'd get up and put on her Shania Twain CD. Too bad she had no honey to come home to.

Just as she'd finished her hot chocolate and was beginning to nod off on the couch, the doorbell rang, making her sit straight up, then cry out at the kink in her neck. Rubbing her neck, she walked almost in a haze toward the front entry and opened the door like a zombie. Yes, she might have looked through the peephole first, but this was Sterling, Montana, where *crime* was a foreign word.

Okay, maybe *some* crime happened. There was the cow tipping, after all.

"Are you Sage Banks?"

"Yes?" She waited.

"I have a delivery for you. Sign here."

Sage took the clipboard and signed, and the man handed her a long, surprisingly heavy box and told her to have a nice day.

Oooh, she couldn't remember when she'd last received flowers. Come to think of it, she never had. Smiling, she took the box to the table and grabbed a kitchen knife, cut it open, then gasped at the aroma drifting upward. Inside were a dozen stargazer lilies, a couple of dozen pink roses, and so much greenery that it looked like a nursery was having a going-out-of-business sale.

After taking the flowers out carefully, she opened up the package inside the box and found a stunning crystal vase.

"Grandma?" she thought out loud before picking up the card.

I look forward to working with you. See you tonight.
Spence

Though she struggled valiantly not to be thrilled, she still couldn't stop the smile from breaking across her face as she filled the vase with water and began arranging the flowers inside it. She'd be sure to have a sore back from lifting the thing, but it was well worth it. She inhaled the fragrance of the flowers as she placed them in the center of the kitchen table.

After admiring them for several minutes, she turned her back and let the smell follow her from the room. The flowers were a welcome surprise, but she was going to have to let Spence know that he was her boss, and nothing more. They would have a strictly professional, working-only relationship. She'd have to discourage him from any further signs of hot pursuit.

A man like him was only out for the challenge, anyway. For probably the first time in his life, a woman wasn't falling at his feet, and he didn't know what to do. There were two possible outcomes for her. She could trip over her own feet in gratitude and he'd grow bored in a flash, or she could continue giving him the cold shoulder.

Either way, he'd eventually get tired of the game and it would end. At least if she shunned his advances, she'd have her pride when it was all over. Heaven forbid that she descend into the depths of obsession with that man again.

As she reached her room, she knew taking a nice long bath was out of the question. The second she climbed into the tub, she'd be out like a broken bulb and would probably drown beneath the water. As appealing as eternal rest sounded right then, she loved her life—for the most part—and had no desire to be found wrinkled, bloated, and blue in a bathtub.

After a quick shower, she dragged herself from the bathroom and practically fell into bed. In about five hours, the whole routine would start again. Work, eat, sleep. Ah, this was the life.

12

Wrapping her coat just a bit more tightly around her shoulders, Sage still shivered as she wandered through an outdoor mall in Billings. It was a day off and she'd made the insane decision to go Christmas shopping instead of staying in her pajamas all day long and alternating between taking naps and eating.

It seemed she never got enough food anymore. Yes, her job burned a lot of calories, but surely not enough to explain her constant hunger. And most of the foods she ate were empty calories, despite the lectures her grandmother had given her when she was young. As a doctor she knew what was healthy—she just chose to ignore all the good advice.

Stepping inside a store, not even bothering to look at the name, she shivered in the entry. This shopping wasn't going to last much longer. She'd found her grandmother a beautiful glass Eeyore that was sure to thrill her—the woman adored *Winnie the Pooh*—and a new cross-stitch project that would keep her busy all year.

Now to find something for Grace and she'd be all set. Why was it the hardest to buy gifts for your best friend? Probably because you always wanted it to be perfect, but you felt like you'd failed every time. Grace would never complain, so she should just grab something and go—make the half-hour drive back home and spend the rest of the night in her jammies, which really seemed to be calling to her. No. Grace would know for sure that she hadn't put forth any real effort. Dang it.

She could have at least gone to an indoor mall. Then she wouldn't feel like she was about to lose her fingers and toes. But the store she'd just entered pleased her instantly. It looked like a country cottage boutique instead of a modern store, and it had a nice selection of unusual gift items. If she wasn't able to find something for Grace in here, she might as well give up.

As she turned down an aisle, totally focused on the treasures in front of her, she bumped into another customer. Before she had a chance to apologize, the man spoke.

"Are you stalking me, Dr. Banks?"

That voice could melt butter on a below-freezing day. Spence was out shopping in the exact same place she was. What were the odds?

"After the flowers, I should be concerned that it's you stalking me," she replied, her heart beating a few paces faster than normal.

"I wish I were. We could have driven here together."

"Well, you know what they say about wishes,"

she said, causing a sparkle to light his eyes. "I'm sure you're very busy, as am I, so I'll see you tomorrow night at the hospital." She turned and bolted in the opposite direction. Grace didn't need a gift after all.

He caught up to her swiftly and followed her out of the store. "Since we're both here, let's have lunch together. I'm starving. Didn't get a chance to eat breakfast."

"I ate a late breakfast. Couldn't possibly have another thing," she lied. Good thing there was a lot of traffic outside or he'd hear the rumbling from her very empty stomach.

"I wanted to give you a performance evaluation. This is the perfect time," he said, playing his trump card.

Though it was her time off, she was curious what he thought about her work. She could cry inappropriate behavior, but something like this wasn't unusual in their community. Well, that he was chasing after her might be slightly unusual, but mixing business with pleasure—more specifically, eating—happened all the time.

"I suppose a cup of hot coffee wouldn't hurt," she said, and before she could change her mind, he had wound her arm through his and was leading her down the festively decorated sidewalk.

The tingling sensation of his fingers wrapping around her had nothing to do with hunger, well, not hunger for food, that was. No matter how much she

tried to avoid this man who she knew was only playing a game with her, he seemed to always be there.
And if the sparks she had felt for him while she was
a teenager had been strong, the passion building inside her as a woman was out of this world.

As soon as he opened the door to the food pavil-
ion, a loud growl broke the silence, and there could
be no doubt that it came from her stomach. She was
almost grateful, though, as it took her mind away
from the fact that she was craving something much
less proper.

"I thought you weren't hungry," he said with a
quiet laugh.

"A gentleman wouldn't call me on that."

Suddenly, his face was only an inch from hers,
and what was burning in his eyes had her feeling a
whole new level of desire. "Don't ever mistake me
for a gentleman, *Dr. Banks*."

Oooh, the man was lethal. Take-me-to-my-grave-
with-a-big-smile-on-my-face lethal.

"My mistake," she whispered, using the last of her
strength to back away from him. Her fingers shook,
so she clenched them together. But nothing was going to stop the wild beating of her heart.

"No, I would fully agree that you aren't a gentleman," she huskily whispered.

"I would be more than happy to show you how a
man treats a lady," he offered, sliding back into her
personal bubble.

"A real man doesn't have to take something that isn't offered," she challenged. If her voice was stronger, then maybe she would be more convincing.

He paused, his warm breath fanning her face and weakening her convictions by the second. But then, he backed away, and she realized she was holding her breath.

"What would you like to eat?" His change of subject threw her off for a minute, and she had to shake her head before she could clear the fog that had infused her brain.

Sage looked around at the different options and found a Cinnabon. That's where her cravings led her, but she knew she should have something with a bit more nutritional value. Maybe if she ate a salad first, she could finish with a big, warm, gooey cinnamon roll. That was a plan. Yes, she'd get a sugar high and then crash, but it was her day off, so she'd be fine.

"I'm getting a salad," she told him, and walked over to a counter with no line in front of it. Of course there was no line—people wanted pizza or Chinese food, not salads.

After she was handed her salad, she glanced over at the pizza place and saw Spence getting something to eat there. She made her way to the Cinnabon counter and placed her order. The two of them finished about the same time; he was carrying a box with pizza in it and a couple of plates on top, plus two steaming cups of coffee.

She thanked him warmly, oddly pleased that he knew how she liked her coffee. It was something silly, but it meant that he paid attention. *Okay, quit reading so much into this,* she warned herself. *It's just a stupid cup of coffee.*

"Nice . . . lunch," he said with a chuckle as he pointedly looked at her massive cinnamon roll and its embarrassing side of extra frosting.

"I have a salad," she said in self-defense as she speared some lettuce. "I even went for the vinaigrette instead of ranch."

"Ah, a good patient," he replied as he lifted a piece of pizza with extra cheese.

Her mouth watered. Pizza was good for you—it had something from all the food groups in it, even fruit if you got Hawaiian. Maybe she should just go get some and give up on the salad. She wasn't a rabbit, after all.

Before she could make a decision, he put a slice on an extra plate and slid it over to her. She knew she should refuse, but it smelled so good. What the heck! Lifting the pizza to her mouth, she groaned as she took her first bite.

"There is absolutely no good pizza in Sterling," she groused. "No pizza at all, in fact, but the frozen kind. Someone should really open up a place."

"I heard that someone turned in a proposal at the last city council meeting, but I didn't follow through or ask any questions. I don't care that much, I guess." He shrugged eloquently.

"How can you not care about great pizza?" She knew she was overreacting, but as she finished her slice, having a nearby pizza parlor seemed of utmost importance. She'd worry about healthier eating when she was in her thirties—heck, maybe her forties.

He looked at her with a supremely serious expression. "I will make sure to take far more notice of all pizza locations within a hundred-mile radius."

Sage realized how ridiculous she was being. Sitting back, she grinned as their eyes met. "Okay, that was a bit extreme. I blame it on working too much."

"If we should be worried about anything in Sterling, it should be the lack of a good barbershop. I mean, I have seen some horrendous haircuts in our town."

"I understand where you're coming from. When I was in California, a bad haircut was grounds for calling in sick and hiding away in your ridiculously tiny cockroach-infested apartment."

The two laughed as they began comparing stories of her time in California and his in Seattle. Sage was thinking that she'd been the one who'd gotten the bad end of the deal. Though Seattle was much colder and rainier than Stanford, at least he hadn't had to deal with the mind-blowing bug population she'd put up with for the last four years.

"Will you go back when you're done?" Suddenly, he was serious, all traces of a smile disappearing from his face.

Sage thought about it. When she'd first arrived in California, she'd been convinced it was where she'd live the rest of her life. And yet now, after being back home for a mere five months, she knew she was a small-town girl.

The saddest part was that the place she'd been living for four years had been more than easy to walk away from. She'd been able to fit her minuscule amount of possessions in her car, and it had taken only a couple of phone calls to change her address.

There were no connections, no friends she'd ever call again. She'd gone out a few times, but the faces would soon fade away. They were temporary friends in a shallow world. That wasn't who she was, wasn't who she wanted to be.

"I would go to the beaches on the coast, but I could never live in California again. It was fun, and I'm glad I got out of Sterling for as long as I did—I hope to take a great job somewhere else eventually, but not in a huge city. It's just too impersonal, too hard to make friends. Everyone seems to be so focused on their own lives and their futures that there isn't time to build real relationships. Living here, I know that if I disappeared tomorrow, a search party would begin almost immediately. It's not like that in big cities, I didn't even tell my roommates I was leaving; I just left them a note with the final month's rent. Not one of them has bothered to call to see if it was legit. That's how much my leaving was noticed." She winced almost imperceptibly.

"Well, it's their loss, Sage, and our gain," Spence said as he reached across the table and took her hand.

For a moment, she was unable to speak, unable to look away from his beguiling gaze as his thumb rubbed across her knuckles. Every moment she was in this man's presence another chink in her armor was chipped away. If she believed this was all real, she would gladly climb into his lap and beg him to take her. But how could it be real? All the rumors spoke of him being nothing more than a playboy, that he liked the conquest and then lost interest. With how intensely she already felt about him, she didn't think she would be able to emotionally handle being one of his castoffs.

"I'm not worried," she finally said, firmly tugging on her hand as she tried to regain her equilibrium. She couldn't keep having these intense moments with Spence. If she continued to get lost in his eyes, he'd never take her word that she wasn't interested in him. His next words proved that.

"Why fight so hard against it, Sage? It's obvious we're attracted to each other. We can keep it professional at work and . . . not so professional afterward. I think we have just the right amount of chemistry to set off some explosions."

She was melting slightly at his words until he finished his last sentence. Then she was fighting a grin. "Explosions? Really, Spence?" It was exactly what she'd needed to hear to clear her head.

"What?" He looked confused.

She finally got her hand free and felt slightly superior. "I have to admit that you were pulling me in there with your suave talk—just a little—and then you said 'explosions.' If that hadn't been such a cheesy line, with little to no imagination, you might have just had my heart racing," she said with a saucy smile.

"I wasn't being cheesy."

"Oh come on, Spence. You're a surgeon, for goodness' sake. Your ego is the size of a small country—no, scratch that, we're talking Russia. I'm amazed you manage to fit through doorways with such a big head. To top that off, you're wealthy and gorgeous, and you have a body that should be illegal to display in public. You can wipe the grin off your face. I'm in no way complimenting you. I'm just saying that with all that going for you, you certainly don't need to chase me to get your rocks off, and you *really* don't need to use cheesy pickup lines. Why don't you just go stand on the street corner and smile? You'll most likely cause a car to crash into you and then be lucky enough to have female paramedics stripping you down to give you a *full* exam."

His mouth was hanging open as she stood up from the table. She gathered her packages and leaned down to encroach on his space. It was nice to feel in charge for the first time since he'd taken the job as her boss.

Shock therapy. If only she'd realized that sooner.

"I have to say that you look even better all wide-eyed and speechless," she whispered huskily before turning and walking from the food court with a self-satisfied smirk. She would give herself ten points for ingenuity and a hundred points for leaving the oh-so-popular Spence Whitman dumbstruck. Surely that was a first.

As she climbed into her car, her smile faded just a tad. She'd doubtlessly face retribution when he had a second to catch his breath. Still, her moment of victory had been well worth it.

The heater actually turned on in her car, and Sage found herself whistling as she made the drive back home. And to top it all off, the roads were clear.

13

"Sage, can you come in here please?" Mo always had a way of making things sound like an order, even when phrased as a question. That was probably why she was so feared and respected at the same time. The thing was that most of the time the woman was right, and had a killer gut instinct about people in general. It was either because she'd been a nurse for thirty-plus years or because the woman was a psychic, or maybe she was just a freaking genius.

Upon entering the room, Sage noticed that Mo had the new male nurse with her who had a habit of *knowing everything* even though he was just beginning in his profession. He'd graduated top of his class and therefore didn't think he had anything to learn. Sage almost felt sorry for the boy, because she knew that Mo was now taking him under her wing and before long, he would be sobbing at the woman's feet.

"Sage, have you been formally introduced to Brian?" Mo asked with her knowing smirk.

"No, not yet," Sage said as she came closer.

"Nice to meet you, Sage," Brian said as he shook her hand a little longer than necessary. Then the boy, who in actuality was only a couple of years younger than her, took it a step too far and began openly undressing her with his eyes. Her sympathy for him washed away as she sent a look to Mo that told the woman to give him everything he deserved. Mo sent Sage a wink.

"If I had known they made doctors as sexy as you, I would have certainly gone to medical school instead of taking the nursing program."

Apparently undressing her with his eyes hadn't been enough. Sage sent him a syrupy sweet smile, and then patted his head before speaking.

"Honey, you couldn't have handled medical school." He looked confused for a moment when the tone of her voice didn't match what she was saying, and then his eyes narrowed the slightest bit before his lips turned up in an arrogant smile.

"Ah, I love a woman with a sense of humor," he chortled, making her want to kick him.

"And I love a man who knows his place," she said back, beginning to lose her cool just the tiniest bit. This kid was a punk.

"Brian, this is John Duncan," Mo said, interrupting what soon would have been an entertaining tirade by Sage. "He's a patient who comes in here frequently after overdosing on narcotics."

"Looks pretty harmless," Brian said as he looked disdainfully at the guy on the table who was in a narcotic-induced slumber.

"Sage, I was thinking we needed to reverse his overdose with Narcan."

It took a moment for Sage to realize what was going on, and then it took everything inside her not to give away what she knew what was about to happen.

"Yes, I agree," she said with a straight face. Any of the staff who had been at the hospital for even a month knew John well as a frequent patient to the ER. It was also well known that he was *very* sensitive to Narcan, and when it was administered he would wake up suddenly and start swinging at whoever was closest to him.

Although Sage's disdain for Brian was growing by the second, she felt guilty about throwing him to the wolves, so the least she could do was give him a bit of a warning.

"Brian, John is very sensitive to Narcan, and when it's given too quickly it will reverse his sleeping state immediately and you may get hurt if you're standing too close." As she was warning Brian she saw Mo leaning up against the wall sipping coffee to hide her smile. Mo always did enjoy a good show, especially on a slow night as this one had been.

"Listen, I may be new, but I'm not stupid." Sage had to control her own temper as he looked down his nose at her before he took the syringe full of medication, walked confidently to John's bedside, and injected it into his IV hard and fast. Then he turned to smirk at Mo and send another leer to Sage.

That was his first mistake.

His second mistake was swiveling his head just in time to catch John Duncan's fist with his face. The sudden punch landed him hard on the ground and knocked him out cold.

Mo's laughter rendered her useless as she was doubled over, spilling her coffee. Sage simply looked at the entire scene in disbelief and then took the next few moments to reassure John that everything would be okay before she decided she'd better check on Brian.

"Mo, that was mean," she said as she kneeled next to the unconscious nurse.

"He was asking for it. The pompous little twerp won't let me teach him and acts like he knows everything. Besides, you did give him fair warning. He ignored you," Mo said between fits of laughter.

"You know, one of these days, you're going to get in trouble," Sage warned, but her own lips were twitching as Brian slowly began to come to on the floor.

"Ah, girlie, I don't do it to the good ones," Mo said, not at all remorseful.

"Wait a minute. Did you do anything to me?" Sage asked as she tried to recollect any mishaps while with Mo in the very beginning.

"That's something you'll never know," Mo said with a wink as Brian awoke fully and sat up, still in a daze.

"You're a terrible woman," Sage said, her words carrying no bite.

"It's what keeps me young and beautiful," Mo said with another wink.

"What in the hell happened?" Brian yelled, making John stir in his bed.

"You didn't listen, that's what happened," Mo said, directing the young nurse's attention to her.

"What the hell? Did that guy punch me?"

"He sure did. And I thought you said he was harmless," Mo said, not even trying to hide her mirth.

"I could sue you," Brian said, hatred flying from his eyes.

"Go ahead and try it, sonny," Mo said, her lips no longer twitching.

Sage almost, not quite, but almost felt sorry for the nurse because she knew he wouldn't be working at the hospital too much longer, probably not beyond the night.

"Why don't we take you to one of the on-call rooms so you can lie down?" Sage said, not wanting to touch the man, but trying to help him stand.

"I don't need you to doctor me. You're just a freaking resident," Brian snapped, no longer flirty.

"That's fine with me," Sage said as she stood upright and backed away from the spluttering kid.

Spence and two other nurses arrived just then to see what all of the commotion was about. It only took a few moments for them to assess the scene, and all three of them covered their mouths as they tried to hide their amusement.

"This woman messed with my training and put me in a situation to be harmed," Brian gushed as he looked up at Spence.

Spence stuck out a hand and helped the nurse up before turning to Mo. "What happened, Mo?" Even though he was asking, it was already pretty obvious.

"John came in again and we woke him up. Sage warned the new nurse what happens when John wakes up, but he refused to listen," Mo said, a twinkle back in her eyes.

Turning to Brian, Spence got a stern look on his face. "I've had several complaints that you refuse to listen. This time, it landed you on the floor." There was no arguing with Spence when he used that tone.

"I'm so through with this Podunk town and this crappy teaching hospital," Brian snapped as he glared at each of them and then stomped from the room.

Spence turned and looked at Mo with a brow raised.

Mo held her hands up in mock defense. "Hey, I was only trying to show the kid the ropes. It's not my fault if he doesn't listen."

"Well then. It looks like you're going to have a new nurse to train tomorrow, Mo," Spence said as he turned and walked from the room.

"I knew the first night that boy wouldn't last," Mo

said to Sage as they followed Spence and the other nurses from the room.

Sage thought that John Duncan must be scratching his head, thinking he'd been admitted into a psychiatric hospital instead of his usual place. Yes, it was crazy, but tonight had been pure entertainment.

"I'm sure glad I haven't gotten on your bad side, Mo," Sage said.

"Ah, girlie, you're too pure to get on anyone's bad side," Mo replied with her cackle.

"I don't know. Spence sure as heck gets irritated with me often enough."

"That's because you're a hot woman," Mo said as she moved toward the exit. "I'm taking a smoke break. Unless the entire town of Sterling shows up, I don't want to be interrupted."

With that, Mo left Sage, and the emergency department went back to its calm setting. At least Sage couldn't say that her job was boring. There always seemed to be something new happening.

14

Standing outside with the snow drifting down while she tilted her face up to the dark skies, Sage laughed in delight. This was something she'd certainly missed while living in the hot sun of California. Yes, it made driving a true pain, but who cared when you got to feel the delicate flakes of snow fall on your tongue and melt in your mouth.

"You seem to be enjoying yourself."

Sage jumped at the sound of Spence's voice and turned to find him beside her. "I'm not playing," she insisted. "It was just really slow, so I thought I'd come out for a breath of fresh air."

"Take all the time you want to stand out here and play . . . er . . . get some air. You're right, it is a slow night."

"Yes. I normally love to keep busy, but after the last couple of shifts, this is perfect. I just hope the newly fallen snow doesn't cause a mountain of accidents."

"Most of the people here are smart enough to not go out unless they have the proper vehicle," he said, then looked pointedly toward the parking lot. "You won't be driving yours home. The roads won't get plowed until morning."

"I'll be fine. I'll just drive really slowly. Besides, I'm out of here in an hour. The roads will be cushioned without being icy," she said as she spun in a circle, causing the flakes falling all around her to swirl in her human tornado.

"As I said, you *won't* be driving home. I looked at that car of yours. It's not fit for the roads of Montana."

"Look, Dr. Whitman, just because I don't have some fancy-schmancy truck doesn't mean I'm a menace to the highways. I'll take it slow." She hated that he felt he had the right to come out here during her moment of peace and say whatever pleased him.

Do this! Do that! Move it, Dr. Banks. In the ER she couldn't complain about Spence's orders, but when it came to what and when she drove, he didn't have a leg to stand on. And since he had such fine legs, that was a shame.

"We can argue more about it in an hour," he said peremptorily.

She looked at him while he stuck out his tongue to catch a snowflake. Despite his last words, for him, the subject was finished. He'd had his say, and in his opinion the conversation was over and done with.

Sage scooped up a large mass of snow and began forming a ball. She was nearly finished when he noticed what she was doing, and he took a cautious step backward.

"Now, Dr. Banks, I would just put that down slowly if I were you."

"I'm not you, Spence. Why so formal all of a sudden?"

"Retaliation will be swift and furious," he warned her with a gleam in his eyes that she should have tuned in to.

But she'd never been able to resist a challenge, and the snowball in her hand and his arrogant smile were just too much to resist. Without giving it much conscious thought, she let the ball fly from her palm. It whizzed through the air, aimed with deadly accuracy right at his incredulous eyes. But he turned at the last second and the snow exploded against the side of his head.

He lifted a hand and wiped the snow from his hair. "I can't believe you actually threw that."

She was already regretting her impulsive decision. She'd started a war with only one possible outcome, and that wasn't her victory. Still, if she was going down, she'd do it fighting. First, she'd attempt escape, but if that didn't work, it would be all weapons set on automatic fire.

"That was my pager," she said, and she immediately turned and began running toward the side doors she'd come through earlier.

"Not gonna happen, Sage. Mine would be going

off, too, but good try," he yelled, his voice seeming to be only inches behind her ear.

She tried to pick up her pace but found herself sliding—beneath the fresh layer of snow was packed ice. She was going to fall flat on her rear if she didn't slow up. Of course, she was going to fall if she stood still.

She'd take her chances with the snow. Speeding up, she saw freedom in her sights when suddenly, strong arms wrapped around her waist, spinning her around and stealing the breath from her lungs, and then she and Spence were launching into the air.

"We're going down," he said, stating the obvious.

Sage cried out, expecting this to hurt, but he somehow managed to turn them around before they fell, and his back landed with a splash in the snow while she bounced against his chest—his delectably hard chest.

"Mmm, now this isn't bad," he said as he brought his hands up to cradle her head.

Finally on the verge of feeling what it would be like to touch him, what his taste would be, what passion he could invoke, Sage almost took his mouth with hers. But before she lost complete control, her hands, almost of their own accord, scooped up another large mound of snow, which she dumped right in his face, leaving him sputtering. He released her in his attempt to clear his air passages.

She twisted off his body and was attempting to rise to her feet when he snaked his arms around her again and she landed in his lap.

"Let me go," she said, but a giggle burst free. She couldn't help it. She hadn't roughhoused in the snow since she was a little girl, and though it was freezing out, she was having more fun than she could remember having in years.

"Not until I get my payback," he said, and she found herself on her back, the snow making a crater around her body. Her ears grew numb with cold.

"Okay, okay, you win," she cried as snow melted and slid into her ear canal. "It's cold as sin out here!"

"I could douse you like you just did to me." One of his hands pinned her arms above her head while the other gathered a huge handful of snow.

"No, no, no! You win!" She closed her eyes and waited for impact. Payback was terrible, but she knew she deserved it.

When nothing happened, she cracked her eyes open and looked up. With the fire that was burning in his gaze, she was amazed there was any snow at all left around them. It should have all turned into steam.

"I have to taste you."

He bent down, and Sage thought about resistance for all of half a second. The moment his lips touched hers, she was lost in a pool of heat and desire so strong she didn't recognize the feelings.

His lips demanded that hers part, and she complied, opening herself to him, tilting her head, squirming beneath his strong, solid, hot body. Oh, this was a first kiss to end all kisses. This man wasn't messing around. When he released her hands, she grabbed his head, holding him to her, wanting more.

When his hand slipped up her side and rested on her shoulder, she pushed against him. Just a little lower, she thought. His tongue sank into her mouth, tasted her thoroughly before retreating, leaving her wanting more.

"Sage," he whispered as he pulled back.

She moaned her disapproval, wanting this to go on, needing him to continue heating her from the inside out.

"Sage, you're going to get frostbite."

His head was too far away. That was her only thought. She needed him to lean down again. Passion burned in his eyes, and to judge from the hardness she could feel pressing against her core, he was also rather excited about their kiss—so why was he pulling back?

It took a few seconds, but once the freezing snow registered in her brain and the fog of passion began to clear, Sage realized what he was saying. Her back was numb where she'd been cushioned against the white powder.

Spence had a thick layer of snow in his hair, and as her vision went past him, she noticed that the stuff was falling down even harder than it had been a few minutes before.

"Oh," she whispered, her mouth opening, making it easy for snowflakes to fall inside.

"Let's get you indoors. We're not dressed for this. We can always finish in the on-call room." He stood up, grabbed her hand, and hoisted her to her feet.

She moved slowly beside him as they neared the doors. Once inside, as a welcome blast of heat hit her, she was racked with uncontrollable tremors. Her scrubs were soaked, and she was glad that he'd come to his senses. *She* certainly hadn't been worried about hypothermia.

"I need to change," she said through chattering teeth.

He walked next to her. "Why don't I assist you?"

"I don't think so. We're at work, Dr. Whitman." She took off down the hall, thankful no one was around. And more than thankful that he'd allowed her to go. She just needed five minutes. That was all.

Sure. Five minutes was really going to help her fight her attraction to Spence, especially when he seemed to have her in his sights for the foreseeable future. While her brain was telling her this was not what she wanted, her body was screaming that it was well past time to take a chance and feel the heat of a lover—to feel the passion so many others had experienced.

With a shake to clear her clouded head, she changed clothes, then hid in dark corners of the hospital for the rest of her shift. If she was lucky, she'd get away without further run-ins with her hot boss.

Of course, when had she ever been that lucky?

15

Sage sneaked around the corner and peeked out. The coast was clear. She'd managed to avoid Spence through the end of her shift—no trauma patients, no one needing her to keep her on the clock beyond her scheduled time.

Now she just had to get out of this building and safely home. After zipping down the hall, she craned her neck to look around the final corner and smiled when there was no sign of Spence anywhere. She was home free.

Once through the outside door, Sage took a step back at the force of the snow blowing toward her. It had been coming down hard less than an hour ago, but right now it looked like a blizzard. The wind had picked up and the snow was pelting her.

But there was no way she'd admit defeat. Determined to make it home on her own, she figured it would take her two hours to make the fifteen-mile trip. Where was a snowmobile when you needed one?

She had to keep her head down as she trudged to the employee parking lot. When she spotted her car, she nearly cried. About eight inches of snow were piled up on the thing, and there was no sign of a road anywhere. Was she really going to let her pride compromise her safety?

As she turned back toward the hospital, unable to even see the building through the thick snow that was falling, she squared her shoulders. Yep. It looked like she was.

After scraping the snow away from the door with her gloved hands, she was nearly a Popsicle by the time she was able to unlock the car. She sat down in the seat, shivering uncontrollably, and missed the ignition on her first try.

Using one hand to steady the other, she finally got the key in. Once the vehicle warmed up, this situation wouldn't look so bleak. She cranked the key, and her car groaned. "Come on, baby. You can do this. Just start for me now and I swear I'll get you to the shop for a full tune-up." She didn't care even remotely that she was speaking to a blasted car.

She turned the key again, and the car coughed but refused to start. "Come on!" she snapped, and slammed her palms against the steering wheel in a mini tantrum. Her fury was suddenly interrupted by the opening of her door, and Spence leaning into her space.

"Well, this is interesting. First, you cajole the car, make promises you most likely aren't planning on keeping, and then you beat it when you don't get your way."

"What are you doing here?"

"I wanted to see if you really were foolish enough to try to drive your little death trap in this weather. I was hoping you wouldn't be so stubborn as to risk your life, but I was sadly mistaken." He propped the door open, allowing a torrent of wind and snow to fall over her lap.

"Spence, you're letting the snow soak the inside of my car," she said as she tried to get hold of the handle and pull the door closed.

He stuck out his hand. "Then grab your purse and let's get out of the cold."

"I told you I could get home, and I can," she replied, refusing to budge. Yes, she knew she wasn't going anywhere, but he didn't have to know that. If she could get the car started, she'd warm up and then figure out a respectable plan B.

"Well then, it will be a long, cold walk, because as of twenty minutes ago, they closed the road that leads home."

"Okay, if that's the case, then how in the heck were you planning on getting home, much less getting me there?"

It looked as if she'd be stuck in the on-call room tonight. That would be almost as pleasant as freezing to death in her car. She weighed her options.

"Luckily, I have a brother who loves me," he said matter-of-factly.

"What does that have to do with anything?" This was a ridiculous conversation.

"Camden just so happens to own a couple of snowmobiles," he said, looking triumphant as he presented the ace up his sleeve.

"Well, they can only carry two people, so unless Camden can tow one behind him, you won't be able to take me anyway," she said, hiding her disappointment. The smidgen of hope of getting home quickly deflated.

"Since Michael is driving one, there will be two extra seats," Spence said. "They should be here within ten minutes. If you don't mind the cots in the on-call room, be my guest. I'm heading home, where it's warm and quiet."

When he turned to walk away, she was filled with panic. It wasn't really so bad to get a ride. It would be a very cold ride, but tomorrow was the start of her first full two days off in months. She really didn't want to be at this hospital when she didn't have to be. Besides, she could ride behind Camden or Michael—she didn't have to be snuggled up to Spence for the ride.

"Wait!" she called out, and he turned. It was probably a good thing she couldn't see his expression. Any smugness she detected there would probably make her change her mind—and she had no doubt he was feeling pretty smug right now.

"Did you need some help back inside?"

His feigned innocence disgusted her. How could she ever have thought that he'd make this easier on her?

"I would . . . um . . . well, if there's an extra seat . . ." The words practically choked her.

"Let's go into the hospital and warm up. I told Michael to bring extra snow clothes so you won't freeze during the ride."

Sage gazed at his blurry image. That was it? No gloating, no dancing in circles of victory? He wasn't going to rub it in a bit that she'd ended up doing what he wanted? Maybe he was just waiting to gloat later because it was so cold out here right now. Sage climbed out of her car and then quickly followed Spence back inside.

It seemed no time at all had passed when she heard Cam call out, "Taxi service is here." He was standing in the doorway holding a large bag and smiling.

"Glad to see you. I've spent enough time on these hospital cots. Don't want to do it if I don't have to," Spence said.

"I couldn't leave you here," Camden said. "The sound of your pleading voice was incentive to come and pick you up."

"Damn, it's colder than a witch's—"

Spence broke in. "That's enough, Michael."

"Here are your clothes, Sage," Camden said. "Get changed so we can head on out of here."

"Thanks. I appreciate it," Sage said, taking the bag and quickly scooting away.

When she came back out, she felt like the Abominable Snowman, and she was already sweating. Maybe she wouldn't end up feeling so cold after all.

"Let's head out," Michael told them, and they all braved the thickly falling snow.

Camden climbed onto one of the snowmobiles, and before Sage could join him, Michael was on behind him.

"Let's go," Spence said as he climbed onto the other.

"I . . . I was going to ride with—"

"We need to go," Spence said as he revved the motor on Camden's toy.

Sage wasn't happy about this, but what could she do? After climbing on behind him, she was trying to sit at a distance when the machine jerked forward and she almost fell off backward.

"Hold on tight, Sage. We won't be able to talk." Then they were shooting forward, through the snow.

Sage buried her face against Spence's shoulder as he maneuvered through the snowstorm. Even with the warm clothes, her body was racked with shivers, and she couldn't lift her head from Spence's shoulder; she was afraid her face would fall off if she did.

Spence slowed and turned his head so she could hear him. "Are you okay?" he asked.

Her teeth were chattering so hard she couldn't answer. Maybe she should have just stayed at the hospital. This hadn't been such a good idea.

"No, you aren't okay. We're going to make a pit

stop," he said, and she couldn't even process the words, she was so miserable.

Vaguely, she heard Spence speaking to his brothers, but it was nearly impossible to hear, so she just held on and prayed the ride would soon come to an end. When he spoke a few minutes later, she let out a sigh of relief.

"We're at my place, Sage. We need to go inside," Spence said, and she noticed they weren't moving through the snow anymore, but still she found herself unable to move. Was she going into shock? Maybe. She tried to assess her own condition.

Before long she found herself inside a place where blessed heat was biting at her face. The bitter wind and snow had disappeared, but she was still freezing.

"You need to warm up quickly," he told her, and she felt herself being lifted. Instead of pulling away, she snuggled closer to him, though with all the clothes between them, the body heat she was seeking couldn't be found.

When he set her down and she felt him tugging on her boots, she didn't resist. Finally, the snow clothes were removed and she felt the heat from the house trying to soak into her frozen skin, but nothing seemed likely to work.

"Where are your brothers?" she asked through chattering teeth.

"They went on to our dad's to check on him."

That was when she realized they were not only at his place, but they were alone. Heat began seeping back inside her, but it was a whole different kind of heat from what she wanted right now. Then again, maybe not. Maybe this was the heat she needed.

Looking up, her eyes connected with Spence's, and she found herself again without words. What was going to happen next? Sage needed to figure out, and quickly, whether she was going to allow anything to happen, because after their earlier romp in the snow, she knew that it would take only the smallest encouragement to get her into Spence's bed.

"This isn't a good idea, Spence." Maybe if she was direct, they could act like reasonable adults.

"The two of us coming together seems like an excellent idea to me, Sage." He began closing the gap between them. When he wrapped his arms around her and pulled her close, Sage still didn't know what she was going to do. When he bent down and kissed her, even her will to think fled.

16

After washing her face, Sage glanced in the mirror and cringed at her mussed hair and glowing cheeks. Spence knew how to kiss—that was for dang sure. He had turned her to jelly in five seconds flat, and then had continued to tease her body for the next fifteen minutes.

And somehow, when she'd finally managed to pull back—she was amazed that her legs had been able to hold her up—he'd let her go. He clearly wanted to make love to her, and she knew she wanted that same thing.

But Sage had never been a stupid woman—she usually lived up to her name. And she'd never been one to make impulsive choices. She was the responsible one, the one who had put school ahead of all else, who had received the best grades. She was the girl who stayed in to study while her peers went out to clubs.

She wasn't about to start making mistakes now. And besides the fact that Spence was currently her boss—who was taking notes on her performances and could determine whether she became a critical-care surgeon or not—he was also the one who'd broken her heart.

To sleep with this man, to have a one-night stand or, even worse, a short affair, wouldn't be wise. So here she was, hiding in his luxurious bathroom while she tried to decide her next move.

Sage could insist he take her home, but since she'd arrived at his place, the storm had picked up even more, and was leaving the wisest decision? If they got lost and froze to death, that wasn't going to do anyone any good. Not that she'd know anything about it later . . .

The real question was whether she'd be able to sleep in the same house as this tempting man without ending up in the sack. She didn't know how strong she was, but she'd soon find out.

Figuring she'd hidden long enough, Sage left the bathroom and made her way back down his curved staircase, her hand trailing along the mahogany railing as she moved soundlessly, cushioned by the thick cream carpeting. Stepping onto the wood parquet floor covered by a stunning Oriental rug, she was surprised to find Spence's home so stately yet comfortable.

He didn't seem the type to have a Waterford chandelier hanging from the sixteen-foot ceiling, or to have a gleaming white marble fireplace as the centerpiece of the room. Stunning ten-foot-high windows offering a gorgeous view of the thick falling snow made this her dream living room.

Spence was sitting comfortably on the leather

sofa, flipping through the pages of a magazine, certainly looking like the king of his domain.

"I wouldn't have taken you for the type of man to have such a . . . um . . . warm and romantic home," Sage said, breaking the silence. He didn't stir, confirming to her that he had known she had entered the room.

"I bought the place last month. I didn't design it," he said.

"Well, you still chose it. It's pretty great. I love the antique fixtures in the bathroom." She shifted on her feet, not knowing if she should sit or not.

"Thank you. My brother actually found them. Michael can be quite the . . . romantic," he said, finally looking up and capturing her gaze.

"Yeah, that's what I've heard," she said, trying to relax.

"Why don't you sit down and join me?" he asked, patting the cushion next to him. Okay, good, he wasn't bringing up their hot make-out session. That was a positive.

"What are you reading?" she asked as she sat and tried to relax. It wasn't easy to forget about the fact that the two of them were all alone on a night perfect for making love.

He was gazing right at her, and his eyes were hot enough to melt her, even though her body still felt frozen. Without his expression changing, he answered, "*WebMD* magazine."

"It seems like forever since I've read for fun," she said with a sigh as she curled her legs up underneath her, trying to get the shaking to stop. She worried she might never feel warm again.

"You have to take some moments for the pleasures in life, Sage, or you will burn out."

"I can't even remember what pleasure is all about," she told him with a humorless laugh.

"That's what I'm here for . . . to remind you."

She froze at the clear look of desire he was directing her way. "Spence, I'm so exhausted and cold that I can't analyze every little thing you say, so can you turn the heat levels down just a little?" She didn't break eye contact as she made her request.

"You aren't warming up, are you?" This time, it was concern in his eyes.

"No. I can't stop shaking," she admitted.

"All right, time for the hot tub," he told her, and she shook her head. "Doctor's orders," he added as he stood up.

"I can't. I don't have a swimsuit," she said, though the warmth of a hot tub sounded like pure heaven.

"Wear your undies. They cover as much as or more than a swimsuit," he told her, and Sage tried to figure out which ones she was wearing. Were they modest enough? "I'll turn around while you get in, and then the water will cover you."

"Fine," she said before she could chicken out. She really was cold.

Spence led her to the bathroom off the back deck, where his hot tub was located. The deck was covered, but a shiver still racked her body when she stepped up to the French doors with only a towel covering her modest underclothes.

She would have to step into the cold before she could enter the hot tub. "Come on. The deck is clear. Just walk quickly. I already have it open and ready," Spence said as he stepped up beside her.

Taking a breath, she rushed through the doors, dropped the towel, and then quickly climbed down into the hot tub, the warm water stinging her frozen limbs as she submerged herself.

"Ah, this is exactly what we needed," Spence said as he climbed in beside her, giving her a glimpse of his impressive chest before the water covered him to his neck.

Scooting to the far side of the hot tub, Sage eyed Spence warily, but he didn't make a move toward her, so she leaned back after a minute, finally beginning to relax as warmth seeped into her skin and the cold finally evaporated.

The coolness on her face and the heat of the water were a perfect combination and she soon found herself feeling human once again. When she began to drift, she felt a wave in the water, and as her eyelids cracked open, she found herself looking into Spence's eyes.

"Want to play a game?"

"I don't think I could win any game against you, Spence," she said. She couldn't back away—he'd left her nowhere to go.

"Come on, Sage. Don't chicken out on me." He brought his hand up and rubbed the top of her shoulder, which was peeking out from the water.

"What game can we play in the hot tub, Spence?"

"Hmm, truth or dare, of course," he said with a gleam in his eyes.

"Fine," she said, shocking herself and him.

"Good. I get to go first," he said as he leaned back, giving her a little breathing room. "Truth or dare?"

"Truth." She hesitated for only a moment before uttering the word.

"When did you have your first kiss?" he asked.

Sending him a glare, she hesitated only a minute before answering him. "I was fifteen the first time. It was with Basal, the foreign exchange student my sophomore year of high school. He could *really* kiss," she said, thinking back with a fond smile.

"Oh really?" His eyebrows went up in shock.

"I'm not always the innocent little girl, you know."

"Come on, Sage," he said in disbelief. "Since meeting you again, I've had a few flashbacks, and I remember your reputation. And from what I've heard recently, that reputation stayed with you in college."

Bluff called! "You were checking up on me?" she asked, irritated, forgetting all about their little game.

"I've learned everything I can about you, Sage."

The way he said it was a challenge. She just didn't understand what the challenge was.

"Maybe I also know all about you, Spence Whitman."

"Do tell." He wasn't at all fazed by her words.

"Some things should remain secret," she said, not wanting to play games with him anymore.

"You can't start this conversation and then just stop," he said, moving closer once again.

"I wasn't the one who started it," she insisted.

"Yeah, but you don't want to run, do you, Sage? You like exactly what's going on between us," he said, his arms coming up on either side of her, boxing her in. The problem wasn't his closeness; the problem was the fact that she wanted him even closer.

Knowing she was falling for him, knowing she was about to cave, she spun around, kneeling on her seat, facing his spacious yard while leaving her back to him.

"Are you trying to hide, Sage?" he asked as his chest pressed against her back.

"Yes," she said, not even recognizing her own voice.

"I don't think I'm going to let you," he said, his mouth grazing her ear and sending shivers down her spine that had nothing to do with the freezing night air.

"I'm not sure I can resist you," she told him, and his lips, which had been grazing her neck, stopped in their tracks.

"Then don't." He resumed his assault on her neck, wrapped his hands around her waist, and pulled her back tightly against his chest. "Tell me to stop if you don't want this to lead where we both know it's going to."

Sage leaned against the edge of the tub, the jets massaging the front of her while his hands trailed across the skin of her stomach and his mouth slid over her neck. Did she tell him to stop, or did she let this take its natural course?

What did she want?

17

"Do you want me to stop?"

Stop? Why would he possibly stop when this felt so good? Somewhere, buried deep in the back of her mind, Sage knew she should indeed call a halt. She just didn't know why. And if she couldn't figure that out, wasn't it time to finally see what all the fuss was about? It was now a bit ridiculous to be a virgin. She could only use school and work as an excuse for so long.

As a doctor she knew how the body worked, knew it was chemicals and hormones. But as a woman, she had no clue what she was experiencing. Whatever it was, though, it was fantastic. And stopping was the last thing on her mind.

As Spence's hands now brushed the undersides of her breasts, her body pulsed with need. When he shifted her, lining up her body in the most perfect way with the pulsing jets, she felt heat building inside, felt something she'd never felt before.

"More," she groaned, wanting to feel his hands come over the mounds of her breasts, to caress her nipples.

"More," he agreed, and then he cupped her, his fingers squeezing her aching peaks through her bra, and a guttural cry of need escaped her throat as she leaned back, her head resting on his chest while he continued his exquisite ministrations.

His fingers found the front clasp of her bra, and then, thankfully, he freed her from the sodden material. Finally his hands were on her skin, his thumbs rubbing across her nipples, making her cry out in pleasure as he twisted them, making them even harder than before.

Spence's hands began moving all over her body, caressing her sides and her breasts again, and then lower, tracing the curve of her hips and proceeding to the inside of her legs. He spread her thighs and centered her core on one of the jets, making her writhe in front of him.

"Spence," she cried weakly, unsure of what she was feeling.

"Enjoy it," he whispered before his lips traced her ear. With one hand he encircled an aching breast, while with the other he reached inside her panties and ran a finger down her folds, spreading them and sliding easily inside her heat.

She wanted more, needed more. Her body knew what it wanted, and she was following the commands it was issuing. When he pulled back, she whimpered until he turned her around and looked into her eyes, his own green depths burning with desire.

"I want to take you now," Spence said.

"Then have me," she said on a sigh before he bent down and captured her lips, needing both to give and to take.

Sliding his hands slowly over her hips, he drew her panties down her slim legs, leaving her naked for his pleasure. She was burning up, both from the water and from the inferno he was building inside of her.

And still it wasn't enough.

He let go of her long enough to discard his shorts, and then she was being lifted to the side of the hot tub. He spread her legs wide so he could see all of her secrets. She wanted to hide, but as his head descended and his hot tongue traced the outer folds of her heat, she lost any impulse to fight.

The cold air on her wet skin made her nipples tighten painfully, while the hot water and steam from the tub rose up to fight the chill. He kissed her core, letting his tongue swirl around her most sensitive area, and then suddenly she was flying, her body releasing in an explosion of pleasure so great she almost lost consciousness under the barrage of fireworks in her body.

As the last of her tremors subsided, she felt herself being pulled back into the water, the gentle heat warming her cooled limbs as Spence pulled her on top of him, her thighs spread over his, his erection pressing against her core, begging for entrance.

She needed to tell him. He should know . . .

But she couldn't say the words. In a blissful euphoria, she waited as he began to press forward, his erection stretching the opening of her heat. "Spence," she sighed as his mouth caressed her neck. All the sensations he was giving her were overwhelming in the most wonderful of ways.

"Oh, Sage, I can't hold back any longer," he cried. He gripped her hips and pulled her down hard on his solid shaft.

Pleasure evaporated. A sharp pain ripped through her and her eyes shot open, her body tensing. Everything seemed to go quiet as Spence froze with their bodies still locked together. He pulled back just a bit and looked into her eyes, his own rounded.

"Are you a virgin?"

Oh, she didn't want to play truth or dare anymore. She didn't want to answer this question. Why did the female body generally have to be so obvious when it hadn't had sex before? Why must there be a barrier for a man to discover?

"Seriously, Sage, are you a virgin?"

"Yes. Or, well, I was a couple of minutes ago," she finally said, trying to make a joke of it. He didn't laugh.

"Why didn't you tell me?" he asked in a calm and gentle voice. "Why did you allow me to hurt you like this?" He began pulling out of her, and she panicked.

"No. Don't stop, Spence. I don't want to stop. I . . . I don't know why I waited so long, but I chose you," she said before she was able to stop the words.

"Sage, this changes things," he said, and then pulled his body from hers, leaving her feeling empty and rejected.

"It changes nothing, Spence," she said, on the verge of crying. "I'm sorry I didn't tell you, but I'm still me, just no longer a virgin."

"I can't do this. I just can't, Sage."

The sting of his rejection was almost too much to bear. She certainly didn't want to look at him. He pulled her back to him as his hand trailed down her back. His touch was no longer comforting, though, it was humiliating.

"I'm sorry, Sage. This shouldn't have happened."

"It doesn't matter, Spence. Please let me go." She was too mortified to sit there and talk about her feelings. She wouldn't beg him to make love to her again.

Without another word, he released her, and Sage climbed from the tub, grabbed the towel she'd discarded, and practically ran inside his house and straight up to the guest room. She wanted to leave badly enough to risk going out on the snowmobile, but she knew better.

It would just be a very long night in his oversized home. She'd spend it facing the humiliation of a second rejection by the man she'd loved for the better part of her life.

THE NEXT MORNING, when Camden showed up to give her a ride home in his truck, she was more than grateful. It was time to start forgetting about Spence Whitman. She had warned herself when he was flirting with her that he only wanted one thing. She just hadn't realized that he'd wanted it with an experienced woman.

18

"Spill the beans right now!"

"Huh?" Sage turned toward Grace and lifted an eyebrow before she faced the tree again and checked it over. It had to be perfectly decorated. The ornaments had to be spaced evenly to give it the best appeal, and everything needed to be in its place. She knew she was ridiculously over the top when decorating, but she couldn't help it. The people around her would just have to deal with her holiday OCD.

Besides, it was something she could control in her life, unlike people. She couldn't control them at all, and that was hard for her to accept. The day after her humiliation in the hot tub, Spence hadn't even bothered to talk to her, let alone call. He'd flown back to Seattle for some high-profile surgery. Yes, he'd been sending a vase of flowers every day since, making her home look like a dang floral shop, but not a single phone call, nor a text, and not a word of explanation. If he really thought flowers were going to make her all warm and fuzzy, he had obviously never tried to court a woman like her before.

Decorations! She needed to focus on the decorations and not think about Spence Whitman or his stupid hot tub, or snowstorms.

As if the stress of Spence wasn't enough, Grace walked over to her perfectly organized table, scooped up a few ornaments, and placed them on the tree all wrong before she scooted around one of the large vases filled with roses and plopped down on the couch.

"You've been moaning in your sleep and I want answers," Grace said as she got comfortable.

"I have not," Sage replied, trying to be sneaky as she grabbed the ornaments Grace had just placed on the tree and repositioned them.

"I saw that, Sage," Grace said, making Sage turn to see the satisfied smirk on her friend's face.

"They looked fine. I just think those branches won't hold them," Sage said, not wanting to admit her need for perfection or hurt her friend's feelings.

"You know, if I didn't love you so dang much, I might be offended that you think I'm a terrible decorator," Grace said before taking a sip of coffee.

"I don't think you're terrible, not at all. It's just that I don't want the branches to break," she said on a sigh.

"I'll let you think that I believe that," Grace said with a wink. "But I will admit that your compulsion to make everything perfect is just one of the many reasons I adore you."

"You know I love you, too, Grace."

"Now, back to why you were moaning in your sleep," Grace said, not letting Sage off the hook.

"I was *not* moaning in my sleep."

"Ha! I caught you," Grace said, sitting up a little taller against the back of the couch. "There's no way you'd be turning so red if there wasn't something you were actually trying to hide. You've been my best friend since the first day of kindergarten. Why in the world wouldn't you spill your guts to me? I'm hurt."

"Wait a minute! You want me to spill, but I spotted you in town with Camden yesterday and *you* haven't said a word." Now Grace was the one blushing, and Sage had the upper hand.

"That was nothing. We were just . . . uh . . . talking. Besides, this is about you right now, not me."

"I'll tell if *you* do, Grace, 'cause right now it looks as if we've both been holding back."

Sage had been having a nice lazy morning getting the tree decorated just the way she liked it—color coordinated and symmetrically appealing—drinking her coffee, and even contemplating reading the paper—not that Sterling had much of a paper. Grace, for once, also had a bit of time off, so it was supposed to be just a relaxing morning. But this was better.

"Look, it's not even Thanksgiving for a couple of days. The tree can wait. Come sit down with me and tell me all. I think my innocent ears may get singed if the ten different vases sitting on every available space in our apartment are any indication. Only a man who is incredibly pleased or incredibly guilt-ridden sends so many bouquets."

"No, I haven't done anything for the flowers," Sage said. And then she stopped, her turncoat face turning scarlet again and spilling the beans for her.

"You *have* done something, Sage! You know I can always tell when you're lying."

"Fine, then." How was she going to speak about this? How could she not? She'd thought of little else since that night in his home last week.

Taking a deep breath, she looked at Grace, her cheeks permanently red, her stomach tied in knots. "It was the night of that huge storm, when I couldn't get home. Spence and I had a few kisses." Okay, this was harder to say than she'd imagined. "Stop looking at me like that."

"And . . ." Grace was sitting on the edge of her seat now, not allowing Sage to look away.

"Well, then we got into the hot tub . . ." She just couldn't admit her humiliation to Grace. It was too horrid.

"Tell me everything now, or I swear, Sage, we will no longer be besties."

"We started to make love and then he jetted off to another state practically before I even arrived back home," Sage said hurriedly.

"Wait! You *started* to make love? How far did you get? What exactly happened?"

"We . . . um . . . went all the way—or sort of all the way—but he freaked when he found out I was a virgin, and neither of us had a happy ending," Sage said, feeling the humiliation all over again. "He just stopped."

"What? You're kidding, right?"

"I wish I were. And he hasn't spoken to me since. He went to Seattle the next day and he's been gone all week."

"No phone calls, nothing, just flowers?"

"Yeah," Sage said, not even wanting to look at the freaking flowers.

"Well, that sucks. What kind of man doesn't even call? Hell, I remember when we were in middle school and you doodled his name all over your note-book: *Sage and Spence forever*," Grace said with an indignant scowl.

"I guess we didn't choose too wisely, because I recall that on your notebook it said *Grace plus Camden equals forever*."

"Yeah, we were supposed to marry the devastatingly handsome brothers and be related for life. Heck, we'd even have our children at the same time so they'd grow up together and be best friends just like us."

"Don't you wish life worked out so easily?"

"Yeah. But the real world never goes the way we

want it to. Enough of that. I want to know how you feel. You lost your virginity. Was it good? Bad? Did he suck? I want details, lots of details."

Sage spent the next fifteen minutes filling Grace in on exactly what had occurred at Spence's house. Even speaking about it again had her hot and bothered. How could an experience that had been so good for her, have been exactly the opposite for him? She felt shamed and humiliated and didn't ever want to see him again.

"You have to talk to him, you know," Grace told her. "You have to figure out what in the world he is thinking. He had to have been shocked. Most women don't make it to your age with the V card still intact. Give him a chance to explain himself."

"He hasn't even tried," Sage said with a frustrated sigh.

"Then corner the man and make him speak."

"I can't even think about this anymore. Please, please, please tell me what is up with you and Camden, and let's not talk about me. You were having lunch together at the diner and your heads were bent together awfully close."

"It's not what you think."

"Sure, sure."

"No, really, Sage. We're just working together on something, or he's trying to work with me on something, but I don't want his help, but the man is a pain in the ass and won't take no for an answer."

"There's no way you are getting away with being so vague, Grace." Sage had lost all interest in decorating the tree.

"There's really nothing to tell," she said, probably hoping that would satisfy her best friend.

Not by a long shot.

"Grace, I know that look in your eyes and I know when you're hiding something from me. I will get it out of you!"

"Look, it's really nothing, but Cam seems to think it's something. I just can't talk about him right now. The man infuriates me."

Sage sat there, looked at the pain on Grace's face, and knew she needed to give her friend a break. Just like Sage didn't want to speak about Spence right now, it was more than obvious that speaking about Camden was too hard for Grace. They would talk to each other when they were ready, Sage had no doubt about that.

"Grace—" Just then the doorbell rang.

"I got it," Grace said hastily, acting as if there was a fire and she was going to be the first out of the building.

"You can run, but you can't hide," Sage called out after her friend.

"We'll see about that," Grace called back before Sage heard the door open.

"My, my, my, looky what the cat just dragged to our doorstep."

Sage had a sinking feeling . . .

"I come bearing treats."

Great. Spence's voice first thing in the morning was almost as sexy as late at night. Of course, thinking of night and Spence's deep voice made her think of beds and . . . Nope, not gonna go there.

"What kind of treats?" she heard Grace ask.

"Fresh hot coffee and pastries from the new bakery down the street."

"New bakery? I didn't know it was open yet," Grace said with suspicion.

"You got me—these are a few hours old. I picked them up before I flew out of Seattle. The coffee did come from the café, though. It was the good barista." He was obviously wearing a seductive smile, and he spoke with his most come-hither voice.

"You may enter," Grace said.

Sage scrambled to her feet. She was wearing pajamas—with little elves on them, for goodness' sake. Bad, bad, bad. No, she didn't want to seduce him, not after being rejected, but *elves*?

"Sage, we have company," Grace yelled two seconds before they entered the living room.

Sage's eyes connected with Spence's and her stomach sank. A week apart from him had done nothing for her libido. And he was clearly still feeling something as well, at least if the smoldering in his eyes was any indication.

Now she was confused, very confused. He could have made love to her all night, but he'd pulled away with no explanation, disappeared, and now was in her home bearing gifts and acting like no time had passed. What in the world was the man thinking? The real question was, did she really want to know?

19

It had been only a week. That was nothing. He'd been in surgeries that had lasted that long. Okay, maybe that was an exaggeration, but still, he'd been through weeks that felt like mere days, but for some reason, this week had felt like a month.

Maybe it was the guilt for not speaking to her after their disastrous night at his place, or maybe it was because he couldn't get her from his mind.

Whatever it was, he knew their story was only beginning. He'd been shocked to find out she was a virgin. Of course he was. Most women didn't make it to twenty-one with their virginity intact, let alone twenty-six. He'd thought he was doing the right thing by stopping, but from the expression in her eyes, he had a feeling he'd taken major steps backward.

It was okay, though. He was confident he could win her back. After all, the two of them shared a powerful connection, and he wasn't going away until he explored exactly what that connection was and where it would lead.

Sage was standing in front of him in what should have been completely unflattering pajamas with freaking elves on them, and he was still ready to toss her over his shoulder and haul her to the nearest bed. He was losing his mind.

Her curves were hidden, though not invisible, in the soft flannel top, but hallelujah for the revealing flannel shorts. Her toned thighs were a thing of beauty, sparking the most inappropriate thoughts of kissing them . . . all the way up to her . . .

Oops. Time to halt that thought. He'd never found such childish pajamas a turn-on before, but they were sexier at this moment than the skimpiest piece of lingerie he'd ever seen. For once, he was seeing Sage's normally tame red hair piled messily on top of her head, and without a trace of makeup she looked fresh, young, and . . . innocent. Dammit. Too innocent for him—they'd already established that a week ago. If he was a good man, he'd turn and walk away before he could corrupt her further than he already had.

Yeah, right. He wasn't strong enough to do that yet. Obviously—he was here, wasn't he? Spence's eyes raked over her delicious body, a body he had felt naked, and he knew he was right where he belonged.

Shaking his head, he jettisoned such mushy thoughts from his brain. This was about conquest, about attraction, about simple animal lust.

He was overthinking this. Time to give her the goodies he'd picked up on a whim, do some light flirting, see if there was a chance of getting her into his bed to complete what they'd begun, and then getting the hell away from her apartment.

"Are you going to stand there all day," Grace asked, "or actually show us what's in the box?"

Feeling as if he was emerging from a deep sleep, Spence pasted on his winning smile again for Grace's benefit. He wasn't a stupid man—he knew that if he wanted to learn all of Sage's secrets, it would help a lot to have her best friend on his side.

"I hope you ladies like chocolate." He opened the lid and showed Grace the fresh-baked goods.

"Ooh, a man after my heart. Are you single, sugar?" Grace reached in and pulled out a chocolate-drizzled pastry.

"Hopefully not for long," he said, and his eyes roamed over Sage again. Her blush summoned images of how she'd appeared as he'd entered her. Squirming in pants that were suddenly too tight, he turned his attention back to Grace. That seemed much safer for his libido.

"Well, take a seat, Romeo," Grace said. "It seems my best friend has forgotten how to speak." She led him to the couch that Sage had just vacated, then gave her a wink. Sage looked as if she wanted to smack her friend, but she remained silent and moved over to the coffee table, where a number of ornaments were lined up. Spence took a closer look and had to grin when he noticed they were separated into groups by color and size. Sage picked one up carefully, walked over to the tree, and stood there in deep contemplation.

"Are you getting ready to perform surgery on the tree?" he asked, then fished out a doughnut and took a bite.

She turned and looked at him. "What?"

"You seem quite focused on ornament placement," he said after he swallowed.

"I like the tree to be decorated according to fixed aesthetic principles," she said defensively. She turned her back to him again and slid the ornament onto the perfect branch.

"What if the tree's branches aren't evenly spaced?"

"I always get a beautiful tree."

"Oh, you must be a lot of fun to Christmas tree shop with."

Sage turned and glared at him before walking back to her table and selecting another ornament. "I happen to think I'm an asset when shopping for a tree. I can gauge the area it will take up, and it won't look too big or too small in its appointed place. I also know which ones will last for the season, and which ones are close to dying."

Spence laughed out loud at her earnestness. He'd never met someone who had a formula for Christmas tree shopping. She was a real treat. He sat back and enjoyed the show when she bent down to pick up a fallen bulb. "Then it's a good thing I haven't bought my tree yet. I appreciate your offering to help."

"I made no such offer." Sage didn't bother to look at him this time.

"Yes, you did. Didn't you hear her offer, Grace?"

Grace gave a gigantic smile and put down her pastry. "It sounded like an offer to me."

"Traitor," Sage mumbled beneath her breath, and sent Grace a stern look.

"I'd love to hang around the both of you and watch the bickering continue, but I have to get dressed and head in to work," Grace said, practically skipping by as she went down the hallway.

"I think you chased her away—and just when all the fun was beginning," Spence said, picking up an ornament and approaching the tree.

Sage didn't tell him he had to unhand the delicate glass elf in his hand; she just stood there watching, waiting. He suspected that this was some sort of test, and he felt the pressure to get it right. Damn. Since when did getting a girl to go out with him depend on his expertise at hanging ornaments?

Since now, apparently.

He placed the little elf in a bare spot and found himself holding his breath as he waited for the verdict. He turned around to pick up his coffee, then turned back to find that the ornament had moved a few inches.

Well, he'd come close. Victory!

He suddenly started laughing. "Let me help you finish up the tree, Sage." And he knew exactly what she was about to say.

"That's all right. I'm going to finish later."

"Come on, I'm really good at it—I'm good at just about everything," he said, waggling his brows at her.

"Obviously not," she muttered as she pivoted back to her tree, studying it the way she would a patient.

"I was thrown for a loop last week and not up to my best performance level, but I've had plenty of time to think, and I have ways of making it up to you. Now, I'm going to apologize in advance for any violations against you."

Before she could speak, Spence turned her toward him and drew her into his arms in one swift movement, savoring for a brief moment the feel of her feminine body pressed against his with the negligible barrier of her pajamas and his sweater.

When he saw the whisper of desire flit across her eyes, he knew she wanted him, knew it wouldn't be long until he had his chance to make up to her for his shock at finding she was a virgin. What surprised him was the warming in his gut, the extra beat to his heart.

"Sage Banks, you have gotten under my skin and you aren't letting me go," he whispered before his lips brushed across hers in the barest of touches.

"I'm not doing anything," she said, her voice husky, the sound rumbling through him.

"Ah, you do plenty. I love the concentration on your face when you're focused, the way your lips so easily turn up to comfort a patient, how eager you are to learn new things, and how willing you are to help others. And I love the way you taste," he said, brushing his lips across hers again, hunger ripping through him. No longer denying the kiss he really wanted, he brought their lips together, throwing away rational thought and restraint.

After sliding his fingers through the glorious tangle of her fire-red hair, he held her head tight, angling it so he could deepen the kiss and take full advantage of the gasp she was releasing into his mouth.

She tasted of sweet coffee and a hint of mint toothpaste, making him think of long summer days and cool spring-fed creeks, and the two of them bare in the sun. He could be content doing nothing but lazing all day and night with this woman in his arms.

She was his—for this moment, she was all his, and he could take her to the highest reaches of heaven. Her seductive groan let him know she had no thoughts of fighting him, so his hand moved down her back, landing on the soft curve of her sweet derrière as he pulled her tightly against him.

Just as he was beginning to reach the point of no return, she stiffened and pushed against him. He knew he could still seduce her, knew he could lift her into his arms and ravish her. But he also knew she'd hate him if he went too fast again.

"Stop."

It was barely a whisper, panted from her moist lips as he eased back. It was all he needed to hear.

"I want you in my bed, Sage. I want you naked beneath me, crying out in pleasure. I want you so much I dream about you and wake up hungry and unsatisfied. I can feel how much you want me, too. Don't keep fighting me. We can be great together." He knew he should leave something to mystery, but, damn, he was aching.

She pushed against him. "No. You proved to me that I'm nothing. I don't want you anymore."

He set her free despite the infernal throbbing below his waist.

"I was in shock that you hadn't had sex before. I'm sorry I left things the way I did. But, here's the reality. We're both single. We're both adults. There's nothing wrong with taking care of basic human needs." Hmm. Did he need a little work on his bedroom talk? Maybe.

"I'm not looking to get involved with anyone, Spence, especially you. I'm a resident, and you know the kind of hours that means. Plus, you're my boss. I am so not going to be a cliché and sleep with the boss. That night was a mistake and I'm glad you realized it, since I clearly wasn't thinking. I think the lack of available women in our small town has you looking for anything near your age. We need to quit this game."

"I may be a doctor, too, Sage, but some things happening in the body can't be explained away so easily. I want you, you want me. There's no reason for us not to be together."

Spence should just leave this alone, should accept her rejection and leave. It's what he normally would have done. If a girl didn't show interest, then why waste his time? But since he couldn't stop thinking about this woman, he knew that he had to see where this could lead.

"You have jet lag. Go home and sleep it off," Sage said, moving over to the couch and sitting down, pulling her knees up to her chest and hugging them, looking so sweet and so many years younger than she actually was.

"Jet lag? Really? It's only an hour-and-a-half flight from Seattle to Billings, and the time difference is only an hour," he said with a chuckle. "No circadian rhythms were harmed in the making of this scene."

"Are you mocking me, Spence?"

"No. Enjoying you."

"Well, I don't give you permission to enjoy me," she told him with some heat.

"My dear Sage, you don't get to decide that." He walked over and leaned down, putting his face just inches from hers.

"I get to decide whom I date," she said, emphasizing the *m* in *whom*—she wished to sound her starchiest—and leaning back as far as she could. It wasn't far enough.

"That's okay. I wouldn't want you to be too easy."

"Did you just call me easy?"

"No, that's one thing that could never be said about you," he said with a laugh, then couldn't resist brushing his lips across the tip of her nose. The move seemed to unsettle her. Good. He wanted her unsettled, wanted to bring a bit of chaos to her ordered life.

"I have to . . ." Dang. She couldn't think of an excuse to make him leave.

He hadn't known what he wanted when he found himself at her door, but right now he felt like singing in the hills. He'd shaken her up and learned she was far more susceptible to him than she wanted him to know. It was enough for now.

He'd let her take a deep breath and rest up, and then the next round would begin. "Have a great day, Sage." He kissed her briefly, then walked from the room. He didn't even try to stop the happy whistle that blew through his lips as he climbed down the front stairs.

20

"There is no way I'm going to that ranch for Thanksgiving dinner."

Sage sat at her grandmother's table with her lips pursed in frustration. Her grandma always cooked Thanksgiving dinner. It was tradition. Eileen always joined them, and they ate a scrumptious meal, then watched the football game on TV. That's what they did. *Always*.

"I'm sorry, darling. I just haven't been feeling well enough to cook a big holiday meal this year, and when Martin invited us over, I just . . ."

Sage instantly felt like the most horrible person on the planet. "I'm sorry, Grandma. I didn't know you weren't feeling well again. I can cook—okay, I can try, at least. I'm sure it wouldn't be that bad."

She *couldn't* go to the Whitman place. No way. She'd managed to avoid Spence last night, since he'd first been in surgery and then she'd been in a roomful of people when he'd emerged from the OR. Thankfully, he didn't attempt to kiss her in front of the rest of the hospital staff. That would have been mortifying.

Now, if he'd pulled her into one of the on-call rooms, slowly stripped . . . No! When had her mind started dwelling in the gutter? She'd been a straight-A student. She was controlled. Cautious. Responsible. Unlike so many others, she didn't have affairs in on-call rooms. That wasn't who she was. She'd screwed up in his hot tub, but no one was perfect. Still, she tried.

Why she was thinking about sex more than she was thinking about surgery was beyond her. She must be losing her mind. Maybe it was Montana. Probably something in the water. The population was so sparse, and because there weren't enough people around, the politicians were secretly drugging their water with aphrodisiacs, making everyone want to mate and bring children into the world.

No! No! No! She would not think about children and Spence—and aphrodisiacs—at the same time. This was getting out of hand. She had to pull herself together. She was strong, dang it!

"I guess we could just stay home and have leftovers. I'll have to break it to Eileen. She was really looking forward to spending the evening with Martin. I think there may be something going on between the two of them. They've been making googly eyes at each other for months now, but neither one wants to admit they have feelings. Oh, yes, Thanksgiving . . . Grace also said she wanted to come with us. You know she's had a mighty heavy crush on Camden for a long time, and she'd never go without you, but I understand . . ."

Sage didn't think it was possible, but she now felt even lower than low. How could she live with herself when she was clearly such a worthless human being? Because she was afraid to be in the same house as Spence, she was going to deprive everyone else of a happy holiday. They might as well call her the Thanksgiving Grinch and get her a green costume—no, make it in harvest colors—and a big bag to steal all the pies and all the paper turkeys and Pilgrim decorations while she was at it.

"I'm sorry, Grandma. I just wanted to have you and Aunt Eileen and Grace all to myself, but if you want to go out there for Thanksgiving, I'm sure that would be fine. I'd better call the hospital and double-check that they won't need me, though. I'm sure if they do, I can at least drive you out to the Whitmans' first," she said, feeling inspired.

She'd just volunteer, whether they needed her or not. That would solve everything. Everyone would then have a great Thanksgiving, including her. Lonely, but great.

"You can't work on Thanksgiving, sweetheart. You already have the day off. I called the hospital to verify before I made any plans. They don't put any elective surgeries on the board on the holidays and they already have an on-call doctor set up for emergencies, so you're free. I'm so happy. This will be a beautiful holiday." Bethel had perked up as she spoke.

Sage knew when she was beaten. It looked like she was going to have to put her acting skills to the test.

"I'd better get to making the pies," Bethel said. "After all, Thanksgiving is tomorrow."

Sage watched her grandma move with slightly too much grace and purpose around the kitchen for a woman who claimed she wasn't feeling well. Then Sage felt guilty again. She was certain Bethel was pushing herself to make sure she had something to bring to the dinner.

Sage would have liked to help her, but she had to leave for the hospital. "Don't work too hard, Grandma. I'll see you in the morning."

As she left, she hoped she could make it through tomorrow without getting burned.

SAGE WATCHED AS all the color left Grace's cheeks. "I did *not* tell your grandma I'd go to the Whitmans' place for Thanksgiving," Grace almost wailed. "I thought we were having it here."

"The car is here, girls. Don't bother taking your coat off, Grace." Bethel shut and locked the door with Sage and Grace still standing on the covered front porch.

Sitting in the driveway was one of the Whitmans' large SUVs, looking sleek and warm as it waited for passengers.

"Grandma said you really wanted to go," Sage

said, looking at the open back door of the SUV. She didn't know what to think now. Her grandma wouldn't have intentionally lied. Certainly not. Bethel was as honest as the day was long.

"I'm sure she just got confused," Grace said, feeling the same way as Sage. There was just no possible way that Bethel Banks would lie. All the kids who'd known her called her Grandma and had been eating her cookies and special lemonade for as long as Grace could remember.

"Well, I'm not going alone, so suck it up," Sage growled through her teeth just as Bethel leaned out the door and called for them again. "Coming, Grandma."

"I have a bad feeling about this," Grace said as she and Sage stepped off the porch and began walking toward the waiting vehicle. They looked as if they were going to a funeral, not to a holiday feast.

By the end of the night, they might be. It very much depended on the behavior of both Spence and Camden, because, with the way those boys were playing with Sage's and Grace's emotions, the two women were likely to team up and off one or both of the men.

21

"I didn't think you were ever going to arrive," Martin called out from the wide-open front door as Bethel and her group made their way up the ornate front steps of the Whitman ranch house.

"You know how girls are," Bethel said, leaning in to kiss Martin on the cheek. "They like to take their time getting all pretty."

"It was well worth the wait. You ladies are stunning, and now we won't have just a bunch of old men sitting around the table," Martin replied, a special light overtaking his features as he glanced over at Eileen.

"Thank you for inviting us, Martin. I'm sure this will be the best Thanksgiving I've ever had," Eileen said shyly, surprising them all when a rosy color suffused her cheeks.

"I know it's already *my* best," Martin said, taking Eileen's arm and running it through his.

"Yes, thank you for having us," Sage said as she followed the group inside.

"I swear I'm going to kill you for this," Grace whispered as the door shut behind them. "You could have warned me or something."

"I couldn't warn you. Up until you arrived at the house, I thought you wanted to come. Besides, you won't have to kill me—I just might take my *own* life," Sage replied. "I'd rather eat crickets than be here and make small talk with Spence."

"Welcome, ladies," Michael said as they stepped into the parlor. "Would you like a predinner drink?"

"Yes!" Sage and Grace said in unison, grinning at each other. They might need five or six to get through the evening.

"Well, then, you're in luck—I've prepared my special eggnog," Spence said as he walked into the room. He was wearing a nice pair of slacks that were custom tailored and hugged his thighs to perfection. The green sweater covering his sculpted chest matched his eyes to a T and looked exquisite. Sage found herself wanting to run her hands over the fabric to see whether it felt as soft as it looked.

She forced herself to turn away as she struggled to find her tongue. She looked to Grace for assistance, but her friend wasn't in a position to provide it. Camden had just stepped into the room and was looking quite suave himself.

When Jackson came in with his new wife and stood side by side with his three brothers, Sage could understand why they'd been considered the cream of the crop during her school years. They commanded the room with their confidence, good looks, and incredible bodies.

What she didn't understand was how three of the four were still single. But men like them seemed to take forever to settle down because they could have anyone they wanted. Why should they choose just one woman when the world was their oyster?

"I'd love to try some," Grace said, and Sage couldn't figure out what the heck her best friend was talking about.

"And you, Sage?"

She turned toward Spence, at a complete loss.

"My special eggnog?" he prompted slowly.

"Oh. Yes, please." Her cheeks colored. She was really going to have to focus if she expected to have any shred of pride left at the end of the night.

"I'll get yours, Grace," Camden said, stepping up to the table with the snacks and drinks. "Come over here."

Grace had no choice but to follow if she didn't wish to appear rude, so she left Sage's side. Soon she and Camden were having an intense discussion in the corner of the room, and not long afterward, they disappeared.

Hmm. Interesting.

"Spence is a mighty fine boy, isn't he?"

Sage looked around to find Martin, Spence's dad, beside her. "Yes, Mr. Whitman. He's wonderful at showing fledgling doctors the ropes," she said, accepting another drink. She hadn't realized she'd guzzled the first one in a matter of seconds.

"Of course he's a fine surgeon, but he's also a great man. That's why the hospital had to have him. The people in this area have so much more comfort knowing top-flight medical care is right around the corner. Before Spence took over the ER, we had a quality staff, but Spence is a shining star and we're lucky to have him here."

"I'm very lucky to have him supervising my training," she said, taking another big gulp from her cup. The last thing she wanted was to discuss a man about whom she was having insanely lustful thoughts with his father. Her cheeks were going to stay a constant shade of red if this night continued the way it had begun.

"I just wish my Maybelle had been alive to see these boys grow up. She would have loved them so much."

"I'm sure she does love them, and she's looking down upon you all and is proud of what a wonderful man she was married to. You are such a great father that the town surely forgets three of them aren't biologically yours. How old were they when you adopted them?" She couldn't quite remember.

"Now that's a story you should hear from Spence." His eyes were suddenly caught by Eileen's, and it became clear that his attention had wandered from Sage, though he stood with her a moment longer.

"I'll have to ask him," she said politely. Martin nodded sweetly at her and then sauntered toward his targeted female.

Now Sage was curious, but what if he didn't want to talk about it? She knew Spence had been adopted, but until now she hadn't wondered why. Did he have any contact with his biological family? So many questions were burning through her, but she didn't know how to bring up something like that.

Sage wandered over to a wall filled with old photographs. The boys were splashing in the creek, riding horses, in football uniforms, and holding trophies of all sorts. Martin was clearly very proud of his sons. To have their pictures be the main focus of his den showed what a family man he was.

"My dad likes photos."

Sage turned and found Spence next to her. He should have a warning bell attached to him. Her stomach dipped as his arm brushed against her shoulder. Did he need to stand quite so close?

"It looks like one of my grandmother's walls," Sage said. "I don't remember a whole lot about my parents—they died when I was only ten. But I have their faces burned into my memory because my grandma has always kept pictures up around the house, beautiful images of them with me at the park, ice-skating, at the zoo . . . all these happy places. I wish I could remember more."

"That's why pictures are more precious than almost anything else. It captures the moment, making us able to relive the memories for an eternity."

Sage had never imagined that Spence could be so sentimental. She had to admit she liked this side of him.

"Are you ready for dinner?"

"I'm suddenly starving," she told him as the aromas of good cooking drifted through the open doorway. Spence held out his arm to lead her into the dining room, and she hesitated for only a moment—probably not long enough for him to notice, she hoped. She was a guest in his home, and there was no need for her to be rude.

"You two sit here," Martin said as Sage entered on Spence's arm.

Sage looked around with suspicion when everyone was seated. This all seemed to be set up a bit too conveniently. What were the old folks doing?

"Do you think your dad and my grandma are up to something?" she asked Spence. She should be irritated, because this seemed almost like a date, but the eggnog was doing its job—she'd already gulped down enough of it—giving her a touch of I-don't-care attitude.

"What do you mean?"

"Never mind, Spence." He seemed to suspect nothing, so she let it go. Almost by surprise, she found herself enjoying a nice meal at the Whitman table, with great food and boisterous laughter.

When the night was over, she couldn't find Grace anywhere. She was just gone, and what was even more suspicious was that Camden was absent as well. Hmm.

"I'll give you a ride home," Spence said.

Sage had drunk a little too much of the eggnog and she was grateful she hadn't driven over, but she didn't need a ride. "I'll just go with my grandma and Eileen."

"I think Dad has plans with them. They're going to be busy for a while," he said with a laugh.

"Oh. Well then, I'd best get home," she said, suddenly feeling nervous.

"There's no hurry. I was just telling you that I'll give you a ride when you're ready." He moved slowly toward her.

"I'm ready now. I have to work tomorrow, you know," she said, turning and moving away from him.

"Not until the afternoon. I don't think you have to be in bed by midnight or risk turning into a pumpkin."

"Are you implying that I act like a princess?"

"You are a princess, Sage, and I think I have just the right slipper to place on your foot."

"Now that's an impressive line, Spence." She let out a giggle, but it dried up instantly when she found Spence cornering her, his warm breath just inches away.

"Then it deserves a kiss. I've been wanting to do this since the moment you walked through the front door."

He leaned down, and all her thoughts of escape vanished when their mouths connected. Spence Whitman really knew how to kiss. Even the foreign exchange student she'd been so fond of was forgotten.

When he pulled back and she looked into his deep green eyes, her stomach dropped. She knew she was in serious trouble. She was beginning to fall for this man again, and he was all wrong for her. She couldn't let this happen. He was her boss, one of the main people who determined if she became a full-fledged doctor. And she didn't have time for an affair. She barely had time for herself, her grandmother, and her best friend.

"I'm ready to go home," she said, and when she noticed he was about to protest, she added, "Please, Spence." He opened his mouth as if to speak, and then she saw when he knew it was useless.

"Of course," he said, and then found her coat.

The day hadn't been bad at all, but the night would most likely prove to be quite lonely. That was okay, though. She had a career to think about, and she had her family—her grandmother and Grace. When she was finished with her residency, then there would be plenty of time for romance, but it certainly wouldn't be with a man like Spence, with whom she would never feel on an equal par.

Thanksgiving was over. It was back to the real world for her.

22

Sage wore a big smile as she slipped outside to the ambulance bay. She'd be off work in an hour, and, rarity of rarities, the sun would still be shining. Sure, it was winter and the ground was covered in snow, but at least it was bright out and she could soak up some vitamin D.

Though Sage really didn't have time for a relationship, Spence had been wearing down her defenses. She wouldn't admit that, but it was the only reason she'd accepted a date with another man to the hospital's annual Christmas party.

She didn't like Dr. Ted Lipencolt—could barely stand him, actually—but she felt it was a much safer move than going alone. Spence would surely be there.

"Dr. Banks, we have a patient in room three. Looks like he'll need stitches."

"Thanks, Tina." She came back inside. This was mindless work, something she could easily perform and still leave the hospital in plenty of time to get ready.

For someone who didn't care about Spence's opinion, she'd sure been putting a lot of effort into this party. No matter how much she told herself it was for her alone, in the back of her mind, she knew she wanted to make an impression, knew she wanted to feel beautiful.

But, hey, that was natural behavior for any woman. It was nice to feel desirable, even if she had no plans for entering a relationship.

"Hello, Mr. Harris. How are you feeling?"

The man sitting on the table was sweating, his face a little green.

"I've had better days."

"What happened?"

She put on her gloves and took inventory to make sure all the supplies she'd need were there. Her aide had done a great job of prepping the area.

"I was hanging the Christmas lights. My wife was really nagging at me, said they should have been hung weeks ago. I work hard, but does she appreciate that? Of course not. All she cares about is that the Dames and Hendricksons have their lights up already. So I go outside, get the ladder out, and start hanging the lights. It was all going fine until the ladder slipped on some ice, and there I was just flying through the air. If I didn't know better, I'd think it was the missus exacting revenge for me taking so long to do the job."

"Do you suspect this wasn't an accident?" Contrary to popular belief, there were a multitude of men out there who were abused.

"No, of course not. I called for her for like ten minutes before she finally came through the front door. Did I get any sympathy? No. She just rolled her eyes and said I wasn't gonna use this as an excuse to not get the lights finished. Hell with that. When I get home, I'm cracking open a can of beer and watching a football game. If she complains, I'll break every strand of lights we have."

"Well, the cut isn't too bad. You were really lucky. And no bones were broken. You should be back to full health within a day or two," she reassured him, trying desperately to stifle her laughter. "So how long have you been married?" She liked to talk to her patients, ease their anxiety while she took care of them. After preparing a hypodermic, she inserted it near the cut to numb the area, then picked up the sterile needle and thread.

"Twenty years this past March," Mr. Harris told Sage. "She thinks I always forget our anniversary until she nags at me, but I don't. I have a drink with the boys after work to mourn the loss of my bachelorhood."

"That's . . . uh . . . nice." Sage really had no idea what to say. If the man was that miserable in his marriage, why didn't he just get a divorce?

"Then I come home and take her out for a real nice dinner."

Okay, Sage was really confused now. Before she could respond, the door opened and suddenly the room shrank as Spence joined her at the table and looked down at her work. Not something unusual.

"Can I help you, Dr. Whitman?" she asked.

"No. You're doing a great job, Dr. Banks." Spence walked around the table and took a seat. It looked like he was planning to stay for a while.

"Hi, Dr. Whitman," her patient mumbled, much more subdued now with a man in the room.

"Hello, Mr. Harris. Another on-the-job injury?"

"No. Christmas lights," he said with a sheepish smile.

"We've had a few of those in the last few days. I bet Mrs. Harris has been anxious for those to go up," Spence remarked sympathetically.

"Yeah, she's real impatient. I don't see the big deal about these lights. Our electric bill just goes up, and they're only on for like a month. It just seems like a lot of unnecessary work," he said, fidgeting on the table.

"Please sit still, Mr. Harris," Sage said as she waited for him to finish adjusting before she started the next stitch.

"I don't know, either, Mr. Harris, but my brothers and I have been hanging the lights since we were kids. We didn't do it one year, and Dad was right—it just wasn't the same. There's something about those twinkling colors that lets you know Christmas is right around the corner."

Mr. Harris smiled at Spence's words. "I never thought about it like that. Maybe if the missus had just said that, I wouldn't have gotten so bent out of shape," he said, as if the good doctor had imparted great wisdom.

"Yeah, we forget to listen every once in a while," Spence replied.

"You got that right."

The two of them spoke about the football game next while Sage finished stitching up her patient. She tuned them out and thought about what needed to be done for the rest of the night. She wanted to ask Spence if he'd be at the party, but that would be too obvious.

All of a sudden, Spence turned his full attention back to her. She almost stumbled on her last stitch when those smoldering green eyes devoured her from head to toe—but *almost* was the operative word. She was far too professional to let a little thing like that distract her from doing a perfect job.

"Dr. Banks, please tell me you don't have a date for the party tonight," he said, a self-confident smile spreading across his features.

"I have a patient here, Dr. Whitman. This isn't the time or the place for you to be asking me about my personal life." She hadn't quite snapped at him, but her voice was cold enough to let him know he was in trouble.

He decided to push it—as she knew he would.

"Ah, this is a work party, so it's appropriate to ask while at work, isn't it, Mr. Harris?"

"I don't see nothing wrong with askin' about it," Mr. Harris replied. Of course he would stick up for the male doctor. Sage was seething now.

"Dr. Whitman, if you wouldn't mind stepping outside, I'll speak to you in a few moments," she said before turning back to her patient. "Mr. Harris, make sure you spread some rock salt along the ground before you decide to climb the ladder again. I'm sure Mrs. Harris would like to have her lights on the house *and* a healthy husband for Christmas," she said with a smile.

"Sure thing, Dr. Banks. You did a mighty fine job. I can tell there won't even be much of a scar," he said as he looked at her handiwork before she covered the stitches with a large bandage.

"See your regular doctor in about ten days to have the stiches removed. If you need a note to miss work tomorrow . . ."

"Nah, I'm a tough bird. I don't need no medicines or anything. I'll just drink a couple of beers and relax tonight. I'll be right as rain tomorrow."

"Mr. Harris, no alcohol tonight, not after hitting your head," she said sternly, though she knew it was a waste of breath to even say it.

"Sure, sure, Doc," he said, not looking her in the eyes.

"I really hope you will listen, Mr. Harris."

He hopped from the table and limped only slightly as he left the room, not saying anything else to her. There was nothing she could do, short of tackling him and keeping him overnight in the hospital, which would never be allowed. Once he was gone, though, Sage's eyes narrowed as she turned on Spence.

"How dare you come into my procedure room and talk about my personal life in front of a patient!" She whirled away from him to dispose of her gloves and wash her hands.

"I'm your boss, Sage. I can be in any room that you're in," he replied, leaning back as if he were enjoying their little spat.

"Yes, you *are* my boss. Maybe you should remember that. It doesn't give you the right to harass me." She couldn't think of a time he'd ever had her so flustered.

"Are you feeling harassed, Sage?" he asked, his voice practically a purr.

"Yes!" she said, then felt guilty at the flinch that crossed his features. In reality, he was professional most of the time at work—though this was certainly not one of those times. It was really what happened after work that was causing her brain to shut down. Yes, she was mad because she was embarrassed— he'd embarrassed himself, too. But she was also angry because of how much she wanted to take him up on his invitation.

"No. I'm not feeling harassed, Dr. Whitman, but you know quite well that you shouldn't have done what you did. It *was* unprofessional, and you have to promise to never do that in front of a patient again."

"So I can do it when we're alone?" he said, and she realized he'd fooled her. He wasn't upset at all. It had been a fake-out. Was this guy utterly shameless?

"No," she said, and turned to leave.

"One date, Sage. That's all I'm asking. If you're repulsed by me I'll stop, but if you're just scared, that's not a good enough reason to say no." He beat her to the door and blocked her exit.

"I'm repulsed by you," she lied, not looking him in the eyes.

"You make me crazy," he said as he ran a finger down her cheek, causing fire to race through her.

"Well, maybe there's a pill I can prescribe for your condition," she said, her voice much more breathless than she would have liked for it to be.

"You're my drug, Sage, and you're all I need," he said, trapping her against the wall.

"Then you're going to have to get used to going through withdrawal."

"Come with me to the party."

"I can't. I have a date already." Her knees were practically shaking, because she had no doubt that date or no date, she was still liable to fall into Spence's arms if the lighting was low and she had too much eggnog again. And if he was close by, she had a feeling she'd need a lot of eggnog to get her through the night.

"Cancel. You won't have nearly as much fun with whoever you've chosen to go with," he said, clearly confident that she'd do just that.

"Sorry. Can't. Don't want to, either. Now if you'll just move away, I want to head home. I have a date to get ready for."

His brow furrowed but he took a step back.

"Good-bye, Dr. Whitman," she said as she opened the door.

"Who's your date?" he asked, stopping her again.

Wow, if she were more of a fool, she might actually believe he was jealous. No. There was absolutely no way.

"His name is *None of Your Business*," she said before turning to exit again.

"I don't like that answer, Sage. I don't like it at all. I don't think this date of yours can in any way satisfy you. I think, as a matter of fact, that I'm the only man capable of bringing you to the heights of pleasure you so desperately deserve to be brought to." He boxed her in again.

"Really? Because you failed once."

She'd obviously left him speechless because she finally managed to get away. Without another word, she left the exam room and waited until she was in the women's locker room before taking in a decent breath of air.

Her last words to him had been meant to hurt, and now she was worried that she'd indeed hurt him. What was wrong with her? Oh, she hoped this night wasn't an utter disaster. As she looked in the mirror and felt the pounding of her heart, she had a feeling that's exactly what it was going to be.

23

Spence sped down the long drive that led to his childhood home. He had his own place now, but he found himself spending a lot of his time back on the ranch, as did his brothers.

This was home, the place he'd received a second chance. This was security. No matter how many years he'd aged, no matter how much success he had, there was always going to be a small part of him that was the frightened boy nobody wanted.

The snow continued to fall as he pulled up to the large ranch house with the inviting wraparound porch, now all decked out in lights that he and his brothers had hung. Yes, there were plenty of Whitman employees who could have done the work, but it was something the four of them took pride in doing each year.

It was time to get some advice from his dad, because he sure couldn't seem to figure anything out on his own. He suddenly felt the insecurities of that young teenage boy who didn't have a thing to his name.

He was falling for Sage and he didn't understand it. This wasn't the right time. His life was mapped out already. He'd planned on finding the perfect wife when he reached forty, and he was only thirty-four, then they'd have two kids—a boy and a girl, of course—and they'd live a picture-perfect life. The emotions he was feeling now were far from perfect. They were erratic and confusing and they didn't mesh at all with his future plans.

For one thing, Sage looked like she'd rather hit him than make love to him. For another, she constantly refused when he asked her out. Was it too much to ask that she return his affection? He was trying to make up for his mistake here. He didn't even know why he still was. There were a slew of women who would jump to go out with him. He'd never had a problem obtaining a date.

So why didn't he just cut his losses and move on? That was why he'd come home today. His dad would have the answers. Spence would walk away from this visit knowing whether he should transfer back to Seattle full-time or if he should throw Sage over his shoulder and take her to some deep, dark cave where he could ravish her repeatedly until she admitted she was attracted to him.

He liked option number two better. A big smile parted his lips as he pushed open the front door and ran straight into Eileen and Bethel. Damn!

With Bethel there, he could hardly talk to his father about ravishing her granddaughter. The woman was likely to hit him over the head with a frying pan, and she'd be smart to do just that.

"I thought I heard a car pull up," Bethel said, and she wrapped Spence up in a hug.

"The weather is so frightful I don't know how anyone is staying on the roads," Eileen said as she stood in line for the next hug.

"The snow is fun to drive in," Spence said. "You just have to have a nice big truck." He kissed each woman on the cheek in turn.

"Well, I suppose for a younger crowd . . . We just got here a few minutes ago. Your father was kind enough to invite us over for supper," Eileen told him.

Spence looked at Eileen's flushed cheeks, the glow in her eyes, and the little squirm as she bounced on her feet, and the lights went on in his head.

"Well then, I shouldn't interrupt," he said, intending on backing away so his father could enjoy his meal and court Eileen at the same time.

"What a great surprise, son," Martin boomed from the top of the staircase as he began his descent.

"Hello, Dad. I was coming to chat, but it can wait. I didn't realize you had company," Spence said, giving his dad a hug when he reached him.

"Nonsense. There's plenty of food, and the ladies wouldn't mind if my handsome son joined us," Martin said as he threw an arm around Spence's shoulders.

"I suppose . . ." Spence replied, but he didn't have a lot of time and he really wanted to speak to his father alone.

"We're going to go into the kitchen," Bethel said, "and see if the cook would like any help." She took Eileen's arm and led her away.

Spence would have to send her some thank-you flowers.

"Let's have a drink while we wait for supper," Martin said, and led Spence into the sitting room. This room was his favorite in the house—the first room he'd entered that day Martin had brought him and his brothers to their new home.

He'd been served the best hot chocolate he'd ever had, and in the fanciest cup he'd ever seen. There was also a tray of tiny sandwiches—with the crusts cut off, which was great since he hated crusts. Martin had laughed and said he'd make sure to have lots of kid-appropriate snacks ready to go. He'd kept his promise, always having chocolate in his secret drawer and fresh-baked cookies daily. This had been a wonderful home to be raised in.

"What has you driving all the way out here in such weather? I can see something's on your mind," Martin said as they both sat down.

"Yes. I needed to talk to you about some personal stuff, and I guess I'd best be kind of quick because I don't want it to be taken the wrong way by Bethel and Eileen." He was hesitating, though he knew he should just spit it out.

"There's nothing you couldn't say in front of those women. They are loyal," Martin said. But suddenly the man's cheeks turned pink. "What have you heard about me?"

For the first time in his life, Spence saw his father squirm before him. "It's about me, Dad," he said quickly. He hardly wanted to force his dad to admit to something he might not be ready to talk about yet.

Martin recovered instantly. "Well, of course it is, Spence. What else could it be about?" He put two fingers of scotch in a glass and drank it down.

"I . . . well, I've been around Sage a lot . . ."

"That's my boy! I knew if I could just get the two of you together, it would all work out." Martin stopped suddenly, and his cheeks colored again, this time for an entirely different reason.

"What?" Spence was dumbfounded. What was his dad talking about?

Martin coughed. "Uh . . . nothing. You go on."

"You have some explaining to do, Father," Spence said, knowing he should sound more firm, but oddly he was only curious.

"Well, you know, my friends and I were just thinking that you boys aren't getting any younger. We weren't trying to meddle or anything. We were just . . . putting two available adults together." His words came out stronger, even huffily, at the end of his small speech, almost as if he felt he was the victim here.

"You're matchmaking?" Spence said, his voice rising sharply.

"I've done nothing of the sort. So what if we kind of pushed for Sage to accept the offer for this hospital? And I *was* feeling mighty ill when you decided to take the ER position here."

Martin kept speaking, but Spence wasn't listening anymore. This had all been a setup—a setup that he'd fallen into quite nicely. So why wasn't he angry? Why wasn't he storming from the house? Why wasn't he reading his father the riot act?

Because the setup had worked—at least for him.

Though the meddlesome five were the ones who'd started everything, the feelings Spence was developing for Sage had nothing to do with his father or her grandmother. They were all-male feelings, and he wanted Sage to know exactly how much he liked her.

"Oh, if Sage knew about this, you would all be toast," Spence said, realizing that he'd better never, ever tell her. She'd skin them all alive, and especially him for going along with the scheme.

"I've known little Sage since she was a small child. I'm sure she would be thrilled to be a part of our family," Martin replied.

"Whoa! Slow down there, Dad. Don't start planning the wedding just yet. I can't even get the girl to go out on a date with me." How he hated to admit that.

"Well then, you have to try harder."

Spence turned to find Eileen and Bethel in the

doorway, both with identical expressions of frustration on their faces.

"What?" He'd been saying that a lot lately.

And why? Had he entered an alternate universe or something? Was this Tag-Team-on-Spence Day? He expected his brothers to join in on the ribbing next. They probably had built-in radar and were on their way there now.

"If you want her to go out with you, you have to make her want to," Bethel said. "A lady wants to be courted, to be treated like she's the crown jewel and like you have eyes for no other woman but her."

"I've never had a problem getting a date before, but suddenly the one woman I want to take out would rather change bedpans than accept an offer from me. I've sent her flowers, told her she's beautiful, made it more than clear that I des—" Oops.

"We may be older than you, sweetie, but we're not stupid. We know when there's chemistry between a man and a woman. Were you going to talk about desire?" Bethel asked, and Spence shifted uncomfortably in his chair. This conversation was going from bad to worse.

"No, ma'am," he muttered, and his father and the two women laughed as he shifted again.

"Well, if you want to get her to accept a date, you need to be more romantic. Yes, flowers are nice, but they're unoriginal. You have to show her that you're putting real effort into it," Eileen said a bit dreamily.

"Effort?"

"Yes, son, effort," Martin said. "I know you don't usually have to work so hard, but isn't Sage worth it?"

"Of course," Spence replied. "She's more than worth it."

"Then prove that to her. Prove that she's worth you using your brain along with your charm," Martin told him.

"Give her the world in the palm of her hand, show her there's still magic in dating," Bethel said, her eyes misting over.

"This isn't helping," Spence grumbled. They were talking in riddles. He needed definitive answers on how to get the girl. A handbook with all the plays diagrammed, maybe.

"Be her Prince Charming," Eileen added.

Was that supposed to make a lightbulb suddenly turn on over his head? It sure as heck wasn't working. But as he stared at the three people in the room with him, his thoughts began spinning. Ahh. Yep. Looked like the light had kicked on, after all.

If one thing was for sure, it was that Spence would make a hell of a Prince Charming.

24

Green and red, gold and silver, garlands and lights—this was no hastily tricked-out break room. The hospital had gone all out to make this a Christmas party that wouldn't be forgotten. Was that an advantage of living in a small community?

Sage stepped into a meeting room that had been completely transformed into a holiday ballroom. The decorations were placed carefully enough to satisfy even her stringent requirements, candles were burning bright, and the smell of Christmas pine, cinnamon, and cloves drifted through the air.

"You are stunning."

She gasped to find Spence behind her, and it took several seconds before she could breathe again. He was resplendent in a black tux with a bright red tie and a sprig of holly on his lapel.

"I could say the same about you," she said, smiling shyly as she lost herself in his eyes.

"I think red is my new favorite color after seeing that number on you."

"Here you are, Sage." Almost in a daze, she turned to find a man approaching with a drink. Who was he? Oh! Her date.

"Thank you, Ted. I'm parched," she said, accepting the glass and taking a deep drink. She only hoped the alcohol level was at least eighty proof.

"I found our table. Would you like to sit down?" he asked, ignoring Spence completely. If she were Ted, she'd do the same. Her date paled in comparison with the guy. All the men in the room did, actually.

"Sage, you are breathtaking."

She turned again, a genuine smile coming to her lips as Martin approached with Eileen on his arm.

"This lovely woman leaves me in the dust," Sage said as she gave each of them a hug.

"Don't be silly. I was just happy to be invited," Eileen said with a giggle.

"Is my grandmother here?" Sage asked. "She didn't tell me whether she was attending."

"No," Eileen replied. "Martin invited us both to come with him, but she wasn't feeling very well."

"She's not well? She didn't say anything to me. I should go and check on her." What had happened? Her grandmother had seemed fine half an hour ago when she's spoken to her on the telephone.

"There's no need to rush off, darling. She just said her feet were tired from all the dancing we did last night."

"If you're sure . . ."

"I'm positive. If you rush out of here, your grandmother would have my hide. You don't want me to get into trouble now, do you?"

"Of course not, Aunt Eileen," Sage said. "We were getting ready to sit down. Would you like to join us?" *Please join us*, she added silently. She had a feeling it was going to be difficult to keep a conversation going with her date if she was left on her own.

"I'd love to join you," Martin said, and the four of them went to Sage's table. "We'll just move the seating around." He grabbed a waiter and had him move some place cards.

She stood at the table, giving Ted the opportunity to hold out her chair. When he simply sat down, she was subconsciously disappointed. Yes, it was old-fashioned of her, but she'd always been taught that a man held out his date's chair, never sitting before she did. When Martin did the proper thing by Eileen, Sage smiled.

Then Spence was there again, his hand on the back of her chair, a smile also on his face. "Ladies first," he whispered seductively against her ear, the warmth of his breath making her heart flutter. Ted didn't seem to notice, the clod.

"Thanks," she murmured as she took her seat and picked up her napkin. When Spence sat on her other side, she knew tonight was going to challenge her self-control.

"Oh! If you'll excuse me, I'll be right back." Ted jumped up and rushed over to a couple who'd just entered the room.

Sage watched as he laughed at something the man

said, and then the two of them walked over to the liquor bar, leaving the woman the other man had entered with standing alone. She didn't seem upset—she was obviously used to being abandoned like that.

"It looks like your date has other things on his mind," Spence said, leaning in too close for her comfort.

"This is a social event. It's perfectly fine to be *socializing*."

"It wouldn't matter if the building started falling down around us—I still wouldn't leave your side," Spence said softly, his deep drawl giving her goose bumps.

"Well, then, you must not be that social—or you just don't have any friends." She knew she was being a bit catty, but she refused to feel bad about it.

"I just know when I have a good thing. And I don't let it go."

"Is that a warning, Spence?"

"It's a promise, Sage."

"Oh no. Will the hackneyed lines never end?"

"Sorry, doll, but it happens to be the truth. I've decided I like you, and instead of just flirting and cornering you in exam rooms, I'm going to say what I think and feel. I want you—and not just for one night."

The sparkle in his eyes told her he was truly enjoying himself. The leap in her libido told her she was in deep trouble.

"And the past few weeks—what was that?" As he hadn't once been holding back from her, she couldn't imagine what he had planned with this new challenge.

"That was simply a warm-up. Now, I'm going to officially court you."

She gazed at him a moment before shaking her head. "Court me? Really? Isn't that what people do when they're planning an arranged marriage?"

"The definition of *courting* is to run after, pursue, chase . . ." There was a determination about him that she was enjoying, though she tried to tamp down the feeling.

"You've got your etymology completely wrong, by the way—rather shocking for a doctor. The root in *court* has nothing to do with the *cur* root meaning 'to run.' *Cur* . . . how appropriate."

"Details, details," he said loftily.

"In any case, Dr. Whitman, you're leaving out one important fact about the verb."

"I think I covered it all."

"*To court* is generally taken to refer to being involved with someone romantically with the intention of marrying them." That would scare him away!

"Hmm . . ." There was a pause as he leaned closer. "I think I like that definition best."

He held her gaze without blinking, making a shudder travel through her. But she finally turned her head, lifted her wineglass, and took a generous sip. No, not eighty proof, so she'd have to improvise.

"I'm on a date. This is highly inappropriate," she finally said when the silence was too much to bear.

"I don't see your date. That makes you fair game."

He seemed to have an answer for everything. "Did you just say that pursuing me is nothing more than a game?" If she could somehow twist his words, maybe she'd get out of this unscorched.

"You can call it whatever you want, but I *want* you, Sage. I want to take you on dates, spend time with you, learn about you, and . . . kiss you. I want to strip off your clothes, run my lips over every inch of your body, and sink deep inside you while you're calling out my name." He ended in a whisper, and she shivered in response.

"It's not polite to be chatting over there and ignoring the rest of us," Ted said.

Sage lifted her gaze, seeing that the entire table was now full, including her absentee date—and all eyes were on her. She wanted to reply that it also wasn't polite for him to run off, but she kept her mouth closed.

Was her skin flushed? It had to be flushed. Was it obvious what Spence had just been saying to her? For the life of her, she couldn't get words to emerge from her tight throat. This man was turning her inside out, and in front of everyone they worked with, too.

"You are absolutely right. We were just discussing work. Anyone have strong opinions about the new oral anticoagulants?" Spence asked.

She was grateful, though she knew the medical joke was at her expense, a sidelong reference to the way words were stuck in her mouth. She could now take a much-needed breath.

"That's my boy, always teaching. I'm sure Sage has a lot of stories to tell from her first few months of residency," Martin said, and he turned his full attention to her.

Sage was relieved by the change of subject. It allowed her to talk of what she knew, what she was confident about. Before long, the entire table was engaged in the conversation. Stories of humorous medical mishaps flew about, laughter spilled out, and way too much wine and eggnog was consumed. The evening had certainly turned around.

When it came time to dance, her date showed once again why he was still single. He stepped on her toes, scuffing her new pair of heels, and, while demonstrating to the world at large that "I Got Rhythm" hadn't been written for him, was boring her to tears with his endless chatter. She wished he'd stayed true to type and had run off with his drinking buddy again.

When she looked out at the crowd and found Spence dancing with one of the night nurses, whose hands were running up and down his arms, Sage felt a searing flash of jealousy. Ridiculous! She was there with her own date, and she didn't want to be with Spence.

So what if it looked like Spence would be taking the woman home for the night? So what if he and that . . . female fell in love and lived happily ever after? She didn't want him—she didn't want anyone. She had to focus on her career, and *only* her career right now.

So did she care when Spence kept his distance for the rest of the evening? She had to admit, after she left the party—Ted dropped her off at her apartment—she felt a dull ache in her stomach, a deep emptiness. Maybe being alone wasn't what she really wanted.

No. She had to shake off these feelings. She was happy with her career choice, a choice she'd always known would lead to a lot of lonely nights. It was worth it because she got to do what she truly loved. Not everyone could say the same thing.

She was also incredibly grateful when she watched Ted drive away without even walking her to her door. It was early, only ten, and he hadn't even asked if she wanted a nightcap. Maybe he'd been just as relieved to get away from her as she was to get away from him.

It was really kind of sad. It hadn't helped that her date, the most boring man alive, had been in the same room as Spence all night. Maybe, before

Spence, she might have had a great time with Ted. Then again, maybe not.

"Stop thinking about Spence," she muttered as she approached her front door. "You don't want him, certainly don't need him, and have nothing in common with him. Just focus on work."

As she reached the top of the steps, she noticed a bright red package sitting there with a large gold bow and a tag with her name in bold cursive letters.

She loved gifts. There was something magical about opening a wrapped present. Yes, she was perfectly capable of going out and buying her own trinkets, but knowing that someone had thought about you enough to give you something he or she had chosen just for you . . . that was special.

Should she wait until Christmas to open it? It certainly looked like a Christmas gift. There was nothing else to tell her who it was from. She shook the snow off her shoulders, then picked up the package and walked into her warm apartment.

After removing her coat and sitting down in the living room with the gift on the table in front of her, she eyed it eagerly. Who was she kidding? There was no way she'd wait. She undid the tape holding the lid down, and when she lifted the lid, she simply gasped.

She picked up the note and held it while gazing at the crystal red apple tree ornament that was sitting on a cushion of bright green velvet.

I have decided to be your fairy-tale prince. It's time for me to wake up my Sleeping Beauty.
    Spence

Her heart melted. Yes, it was silly. Yes, it was a bit cheesy. And, yes, she was in trouble—total-and-complete-meltdown kind of trouble. She was falling for this man even though she knew she shouldn't, and knew it could be disastrous. But how could she not when he was claiming to be her very own Prince Charming?

25

"Is it normal to have sharp, shooting pains running up and down my legs and spine?"

"Yes, unfortunately, and it's nothing that can be helped. When you're on your feet for twelve hours straight, that tends to happen," the nurse said with a laugh before trudging off down the hallway. Sage already knew that, but somehow it felt better to voice a complaint.

Sage had been working long shifts for five days in a row and she felt—and looked—like the walking dead. She had the next two days off and she wasn't going to leave her apartment the entire time. Bed, food, and romantic comedies on the television screen—she didn't care in what order.

When she turned a corner and saw Spence walking toward her, her heart did a little flip-flop and she couldn't prevent a smile from popping up on her face. The man was a gift-giving genius. She wanted to not like them, but she couldn't help it. How was a woman to resist when she kept getting packages on her front doorstep and in her locker at work?

She knew she should tell him she couldn't accept these presents, but each one was so unique, so special, that there was no way to give them back. Grace was green with envy each time Sage showed her the newest installment in Spence's recurring gift club.

He'd left her the crystal apple, two silver bells, a miniature dragon, and a single red rose. All of them had a theme from her favorite princess movies, all had a meaning, and each came with its own note.

This man was flipping her world upside down and she was so ready to pull him into the nearest broom closet and show him her appreciation—and maybe, just maybe, relieve the constant ache in her body, which grew worse every time she saw him.

"How did your last trauma case go?" he asked, standing well within her personal space.

She didn't care.

"It went well. I have to admit I was a little disappointed when I had to come back home for my residency, but I'm learning a lot and logging massive hours. And not only is it excellent training, but it's been good to be home." Sage started walking toward the locker room, because, as much fun as it was to stand there and chat with Spence, she really was exhausted and more than ready to get back to her apartment and put her feet up.

"Yes, it's been a slow season, too, so imagine what you'll learn when things start heating up."

"Is it awful to hope for disasters?"

"It is if you want people hurt, yes, but not if you want to learn how to save more lives."

"Well then, I shouldn't be in too much trouble. I do want to learn how to be the best doctor I can."

"You're off work tomorrow, right?"

Of course he knew her schedule. He was asking, but she knew he was planning something. She waited, not bothering to answer.

"It's time I get my tree, and if I do recall, you offered to help me."

"If I remember correctly, you pretended I offered to help," she informed him.

"That's not what Grace said."

There goes my lazy day off, she thought. And still she couldn't feel a hint of regret. Spending the day with him and picking out the perfect tree sounded pretty darn great.

"Why don't we go get some coffee and discuss our strategy? Better yet, let's get some dinner. You're off the clock, right?"

"Yes, my shift is over, but it's been a really long day. I was planning on heading home, sinking into a deep, hot bath, and not emerging from the apartment until I have to work again," she said, though she knew he wasn't going to be discouraged that easily.

"Then it's my mission to make sure you are well fed, and that you get out to see the sunshine. Being cooped up either in the hospital or in your apartment for too long will turn your skin white and endanger your health. Doctor's orders."

"Oh, I see. You're just a concerned doctor?"

"Of course I am. As the head of the ER, I have to make sure all my patients are well taken care of."

"You're now *my* doctor?" she asked, and was greeted with the instant image of the two of them playing doctor. Bad move, but she was having trouble feeling disgusted.

"I'll be your doctor anytime you like. I have all the tools I need—right on me," he said with a wink. When he saw her eyes straying involuntarily down his body—however convenient in general, scrubs weren't good for voyeurism—he had to ask, "Like what you see?"

Her head snapped up to meet the devilish smile on his face and the small box in his hand. "What's that?" She wanted to reach out and grab the package. But though she knew it was for her, she also knew she should refuse it so she wouldn't encourage his behavior. That wasn't going to happen, though, because she loved presents too dang much.

He held out his hand. "Just a little gift."

"You've got to quit getting me things," she said, but, after looking around to make sure that they were alone, she reached for the box.

"I like getting you gifts, Sage. Open it."

"It's not even Christmas and you've already left several packages at my place and at work. People are going to talk." Damn. Even the packaging was beautiful.

"Let them talk. I have nothing to hide."

"The other staff will hate me if they think you're playing favorites, you know."

"Everyone in this hospital knows already. As a matter of fact, if you want to earn a few extra dollars, you can sign up on the big office betting pool. People are laying down wagers on the date they think we'll get married."

Sage's mouth almost hit the floor. Marriage? Ridiculous. No way. She was so not ready for that. She hadn't even gone out on a real date with this man. Yes, there'd been a lot of flirting, and then, of course, their night in his hot tub . . . Add the fact that they kept running into each other—it was a small town, after all—and she was with him more than anyone else she knew. But still, they weren't a couple, and certainly weren't anywhere near having him proposing marriage.

"You have to stop saying things like that," she whispered as they reached the locker room.

"I like shocking you. I love the way your mouth opens into a perfect circle, love the way your skin flushes. I love watching you, love waiting on you. I don't think there is anything about this unusual relationship we have that I don't love." He leaned in even closer as he spoke.

Sage's heart fluttered again. The word *love* was sure coming from his mouth a lot. They weren't in love. She knew that. But, oh man, was she falling for this guy—falling hard.

Lifting the lid on the box, she sighed as she looked inside at the jewel-encrusted comb.

"Every princess needs a special comb," he said into her ear, making her heart beat faster.

Unfortunately, she had no doubt the gems on the handle were real. "I can't take this, Spence. It's far too expensive," she told him, though she wasn't putting much effort into handing the gift back to him.

He closed her fingers around the comb. "You will take it, use it, love it, and . . . think of me."

And he was right—she would.

"How do you know what to get? How did you know how much I love princesses?"

"A lot of determination and research on the perfect gifts. I'll have you know that I had a Disney movie marathon and watched *Cinderella*, *Beauty and the Beast*, *Mulan*, *Sleeping Beauty*, *Tangled*, *Frozen*, and a few others. I wanted to make sure you were fully enchanted."

She looked at him and knew he was speaking the truth. How could he be wrong for her when he was doing all the right things? Why had she decided dating him was a bad idea? The reason was beyond her right now, because at least in this moment, he seemed more perfect than humanly possible.

She was in a fog as she gazed up into his eyes.

"Why? Why me?" she asked him, letting the walls tumble down and opening herself up.

"I like you," he said as he got even closer, his body brushing against hers in the most sinful of ways, his lips grazing her ear before he continued speaking. "I want you. You're all I think about. Right now, I plan to take you for a nice meal, and then I'll take you back to my place, where I'm going to make love to you all night long, sleep with you in my arms, wake up to a nice brunch, and then go Christmas tree shopping."

He ended his little speech by connecting their lips, kissing her gently, and wiping away the last of her defenses. One night wouldn't do any harm. One night—that was all he was asking for.

"I can't seem to think around you . . . breathe around you."

"Good. Don't think; don't breathe. I'll provide the oxygen for both of us," he said, his hand wrapped around her, pulling her tightly against him. "All you need to do is say yes."

But he didn't give her time to say yes. He just devoured her mouth and claimed her body with his hands. Just when she was ready to give him her full surrender, her pager went off, making her jump as the blood continued rushing straight to her core.

"I need to check this," she whispered, barely able to get a word out.

"You're off the clock."

"We're never off the clock, Spence, and I can't believe *you* of all people would say such a thing." It was quite amusing, really, that her boss was the one trying to talk her out of work.

He pulled back, the glaze over his eyes starting to clear up when he noticed that his own pager was going off. "Crap! I need to check on this."

Overhead, they heard "Trauma alert, ER" come over the hospital speakers. Both of them headed straight there.

"Dr. Whitman, we have a six-year-old female, auto versus pedestrian. ETA, one minute."

Sage tensed instantly. She hated cases involving children. She knew it was a reality of her job, but she hated it. All traces of passion were long gone as she stood side by side with Spence and waited for the huge bay doors to open. It would be any second. The sirens had been blaring and now were silent.

"Let's go," Spence called as the doors opened and the paramedics rushed in with a small girl on the gurney. Sage moved to one side, listening as they shouted out important information. Spence was on the other side of the gurney, doing his own assessment of the child as the paramedics spoke.

"Female, age six, run over by mom's half-ton pickup. Found unresponsive and apneic, with unstable pelvis. Abdomen tight and distended. Placed two eighteen-gauge IVs to bilateral ACs with IV fluid wide-open, but girl's blood pressure keeps dropping. Has been intubated, and we needle decompressed her left lung. In full C-spine precautions. Vital signs are BP sixty over thirty, HR one forties, no spontaneous respirations, oxygen saturation eighty-two percent."

"We can save her," Sage said beneath her breath, determination shining in her eyes.

"My daughter!" a woman screamed as she rushed into the room. Sage took only a second to glance up at the hyperventilating woman. The poor mother was held upright by her husband; her face was red, and her body looking almost lifeless in her despair. "Please! My baby girl!"

The woman suddenly started writhing in her agony, and when her husband lost hold of her, two nurses had to grab her before she fell to the floor. Sage tuned everything out as they moved the child to the trauma bay, everyone doing their job like well-choreographed dancers. The nurses cut the rest of the child's clothes away and began looking for the damage while Sage began her exam at the head of the table.

She assessed neuro status, pupils, airways, calling out orders to the trauma nurse, making sure it was all getting documented. "Pupils are fixed and dilated." The girl had severe head trauma. But Sage wouldn't lose this child—she couldn't!

No. She had to keep her cool, had to do a full assessment. She couldn't think about losing the child; she just needed to look at each individual piece that had to be fixed. "I don't hear any lung sounds on the left side, and her ventilator pressures are high. We need a chest tube set up, stat."

As Spence placed the chest tube, Sage continued her assessment of the girl, and it wasn't looking hopeful, but she wouldn't think this way.

"She has a flail chest to her left side with multiple rib fractures bilaterally, distant heart tones indicating possible cardiac tamponade," Sage reported.

"Left side hemothorax," Spence called after inserting the left-side chest tube.

"I need two units of O negative. PRBC's, stat. Abdomen is distended with ecchymosis noted to bilateral flanks. Pelvis unstable; place a pelvic binder now to reduce internal bleeding. No obvious deformity to her lower extremities. Get me the fast scan so I can take a look at internal bleeding."

People continued moving and Sage wanted to shake, wanted to weep, but she wouldn't. There was a job to do and they would do it. There was no time for weakness.

Sage was on autopilot, calling out commands and working furiously with Spence to save the child. Then the room seemed to slow down as she looked up, his eyes connecting with hers. When it seemed there was nothing else she could do from her end, he spoke.

"What do you do next, Sage?"

What? What did he want her to say? She didn't know what to do. This wasn't a training moment. He needed to save the child. "We need to get her to surgery now, save her," she said.

"How, Sage? How do we save her? Take over," he commanded.

The force in his voice shifted something inside her. Not knowing how it was happening, she moved, shouting out orders, doing everything she could to heal this child's broken body.

The scan showed significant internal bleeding. "I can't see the source of this bleeding. It could be her spleen or liver. We need to get her to the OR, stat!" Sage commanded.

"They are ready for us, Dr. Banks," the ER nurse Mo said, the look in her eyes making her opinion obvious. She didn't think the girl would make it.

"Don't look at me like that, Mo. Don't give up on this girl."

"Please don't let my baby die. I didn't see her. I didn't see her," the mother wailed. A couple of nurses were holding her and whispering soothing words. Sage didn't have time to address the mother yet. All she had time to do was take care of this child.

Suddenly, the endotracheal tube disconnected and a groan came from the girl's throat before she coughed, spraying blood all over the front of Sage's gown.

"Suction her ETT now and tell the OR we are en route. Get two more units of O negative to the OR to prepare for surgery and keep those fluids wide-open," Sage commanded. "Let's go!"

They began moving and Sage noticed that Spence wasn't following. Why wasn't he doing something? He needed to help this girl, and he needed to do it now, before it was too late.

"Go, Sage. You have this," he said as they reached the elevator and rushed inside.

Sage looked back, seeing Spence standing in the hallway, watching them leave the bay. She didn't have time to analyze the look in his eyes—but it looked like sadness.

No!

He wouldn't be sad for this child, because she would live. Sage wouldn't allow her to die.

26

Nothing but a long, eerie tone could be heard in the room as the heart monitor indicated the patient's heart had stopped.

Sage stood there, her hands and scrubs bloodied, a single tear falling down her face. "Time of death, 6 p.m."

She turned and walked from the room. Despite all they'd done, nothing had worked. The little girl kept on fighting, kept on struggling to live, but where one problem was fixed, another had appeared. Her little body hadn't been able to endure any longer.

Finding her way to the locker room, Sage sat hard on the bench, no emotion, nothing able to break through. Spence had told her to save the child, and she had failed.

This little girl had her whole life ahead of her, and because of a stupid accident, her parents were being told right now that they wouldn't be taking their daughter home, but instead, they'd be saying goodbye to a cold corpse.

Finally, Sage stood up, moved to the showers, and stripped, then climbed in, not even able to tell whether the temperature was right. On days like this she hated her profession. This was when she wanted to quit. Why put herself through the hell of medical school and residency if she couldn't save the life of one small, precious child?

She didn't know how long she stood beneath the spray, but she eventually stepped from the shower and dressed. She couldn't say what she was wearing. Her night, which had looked so promising, had just crashed around her.

She just wanted to go home, curl into a ball, and let the tears out. She'd get over this—she had to. It might take a little bit longer than normal, of course. She could still see the bright blond curls, the pink jumpsuit. In her years in the medical program, she'd seen death, but it always seemed so much harder when it was a child.

As she emerged from the locker room, she spotted Spence, changed and ready to leave. She walked past him, not wanting to talk. Not wanting to talk to anyone. She just needed to escape from this place, get away before it consumed her.

"Sage . . ." He was following her, his voice quiet, hesitant. She didn't want his sympathy, didn't want assurances that everything would be all right. She just wanted to go home and forget everything.

"Leave me alone," she said, moving into the snow-covered grass beyond the parking lot. She gazed out at newly falling snow and wished she could just drift away in the wind.

She'd been trained for this, and had been told over and over that she mustn't and couldn't take it personally. There were more lives she would save than lose. And yet if all of that was true, why did her heart ache so badly right now? Had her instructors been lying to her? It sure as hell seemed like it.

"I'll give you a ride home," Spence said, his hand grazing her shoulder.

She shrugged it off. "I can get home myself." She didn't need him to look after her. She didn't need anyone. She was strong and independent. She was a doctor, a woman, and a person. She would survive.

Unlike the small child.

"You can't drive right now, Sage. This was a hard case," he said, wrapping his arms around her from behind. She tried to push him away, but he wasn't allowing it, wasn't letting her grieve. Damn him!

"I'm fine, Spence. It wasn't like this was a natural disaster with thousands of lives lost. This was one person—one . . . child. Yes, it's harder when it's a child, but it happens. Isn't that what we're taught? Of course, they can say what they like about not blaming yourself. They're teaching, not trying to save a life. I know we did all we could. I know we tested her, and fixed things. I know she was beyond help. None of that makes a difference, though, does it? Nothing we did saved her. Right before Christmas and she's gone forever. Her parents will get up on

Christmas morning, wait to hear the sound of her excited voice, and only hear silence."

Sage tried desperately not to yell, not to cry, not to feel this all-consuming rage. It wasn't working. She was pissed and sad, and felt wretchedly vulnerable. She wanted Spence to leave, and she wanted him to hold her. Ultimately, she really didn't know what she wanted.

"Come on. Let's get you out of this cold," Spence said, his voice still low and level.

She allowed him to lead her off, and when they got to his pickup, she panicked. She didn't want to be inside a vehicle. What if the brakes failed? What if she fell out? What if she were run over and no one heard her cries?

She pulled back from him, slipped on the ice, and before he was able to turn back to her, she fell to the ground, her back stinging as she landed hard.

"Sage, I'm sorry," Spence said, immediately crouching down.

"I'm fine," she said as the sob bubbled up and escaped through her tight throat.

"You are nowhere near fine," he said as he opened the truck door and got her inside. She didn't want to be in there but somehow found herself shivering on his front seat.

"I don't want to drive anywhere," she told him, nearly eaten alive by panic.

"Then we'll just sit here and keep warm."

She could handle that. "I wanted so badly to save her," she said, anguish clearly coming through.

"She couldn't be saved, Sage. As soon as I did the first assessment, saw the damage, I knew we wouldn't save her," Spence said, making her head whip around as she replayed his words.

"Wha—what? What do you mean?"

"She wasn't going to make it. The internal damage was too great. A rib had pierced her heart and both lungs. She was hemorrhaging. With the condition of the roads and the delay in the emergency call, it took too long for her to get here. Nothing we did from that point forward was going to help."

"Then why did you tell me to save her, damn you?" Sage was seething. She needed somewhere to direct her anger, and Spence had just given her the perfect target.

"Because that's what we do, Sage. We work on the hopeless and sometimes there's a miracle. We work until we can't work any longer so we can tell the parents we did absolutely everything we could. We work until that child is no longer with us, even when we know it's of no use."

"Why didn't you keep working, then? I'm just a resident—a freaking first-year resident. I've only been in training for a little over six months. I don't know everything, not at all. You gave up. You shouldn't have given up."

"It's something you had to learn. You had to know

that you can fight to the death if you have to, but that you will survive when the worst happens. And you will, Sage. You'll hurt for a little while and then you'll come back in and do this all over again. Sometimes you'll win and sometimes you'll lose, but the point is that you *will* survive."

When Spence reached toward her, she jerked away, angry with him even though she could see some logic to his words. He was, in essence, her teacher—and to do his job right, he needed to teach her everything he could. But this lesson hurt too badly—was still hurting her too badly—for her to forgive him just yet.

"I'm going to drive now, Sage. I know you haven't eaten anything all day, and you need to get something in you before you make yourself sick." He put the truck in reverse and started moving.

Sage should have left, stepped from the truck, but though she was mad at him, she also wanted his comfort, wanted not to be alone. They drove for a while, heading toward the city instead of Sterling. She watched fat snowflakes fall against the windshield as she and Spence reached downtown Billings, where lights lined the streets and people rushed from vehicles to restaurants and stores. The city was alive even with the snow. It continued forward even if one of its residents had been tragically taken from them.

"If you let it, this will kill you, Sage. If you get too attached, start blaming yourself, you will fail again and again. You can't grieve over your patients, and you can't hold yourself responsible. You have to work as hard and as fast as you can, but you have to remember that you're only human—there's only so much you can do. Sometimes, God has a different plan."

It was odd, but the sound of his voice was soothing her, making her feel somehow just a bit better. He wasn't saying anything she hadn't heard before, but when faced with life and death and coming out on the losing end, she'd found it difficult to remember what she'd been taught.

"I understand that, Spence. But it's still easier said than done."

"Yes, but you can find the balance you need to find. You'll know how to care just the right amount, enough that you'll work your hardest, but not so much that you lose yourself. You're a fighter, Sage, and you'll be an advocate for your patients. That's all anyone can hope for from a doctor. Be strong, but don't be afraid to lean on others."

"I guess the hardest part is that so many people live who will go back to abusing drugs, or cheating on a spouse, or beating their children. So many people get their lives saved who turn around and throw that life away. And then, suddenly, there's this six-year-old girl on your table who woke up that morning to ask how many more days until Christmas, who might have gone outside and built a snowman, who'd just begun school and had an entire future ahead of her. And she's the one who goes. It's just not fair."

"No, none of it's fair, Sage. All I know is that we take an oath to help everyone who seeks us. We take an oath not to judge, to do all we can. Sometimes we do have to help people who the world might be better off without. You can never know that, though, and sometimes we lose someone so precious I don't know how the world can survive the loss. Sometimes the day doesn't bring us anything at all. This is a job—a job we love, a job that helps people, but it *is* a job. You have to leave it at the hospital when you step through those doors. You can't carry it home with you, and you can't shoulder the burden all alone."

He was right. Of course he was right. And it was helping to talk it out, but she couldn't think about it anymore, couldn't keep focusing on this loss. She had to get her mind off it or she'd be weepy all night.

He stopped the truck, and the snow quickly enveloped them in a cocoon, invisible to the people passing by as it piled up on his windshield and the side windows fogged. It felt like they were the last two people in the world.

"I'm sorry I didn't warn you—sorry I put you through that," he said as he pulled her close to him and wrapped her in his arms.

"I'm sorry I yelled at you," she said, though she felt only a smidgen of remorse.

He chuckled softly as he laid her head on his shoulder. Then he was rubbing her back, moving his hand in slow, easy motions that were draining the last of her tension.

"I care about you, Sage," he whispered in her ear.

She was too vulnerable right now to hear this. She might actually believe him if she wasn't careful.

"Ditto, Doctor," she said, trying to lighten the mood.

"Good. Because I plan on being around for a very long time." He pulled back so he could look into her eyes.

What was he trying to say to her? Were they now officially a couple? It wasn't as if grown-ups tended to define this sort of thing, which could really make it confusing. If he kissed her in the backseat of his car, or in this case, the front seat of his truck, did that make them an item? It was all so confusing, but she was grateful to focus on their relationship—or nonrelationship—instead of her patient's blond curls.

"Take me home with you, Spence." She was a bit shocked that the words popped from her mouth, but as soon as they were out, she didn't regret them. He'd invited her to spend the night, after all, and she was ready to do that. Ready to feel.

"Oh, Sage, you're killing me," he groaned. He lowered his mouth and kissed her, a gentle, sweet kiss that had her sighing into his mouth. "This isn't the right time." He drew away, breathing heavily.

Hurt flashed through her. "I thought . . . you wanted me." Was she actually going to be rejected *again* by this man? Had she not learned her lesson? He'd been pushing her for so long now, and when she was ready to accept what he was offering, he suddenly wanted to take the offer back. She didn't think she could endure anything else today. Tears were so close to the surface.

"I want you more than it's possible to say, Sage. I could show you, but I don't want to embarrass us both. I could tell you that I'm just following through on our date, or that it would be better for you not to be alone, but I'd know that it was my own selfishness, that I was taking advantage of you when you've just gone through a seriously traumatic experience. I'd be the worst kind of subhumanoid if I took you to bed tonight."

She looked at him with surprise. Was he really a prince come to sweep her off her feet? What man was this noble? It couldn't have been rehearsed. There was no doubt now that she was falling in love with him. And it didn't bother her one whit.

"I want to make love to you, Spence. I want it more than anything," she said as she boldly ran a finger up his chest and across his hard jaw. He shuddered, which gave her a measure of satisfaction.

"It can't happen like this, Sage. It has to happen because we are consumed with desire. I want you to be making love to me, not trying to escape your pain."

He wasn't being cruel, but he was still ticking her off. She wanted to forget what had happened today, and she was sure that being in his arms would be just the right antidote. He'd told her earlier, before the poor little girl was wheeled in, that he wanted her. So why wasn't he stripping her right here in his truck?

"Fine. Then take me home." Just great. She was now embarrassed on top of everything else. She'd thrown herself at him and was rewarded with a nice, fat rejection.

"Nope. That's not going to happen, either. I'm going to feed you a good, healthy meal, then I'm going to bring you back out to my truck and drive you home—your home. And once we're there, we'll park out front and steam up the windows. Then, when I can't stand another second without ravishing you in the most disgraceful way possible, I will walk you to the door, kiss you one last time, and then run like crazy back to my truck before I do something foolish like follow you indoors and taste your body like I so desperately want to." His voice had grown huskier the longer he spoke.

For her part, Sage felt her breathing rise a few notches. This man could turn her on with nothing but words.

"I don't think I can eat anything," she said, deciding for now to ignore the rest of his declaration.

"Then eat for me." With that, he turned off the

truck and pulled her with him out the driver's door. After being in the heat of his truck for the past half hour, it was a real shock to step outside into the freezing snow.

"Fine," she said. Not that she had much choice.

The sooner they got through the meal, the quicker they could begin their make-out session in his truck. That, more than anything else, made her more than ready to eat.

Later, the night did end the way he'd described it, but with just a little more moaning on his part than he'd led her to expect.

27

"Get in here and open this package right now!"

Sage turned from the front door to find Grace sitting on the couch with a long box in front of her on the coffee table, practically salivating over the thing.

"I've had a long day at work, Grace. What's got your panties in a bunch?" But Sage knew. Grace was just as excited to see what was in the package as Sage was.

"Don't play dumb with me, roomie. It's only because I'm such a loyal friend that I haven't ripped this box open. This is a different shape than the others and I'm dying to see what's inside. So hurry up and end my misery."

Sage walked over to the couch and sat down. To be truthful, she wanted to open the package, but it was so much fun to torment her best friend. She wasn't sure which of them could hold out longer, but she was going to try.

"I'm so tired," she said. "These long shifts have got to end at some point." She slowly pulled off her shoes and began massaging her feet.

"I'm sure you could find a highly qualified surgeon who would love to rub those feet for you if you'd quit avoiding him like the plague. I swear that he left fifty messages on the machine a couple of days ago. You'll have to tell me what happened eventually. I'm not above using Chinese torture methods."

"If you were ever home, Grace, maybe I'd be more willing to talk to you."

"I'm home now, sweetie."

"I lost a patient, then offered myself to Spence, and he turned me down. So I avoided him during my two days off, ate a lot of Chunky Monkey, and slept for hours on end. It was horrifically boring."

"Well, then, at least you were nice and rested." Grace did have a way of looking at things from a brighter perspective.

"Not anymore. And though I *was* nice and rested, I had nowhere to go," Sage said with a lopsided grin.

"If you'd answer the phone, I'm sure you'd have somewhere to go all the freaking time. For now, let's open this box." Grace jumped up, grabbed it, and tossed it into her friend's lap.

Sage had no choice now but to open it. She took the card off the top and read that first.

Please wear this tonight.
  Yours, Spence

"Ooh, I can't stand the suspense," Grace said as she rocked from foot to foot.

Sage opened the lid and didn't know what to say. Inside was a dress, a delicate hunter-green chiffon gown with long, flowing sleeves and a slit that was indecently high on one thigh.

"I couldn't wear this," Sage gasped.

"Oh yes you can, and you *will*. I am so jealous," Grace said as she stood up, took the dress from Sage's fingers, and held it up to her body with great drama. "You'll definitely look like a princess. I guess he really is keeping that whole royalty theme rolling, isn't he?"

And she proceeded to twirl around the living room while humming a Disney tune.

"Do you want to go on the date with Spence?" Sage asked with a laugh.

"Don't tempt me. It's been way too long since I've had sex," Grace grumbled. She handed the dress back to Sage and slumped down in her seat.

"From what I've seen, Camden wouldn't mind getting underneath your skirt," Sage said with a waggle of her eyebrows.

"I don't think so. We can barely stand to be in the same room together. That man runs hot and cold like a kitchen faucet. One minute he's all charm and the next he's Mr. Brooding. I don't get it. Not like I care or anything."

"If you'd just spill your guts about whatever deal you have going on with the man, your troubles would evaporate," Sage told her.

"There will be no spilling of my guts. It's a national secret," Grace said with a wink.

The frightening part was that Sage could see Grace mixed up with some ultrasecret mission. It was the sort of thing that fit perfectly with her best friend's personality.

And as usual, Grace changed the subject. "Okay, if you're going to wear that dress, Sage, we have to go shopping right this minute for the most shameless panty set we can find. You have to be sexy as sin when that thing comes off."

"I haven't even decided whether I'm going," Sage said, but Grace just jumped up and grabbed pen and paper.

"You are so going, Sage. I can see it in your eyes. Besides, you'd be a fool not to. I can already tell that this is going to be the best date ever."

"I don't know . . ." She'd offered her body and he'd turned her down flat. That still stung, despite all his fine talk about being a gentleman or whatever.

"Oh, quit being a martyr. If anyone needs to loosen up, it would be you. You've always put everyone and everything in front of your own happiness. Yes, getting good grades and excelling in everything academically is great and all, but you have to live a little, too. Otherwise you'll never have a well-rounded life. Trust me on this one. Let's get the sexy undies, go and get manis and pedis, and then knock the socks right off of Spence when he shows up tonight."

The pleading in Grace's tone was her undoing. Not only did Sage want to do this, but having a girls' day out sounded perfect. With the number of hours she had been working, a night off was always good. And she couldn't remember the last time she'd had a pedicure. That was exactly what she needed. The week's stress would float away the minute she put her feet in the hot, massaging water.

They left immediately, since it was an hour to the nearest mall. Peggy's clothing store didn't carry the kind of lingerie Grace had in mind. Living in a small town was great until you wanted to do some real shopping and have a gourmet meal. Sage wasn't complaining, really, but she did love the convenience of a big city.

The first store they hit was Victoria's Secret, and Sage found herself blushing at the things Grace was holding up for her to examine.

"Are you crazy? I can't wear that. He'd think I was a hooker," Sage said as she looked over her shoulder to make sure no one was paying attention to them.

"You'll make him so hard, he'll drop to his knees and beg you to be his forever," Grace said, holding out a bright red corset and garter belt. "Besides, you definitely want to be wearing a garter belt for much easier—and faster—access." She offered up her best wolfish grin.

"Why don't we just buy the split undies and make the access instantaneous?" Sage snapped.

"Now that's an idea . . ."

"Look, Grace, I've never worn a corset or a garter belt. I don't know if I can even make the dang things work. I'd probably mess everything up." Sage eyed some pretty bra and panty sets that weren't quite so wanton.

"You will wear this, and then you will report to me how far his jaw drops when he sees you in it. Got it?"

Grace grabbed Sage's hand and the lingerie and led her to the dressing room in the back. Sage was absolutely mortified when an employee had to explain to her exactly how to wear such a getup.

"I CAN'T BELIEVE how innocent you are," Grace said as they drove back to the apartment that afternoon. "You missed out so much on crazy, down-and-dirty college romps."

"Um . . ." Sage wasn't used to this sort of banter and had no idea how to respond.

When Grace swung her head around to stare intently at Sage and say, "We are going to take your innocence, stomp on it, and toss it in the trash, as of tonight," the car swerved violently.

"Watch the road!" Sage squealed, her heart pounding triple time. She'd never make her date with Spence if Grace went on like this.

"Oh, the roads are fine. The rock trucks came and got them nice and clear," Grace said, waving her hand.

"Well, they aren't deicing the ditches, Grace, and that's where you're headed if you don't pay attention."

"Quit being responsible for five minutes straight, Sage Banks. I want confirmation that you're going to let it all go and live a little, and I swear I *will* land us in a ditch if you don't agree to this date with this guy."

"I'm worried, Grace. We had that epic failure at sex once, and then I threw myself at him a second time, and what if it's all me and I'm just horrible at the whole sex thing?"

"Oh, honey, you will rock his world. He was in shock at finding you a virgin. That's understandable. And then he was doing the right thing the other night. Only a cad would have taken you to bed when you were so vulnerable, so upset at losing that little girl. But tonight, you both know what's going to happen, and it will be beautiful. The reason it will? Because it's obvious that you're in love with him."

"I think I am falling in love with him. It's just that he's so . . . so . . . I don't even know how to describe it. He's romantic, funny, sweet, understanding. He always knows what to say, and he seems to know exactly when I need him the most. I've really started to fall hard for him. I hope it's not all just a big joke on his part."

"There's no way, sweetie. He would be a total and utter fool if he dared to play a game like that with you. I'd most certainly have to kick his ass right into Idaho!"

When they arrived at their apartment complex— safely, somehow—Sage practically floated up the steps with her purchase clutched tightly in her hands.

"We only have a couple of hours until he gets here," Grace said. "It's time for me to work my magic." She led Sage to the kitchen and sat her down.

It didn't take long for the curling iron, flat iron, and Grace's huge cache of makeup to come out. Sage had a feeling she'd feel like a Barbie come to life by the time her best friend was done. Maybe Spence wouldn't even recognize her. But she had to admit that, for tonight at least, she rather wanted to feel like an entirely new person.

28

The dress fit like it was made just for her. Of course, this was from Spence, so it most likely had been. She didn't want to know how he'd gotten her exact measurements. Still, the image of him sliding his hands around her body and sneakily writing down the details was far from an unpleasant one. Heck, the thought made her sigh and giggle at the same time.

Once she was all dressed up and ready to go, Sage looked in the mirror with a critical eye. But there was nothing to be critical about. *Beautiful* wasn't a word she often associated with herself, but right now, at this exact moment, that's the way she felt.

Her wavy red hair had been tamed—not an easy task—and her makeup, though subtle, highlighted her eyes, cheekbones, and lips. She looked ready to walk the red carpet and hoped Spence didn't think she was trying too hard.

Knowing that she was wearing the sexy lingerie underneath the dress made her feel even bolder. This was the night—she could feel it to her very bones. They were going to make love and it was going to be spectacular.

"You are a vision, an absolute vision," Grace said from the doorway, her eyes tearing up. "I take full credit for the hair and makeup, but the total package is indescribable, and it's all you."

"Thanks, Grace. I never could have pulled this off without you." Sage gave her best friend a hug. "He'll be here anytime. I'd better get downstairs." She took one final look in the mirror and headed toward the living room. The doorbell rang just after she slipped on her borrowed shoes from Grace. Right on time—something she appreciated in a man.

When she opened the door, Sage lost her breath. Literally. It just whooshed right out of her. The same thing had happened last time she saw Spence in fancy clothes. And here he was in his black tux with his hair smoothed back, a single red rose in his hand, and a smile on his lips—male perfection personified. The added sparkle in his deep green eyes completed the look.

"I am one lucky man," he murmured as he stepped over her threshold and pulled her into his arms. "The dress has come alive with you in it." He bent down and kissed her, and she forgot the rest of the world existed, thought only of him and what they would do later tonight.

"What are the plans?" she asked when he finally pulled back. She'd half wanted that kiss to go on forever and couldn't help feel a twinge of disappointment when it didn't. But if they were ever going to get out of her apartment, his lips would have to detach from hers.

"That's a surprise," he said. "But don't plan on an early night. As a matter of fact, don't plan on being home until tomorrow night," he said as he took her jacket and placed it over her shoulders. She'd much rather wear a pretty shawl or wrap, but the weather wasn't going to allow that.

"What about work?" She'd gotten off a ten-hour shift a few hours ago, and she was scheduled again tomorrow.

"The boss gave you tomorrow off," he said with a wink. She knew she should be upset that he hadn't consulted her about that, but she was too excited to scold him.

"Well, then, I guess I'm in your hands until tomorrow," she said, feeling a wonderful freedom at letting him take over. When she was the one always in control, it tended to get a little draining. This letting go could become addictive.

Spence led her to his truck, and soon they were traveling down the plowed roads. Snow was still threatening, but the night was clear for now. When they turned into the small airport, she looked over at him.

"What's going on?"

"You just have to wait," he said with a sly smile.

They pulled up to the terminal and he parked the truck. Walking through the one-room building, they came out on the other side, where a private jet was waiting.

"Okay, Spence, you *have* to tell me something," she said, looking from the jet to him.

"I'm taking you to dinner," was all he said before leading her to the stairs.

"Welcome back, Dr. Whitman," a flight attendant said when they reached the top of the stairs and stepped inside.

The jet was decorated in creams and cherrywood. It had a sleek leather couch along one wall, and a couple of matching chairs along the other. A television console was on the wall with a small bar beneath holding snacks and drinks.

"We'll sit in the chairs for takeoff," Spence said. "If you'd like, we can then move to the couch."

"That sounds fine," she said, though she was out of her comfort zone in his jet. She knew the Whitman family had a lot of money, but she wasn't used to seeing things like this. "Is this yours?"

"My family owns a couple of jets. They've come in handy with all the trips to Seattle. Plus, the nearest commercial airport is almost an hour away. That's far too much commuting for me," he said.

The flight attendant approached and asked them what they'd like to drink.

"I'll take a red wine, Laura," Spence said.

"I'll have the same," Sage said as she sat down.

After the plane had taken off and had reached cruising altitude, Sage turned to Spence and asked, "So, are you going to tell me yet where we're going?"

"Nope. You'll soon find out."

"You're just lucky that I'm finding this all very exciting. I normally need to know everything in advance."

"I'm incredibly lucky that I get to spend the evening with you, Sage. You take my breath away—and I don't mean just with your spectacular looks. I really enjoy our time together. I've just never been with a woman like you."

She gave a nervous laugh. "I don't know if that's a great line or not, but I have to tell you, it's working." If the guy was playing games, he was clearly the winner.

"I wouldn't do that to you, Sage. I'm falling hard."

"I think this jet's temperature just rose a few degrees, Spence."

"Then I better stay where I'm seated, because if I come over there, I'll mess up your glorious hair."

"Grace would get more than a little upset with you. She worked hard on it," Sage said, then winked. "I, on the other hand, wouldn't mind at all." He began to get up when Laura came back in to refill their wineglasses.

Spence's eyes burned with hunger, but he remained where he was, and not long afterward, the jet started making its descent into Seattle. Their night was just beginning, and the need ripping through Sage's stomach was rising degree by degree.

29

"Where are we?" Sage asked when the car finally stopped. They'd landed in Seattle over half an hour ago and were now somewhere downtown. She'd never been to Seattle—she'd only seen pictures of it, or images in some of her favorite movies, like *Sleepless in Seattle*.

"Dinner and dancing at the Vault Nightclub," Spence told her.

"I haven't heard of it," she said, wondering whether she should try to act a bit more worldly. At her age and with her level of education, she should know more about culture and entertainment, but she'd studied just medicine so intensely and for so long that she simply didn't know what the outside world was like—let alone what the dating world was like.

"It's a cozy place with the best chef in the west, but only the best of the best are in on the secret. Otherwise the location would become too crowded. There is nothing like warm food and intimate dancing to heat you up in the thick of winter. We're going to have a nice romantic dinner and then listen to soft music while I hold you close," he said as he led her from the car to the club.

After stepping inside, they were seated immediately, and Sage discovered that Spence hadn't been kidding. The place was dark, small, and romantic, and their table was near the stage where a band was setting up.

"They won't start playing for another hour. We have plenty of time to enjoy a nice meal, then sit back and enjoy a drink before dancing."

"I bet you've been here a lot," she said after they ordered and waited for their appetizers. He looked at her for a minute as if trying to decide what he should or shouldn't say.

"Sage, people like to play a lot of games. It's natural and it comes to us easily. I like the occasional game myself, and I won't lie to you about it. I've dated a lot, but what we have right now is fresh and new. Maybe I shouldn't have brought you to Seattle, where I lived for so long, but this is one of my favorite places on earth. While I have taken many a date to dinner and dancing before, it wasn't here. Most the women I dated in the past—let's just say that this wouldn't have been their cup of tea. I tended to date more . . . shallow women. One of the reasons I like you so much is because you're so real—because you're the type of woman a man wants on his arm forever, not just for a night."

Should she be offended by anything in his speech? Sage didn't know. Was he saying the other women he'd dated were all show and no substance? Maybe.

But was he also saying she was all wholesome and good for bearing kids, but not exactly a seductress? That should please her, but, heck, part of her really wanted to be femme fatale. Didn't all women want the guys they were dating to think they were the most amazing creature ever? Didn't they want men they cared about to be reduced to a drooling pile of mush in their presence?

Okay, maybe not. She never used to feel that way before.

"I agree about the games," she finally told him. "I've seen a lot of men play them—and a lot of women, too. I don't want to be dishonest. I was so focused on studies that in my downtime pretty much all I did was observe the world around me without actually living in it. I'm a little sad about that now. Yes, I'm proud of my education, but there's more to life than just work and school."

"I agree, but I don't play as much as you might think. The game has changed anyway. This has gone from my being fascinated by you to my not being able to go one hour without you on my mind. If this were nothing but an act, you'd be able to see it. When I was younger, I wasn't interested in women for much more than a night. I hate to admit that, but it's true. Now . . . well, my feelings are different. Now I never want to let you out of my sight."

"Should I be afraid? Maybe get a restraining order?" she asked, chuckling.

"Afraid? Yes," he said with a gleam in his eyes.

Her stomach tightened with need. "I could skip the jazz," she said. She was ready—more than ready—to go to his room.

"I'd love to take you right now, Sage. But I'm not going to. I'm giving you a full first date before I take you to the hotel and ravish you."

"Fine. Then we had better talk about something else, because right now, even this thin material feels like a straitjacket."

Just then, the waiter appeared with their appetizers. He didn't act as if he'd overheard, but Sage's cheeks heated anyway. They definitely need to put the sex talk on the back burner.

"I'm an open book. What do you want to know?" he asked, leaning back and opening his arms.

"Tell me about your family. You were all so much older than I was, so I don't know much about your brothers. Yes, I had a crush on you, but let's not dwell on that, please," she said and paused, but when he said nothing, she continued. "My grandmother and your father have been friends forever, but all I know is that you were adopted."

His eyes clouded, and she regretted asking him to open up about his family. Maybe it was a touchy subject.

"I'm sorry. I shouldn't have asked," she said.

"No. It's fine. I love talking about my family. My brothers and father are the most important people in the world to me. It might take a week or so to fill you in on everything, though."

"It's a good thing that I could listen to you talk all day and night for months on end," she replied, then blushed again at how much she was revealing about herself. Luckily, he let that one pass.

"Some of this you probably already know, so I hope I don't bore you. Michael is the youngest—the baby, as we like to call him when we're teasing him. He's also the most sensitive, but don't push his buttons, because I've seen that boy explode. He's always jetting off somewhere—he buys and sells commercial real estate. I've noticed lately that he's been home a lot more, though. We all have since our dad got sick."

"I didn't know your dad was sick."

"He didn't want to upset anyone, so he didn't say anything, but since we've been back, he's doing a lot better." Spence kept his suspicions to himself. He'd feel horrible if he'd been thinking his dad was faking and then something really did happen. "Onward then. Camden is next in line. He's the family lawyer, and we make fun of him because he's always searching for unusual cases. I don't know what he's working on right now, but he's pretty excited about it."

"Grace is doing something with Camden and she won't tell me about it. It's driving me crazy. Do you happen to know?"

"I will do some investigating and see if I can find out."

"I guess that's a start. This is the first time she hasn't shared with me."

"Now you have my curiosity piqued."

"Well, there's nothing we can do about it right now, so continue. I believe we are up to Jackson," she said, and sipped at her wine.

"Ah, Jackson. He's had some rough patches over the years. He was married and then lost his child. To this day, it's hard for him to talk about, but since he got married to Alyssa, he's a new man, and I'm enjoying time with my brother more than I can express. He's a good man."

"I can't imagine losing a child. How did he make it through all of that?" she asked.

"I really don't know," he said with a sigh. "It took a lot of time. He'll open up eventually and share it all with his brothers, but for now, I'm just glad to see him happy again."

"It doesn't always help to open up. I know everyone says that we need to talk about our feelings, but sometimes it's just too painful to share them with anyone—like reopening a wound. It's hard when you think the rest of the world can't possibly understand." Sage was remembering how alone she'd felt after losing her parents and grandfather.

"It sounds like you might know something about this subject."

"Well, you know . . . girl problems," she said flippantly, hoping he wouldn't push this subject. She didn't want to be mousy and pathetic tonight. Besides, she found it far more interesting to talk about him. "Do you know anything about your birth parents?"

Spence paused for a moment before answering her. "My dad and my brothers don't know about this, but I did find my biological mother about ten years ago."

"Do you still talk to her?" Sage asked with surprise.

"No. I thanked her for giving me up for adoption, for allowing me to have a better life. She was so high, I don't think she even knew her own name, let alone had any clue who the man was standing before her. I was just a baby when I was found at the doorway of a fire department."

"Oh my gosh, Spence. I can't imagine what you must have gone through to stand before the woman who willingly gave you up," Sage said as she took his hand and squeezed it.

"I'm not angry with her, Sage. She did the right thing. She was too weak, and too addicted to take care of a child. Yes, my early years in foster care weren't pleasant, but ultimately it led me to Jackson and Camden, and then Martin and Michael. My brothers by choice are my best friends, and with Martin, I learned that someone doesn't have to share the same blood to be family. He was and is a great father, and I'm the man I am today because of him, so I'm grateful to the woman who birthed me."

Sage found herself fighting tears as she listened to this man who was so much stronger than she was. If she hadn't lived with her grandmother after her parents died, she didn't think she would have been as strong. She didn't know what to say.

"I've shared with you," Spence said, and then waited. His opening up gave her the courage to share with him.

"I lost my parents when I was ten. My grandfather was taking my mom and dad fishing and their tire blew out over a bridge. They crashed through the guardrail into the river, and it took the rescuers eight hours to pull the car out. I still have a hard time discussing it. I was supposed to be with them but wasn't feeling good that day, so I was home with my grandma. She told me it was the angels protecting me, but if that's the case, why didn't they protect my parents and my grandfather?" She knew she'd never have an answer to that question.

"We don't always get to know the reason something happens, but I do believe our lives are shaped by every experience we go through. Maybe that feeling of helplessness is what shaped you into who you are, is what gave you the drive to be a doctor. No, it shouldn't take losing your parents to find yourself, but everything really does happen for a reason."

Spence reached across the table and took her hand, offering her the only comfort he was capable of giving right then. It wasn't enough, and at the same time, it was exactly what she needed. She didn't want to speak about it anymore, and he seemed to get that.

"Okay, we're going to shelve conversation for now. The band is about to start, and I want to hold you." Spence stood up, escorted her to the corner of the dance floor, and put his arms around her. Couples were already swaying to the recorded music coming from the speakers. When the live band started, the floor would be packed.

"Thank you for sweeping me off my feet tonight, Spence," she said against his neck.

"Thank you for giving me the chance to do it, Sage." He kissed her gently, giving her a taste of the way their night was going to end.

30

Well after midnight, Spence opened the door to their rooms at the Fairmont Olympic Hotel. The hotel was beautifully designed and appointed, with an ambience of high style and exclusivity, but this corner suite still managed to surprise Sage. They entered the living room to find a fire burning and soft lights. On every table sat a vase holding roses and lilies in colors and shapes she'd never seen before. It was romantic. It was perfect.

She walked to a window and looked out at the beautiful green hotel grounds through the bright lights that illuminated the area. Even after her years in California, she never ceased to be amazed at the beauty one could find in the middle of a metropolis. When she'd imagined cities as a child, she'd thought only of pollution and garbage. Thankfully, there were always oases to be found.

As Spence's arms wrapped around her, she closed her eyes and leaned back against him, feeling perfectly happy just as they were. Yes, she wanted to get to the lovemaking, but at the same time she wanted to freeze this moment, this feeling of bliss from the first truly romantic day she'd ever experienced.

"I don't know how you arranged all of this, but thank you," she whispered, afraid of breaking the spell she was under if she spoke too loudly.

"I just made a couple of phone calls. The staff here did the rest."

"Well, they were great phone calls. Thank you again, Spence. You've made me feel special."

"I want you to feel special because you are. Everything I do for you, I do because it pleases me so much to see your eyes light up with happiness. A smile from you brings me joy unlike any gift ever has." He punctuated his words by caressing the side of her neck with his lips.

She found herself tilting her head to give him better access to that sensitive skin.

Spence drew his head away momentarily. "Would you like a drink before . . . ?"

Sage was glad he didn't finish the sentence. She was ready for this, but to talk about it . . . no, she didn't want to. Talking might give her the opportunity to back out, and that's the last thing in the world that she wanted. *This* was what she wanted. If she could just manage to fight off the nerves that kept threatening her.

"A drink sounds good," she said, and nearly whimpered when he released her.

He walked over to a wine bucket, lifted out a chilled bottle, and prepared it for the corkscrew. "From the moment our eyes connected, I wanted you. It soon became an all-consuming passion, a need to have you. Now . . . now, it's so much more." He drew out the cork smoothly and then poured the wine into crystal goblets.

She accepted the glass he offered and moved back to the large window. "It feels like I've wanted you forever. I'm sorry I didn't tell you before about . . ." No. Why belabor their fumbled night? It was something best forgotten.

"I have this strong impression that I need to guard you—or rescue you. Am I the one you need rescuing from?" He was joking, but not entirely.

His uncharacteristic moment of insecurity gave her strength, wiped away the nerves that had been gnawing at her most of the night—heck, most of the time since being back in Spence's presence.

"I think I need to be rescued from myself—from the protective ball I've placed around myself. I think you really are my prince come to life," she told him, setting down her wine and walking over to him, feeling the material of her dress swirl delicately around her legs.

He set down his own glass and raised his hand to her cheek. "I can do that. I can be anything you want me to be. I want to be a better man when I'm with you." He bent down and took her mouth gently, showing her his need in a slow, sweet kiss.

Sage broke away only long enough to say, "I just want you to be you. I just want you, Spence," and then returning to the kiss, she got lost in his arms. If this was a preview of their night to come, she thought she might never float back to earth again.

"We won't rush this, Sage. I want to build the fires, make sure you know that lovemaking is about pleasure, not pain. I don't want to push you, and I don't want to ever stop. Tell me what you want, what you desire. Let me please you."

"Don't treat me like a porcelain doll—that's all I ask. I want you to lose yourself," she said, crying out when he gripped her hips and pulled her against him, showing her that he was thick and hard.

"I can do that," he said, the low growl in his voice stoking an inferno inside her. "You are mine—only mine, Sage Banks."

Lifting her up, he moved to the bedroom, making her breath catch and her heart race. Yes, he was her Prince Charming, claiming her, owning her, taking what he desired. She was more than willing to be his partner—to be whatever he wanted her to be.

She was seduced, and from the look in his eyes, he was just as much hers as she was his. They were made to come together like this, made to catch fire in each other's arms. She hoped time would stop and the night would never end.

Sage hardly noticed the low lighting in the room, or the flowers on the nightstand. She barely registered the silk sheets, or the rose petals covering them. She seemed unable to notice anything but the sultry look in his eyes.

Setting her down next to the bed, he stepped back, making her hunger to be in his arms again, but he just stood there, his eyes roaming up and down her body as he removed his jacket and then began undoing the buttons on his crisp white shirt.

"Spence?" She wanted to be bold and reach for him, but the secretive smile flitting across his mouth told her to be patient. She was—but just barely.

When he'd cast his shirt aside, her mouth watered as she gazed at the golden smoothness of his chest. Taking a step forward, she reached out, ran her finger along the hard lines and down the planes of his stomach.

"Oh, Sage," he groaned, making her feel bold, making her want to move her fingers even farther downward. He grabbed her hand and drew it up to his shoulder, then wrapped his arm around her back.

He kissed her now, this time with so much more heat, possessing her, leading her to what was coming. His hands splayed across her back, moved down and gripped her behind to pull her against him, press her against his pulsing arousal. She groaned into his mouth, opening even more for him, feeling completely devoured.

She felt his hands at her shoulders, felt him removing her dress, but she could barely register the material falling away as he pulled back just enough to let it drift down her body. When he saw the sexy lingerie she'd almost chickened out on wearing, the pure lust in his eyes made her glad she'd bought it.

Then his mouth was teasing the sensitive skin of her shoulder, skimming over the swells of her breasts, while his hands found her nearly naked behind. He paused and brought his head back up to hers, his eyes smoky with passion, his mouth moist from their kisses.

"You are . . . all my fantasies come to life," he told her, his hot breath rushing over her neck as he leaned forward, his mouth running along her collarbone.

She couldn't speak, couldn't respond no matter how much she wanted to.

Spence took his time, running his hands all over her, tracing the edges of the undergarments she was wearing. She loved his obvious lust, loved that the lingerie spurred it on, but now she wanted the frivolous lace gone. She didn't want any barriers between the two of them. She wanted his hands and mouth all over her, her skin pressing against his.

Shivering, she arched into him, pushed against his arousal, pressed her breasts against his chest, tried to find relief for the aching that was consuming her. His hand came up and cupped one of her breasts, his palm rubbing against the aching peak before both hands moved to her back and he began undoing the tiny clips in the back of her corset. She held her breath as he moved inch by excruciating inch until the garment finally came undone and then only their bodies held it in place.

He moved back just a bit and the material fell away. She thrust her naked breasts against his chest, her nipples aching even more for the touch of his hands, his mouth. He didn't make her wait long. He bent down and captured one peak, sucking it deep into his mouth, making her cry out in pleasure. He moved to the other, licking it before blowing on the area, making her twist her back so she could get closer.

When he suddenly kneeled down in front of her and caressed her stomach with his tongue, her legs trembled, and she didn't know how much longer she'd manage to stay standing before him. This was too much, all too much. So many feelings were rushing through her body. How could she survive the night?

His hands skimmed up her legs, starting at her ankles and moving upward until he reached the clips of the delicate straps on her garter belt and he began undoing them, one at a time. When his hand caressed the sensitive skin at the inside of her thigh, she cried out again, her core moist and eager for his touch.

With the garter straps unattached, he began slowly peeling off her stockings, everywhere he touched feeling like fire on her skin. When he next removed the lacy belt, and then pulled her panties off with his teeth, her entire body shook.

Standing before him completely nude, her body

was a playground of pleasure for both of them. When he stood back and looked over her as he undid the button on his trousers, she found her heart thudding rapidly.

Oh yes, she wanted to see what had been pressing so pleasingly against her. When he revealed himself in the low light, her mouth formed a wide circle. "Oh my," she gasped. Yes, she was hot; yes, she was turned on, but slight fear filled her, too, because she remembered how badly it had hurt when he'd thrust inside her in the hot tub. Would it still hurt? Or would this time be nothing but pleasure?

Then she didn't have time to think, because he laid her down and then he was on the bed with her, his body covering her, his mouth capturing hers. There was a new urgency in him and his movements were more forceful.

Her fear evaporated, replaced by consuming desire to be taken by this man. She wanted more. When she was desperate for him to thrust inside her, he pulled back, his mouth growing gentler, his hands slowing down. No! That's not what she wanted. She wanted passion, heat, hunger, fire.

His lips moved to her neck and sucked on her flesh, and he nipped her with his teeth. His hands caressed her, up and down her body, molding her, shaping her, preparing her. Spence worshipped her breasts, then her stomach, then the sensitive flesh below her navel.

He tasted every inch of her, and had her begging him for more. She forgot her fear. He wasn't giving her time to be afraid. He was only giving her time to beg—to beg for more and more and more.

She moved her hands into his hair, guiding his head, leading him across her body, feeling the softness slip through her fingers, and then, as he moved his mouth upward along her body again, she ran her fingers down his back, over the solid muscle that flexed as he moved, as he returned his attention to her mouth.

He shifted his body to the side, ran his fingers between her breasts and lower, until he was at the juncture of her thighs. She opened for him without hesitation, opened and urged him to touch her there. He didn't keep her waiting, but slid his fingers inside her, plunged into her wet heat, making her scream as her body built to a level of pleasure she'd only dreamed about.

She arched into him, instinct taking over as she sought what only he could give her. "Yes, Spence, please," she begged him, the pressure almost unbearable.

Pure sensation overtook her. She was a giant stream of lava, her body melting as she peaked, as fire consumed her and she let go, her body flying. She knew there was no coming back from this. Before she could even think of recovering, Spence was above her, the weight from his body a welcome anchor to this world, his legs spreading hers even wider apart.

"Are you ready for me?" He asked the question through clenched teeth as he tried to slow himself, tried to ensure he didn't hurt her. It only made her love this man more.

"Oh yes, more than ready, Spence." The quivering flesh of her core was more sensitive than ever, and finally she felt him pressing into her, filling her, completing her. She groaned as his lips took hers again.

"Oh my, Sage. You are so hot—so tight," he groaned as he pulled back, making her whimper until he thrust forward again. No pain this time, nothing but unalloyed pleasure as he got into a sublime rhythm, moving in and out of her, building her higher and higher again.

One hand gripped her hair, holding her in place, while his mouth devoured hers. The other grabbed her hands and trapped them above her head, holding her captive.

"Open your eyes," he commanded.

Though it felt like weights were holding them down, she cracked them open, looked into his passion-filled eyes while he continued his erotic dance. Time stopped. She'd gotten her wish. This moment was forever frozen in time, and she would never have to leave it.

"Let go, Sage," he said, and she did. She flew over the cliff—this time with him, and it was even better than before. It was better than she'd ever imagined it could be.

Silence reigned for several moments. He withdrew from her, making her groan her disapproval, but he didn't go far. He simply turned onto his side, pulling her into his arms as he kissed the tops of her breasts, her shoulder, her neck.

"You're amazing, Sage."

"I could do that forever," she said with a sigh, making him chuckle.

"I may need a few minutes to recover before we try again. And again. All night long."

"Ah, but I want more now." In her newly found passion for this man, she felt bold and strong.

"Woman, we will never leave this suite," he told her. He captured her nipple and sucked, making her writhe against him.

"That's a promise I'll hold you to," she said, and pushed his head closer against her breast. And then she urged him upward. His mouth returned to hers and her body caught fire once again as he began caressing her in all the right places.

Sage was forever lost in Spence's arms, and for now, at least, she never wanted to be found again.

31

Spence woke Sage up by stroking the flat planes of her stomach. "I know I promised never to leave the suite, but I do have a full day of fun planned," he told her.

"Mmm, how about this? Our fun day happens right here in this bed . . ." What a wanton woman she was turning into. This was so not her.

"You aren't going to be able to walk if we make love again, Sage."

When she shifted, she finally felt the ache. And she had to groan when she sat up.

"Oooh, I think you're right," she said, chuckling as she moved to the edge of the bed. She stood up in front of him completely naked, shocked she wasn't embarrassed. Maybe it was because she'd suppressed her sexuality for so long, and now it was coming out in spades. But when she took a step, she winced. Yep, she was sore.

"I changed my mind. A day in bed is all the fun we need," he said, making her turn toward him. Pure lust filled his eyes as he looked at her body.

"Sorry, that offer has expired," she said with a smile. "The doctor has ordered a superhot shower."

With that she turned and walked to the bathroom, adding an extra sway to her hips because she knew his eyes were glued to her derrière. His moan gave her immense satisfaction.

Somehow, they managed to get out of the suite—*after* he joined her in the shower and helped wash her back, and then the rest of her. Sage felt she was on an all-time high, and the day couldn't possibly get any better, even if it was cold and foggy outside and a serious chill crept through her body. At least it wasn't snowing or raining.

"Are you going to tell me yet what we're doing?" she asked as the two of them climbed in the rental car.

"We're meeting up with my good friend Austin and his wife for a day on the water," Spence replied.

Sage looked doubtfully at the foggy skies. "Um, won't that be cold?" she asked.

"If people in Seattle waited for the clouds and rain to go away they would never make it out on the water," he said with a laugh. "Just consider it all a part of the atmosphere."

"I think I could be happy doing just about anything with you," Sage said as they pulled up to the marina and parked the car.

A couple was walking toward them, and Sage recognized Austin Anderson, whom Sage last saw at the party at the Whitmans'. "I wasn't sure if you were going to make it," Austin said. "When you said you were staying at the Olympic, I figured you'd never get out of bed."

Sage blushed scarlet as Austin smiled with no remorse.

"Austin, that is no way to talk, and you know it," the woman on his arm said. "Why do you Anderson men think you can run roughshod over people's feelings? You've embarrassed this nice woman. I'm sorry about my husband's behavior. I'm Kinsey, by the way."

She stuck out her hand and Sage grasped it, feeling ridiculously shy. "I'm Sage Banks," she said after a long pause.

"Are we going fishing, or gonna just stand here?" Spence asked as he clapped Austin on the back.

"We'd already be on the water if you hadn't taken your time getting down here," Austin replied with a grin.

"Well, I had a late night," Spence said with a waggle of his brows, making Sage blush even more.

They boarded Austin's boat from the private marina on Puget Sound and were soon gliding across the foggy but calm water.

"It's been a great fishing season," Austin told them. "Dad and I have come out a few times. We've even managed to pull my cousin Lucas from the office for a trip or two."

"That's a miracle," Spence said as their boat moved slowly through the no-wake zone, allowing

Sage to see everything. This was her first boating expedition. Spence seemed to be treating her to a lot of firsts.

"I know. He's a workaholic. Still, he's slowed down since marrying Amy and having his kids. Our trips nowadays are largely of the park variety," Austin said with a laugh.

"Careful, Austin. You don't want the world to hear that a playboy extraordinaire has been domesticated," Kinsey said before leaning over and kissing him on the cheek. He turned quickly and hauled her into his arms to kiss her properly. When they came up for air, Sage was blushing yet again.

"Sorry. The kids were sick all last week, and I was lucky to get out of my pajamas. This is a real treat, and some much-needed kid-free time was warranted," Kinsey said with a grin that said she wasn't sorry at all.

"I look forward to those days," Spence said, shocking them all into silence as they turned and looked at him. "Hey, I'm not as bad as Austin was before you, Kinsey. I want kids."

Sage's heart grew a bit bigger for this man she was sharing the day with.

Austin pointed. "Over there is where Uncle Joseph lives."

Through the fog, Sage could just make out a couple of large towers. "Is that a castle?" she asked when they got closer.

"Pretty much," Kinsey said with a laugh. "And while it looks intimidating, I've never felt as at home as in that house. Except at home, of course."

"Impressive," was all Sage could say.

"We'll stop in and say hi a little later," Spence told her.

They pointed out several huge homes, making Sage's mouth hang open. She wasn't a novice to wealth, but this area was a whole other world. "Are there any normal-sized places out here?"

"Nope. I don't think so," Kinsey said with a giggle.

When the boat turned south and they began moving toward the Nisqually Indian Reservation, the fog cleared, and Sage could finally take in all the marine life. The air smelled sweeter, and the birds seemed to sing more melodically. It didn't take the four humans too long to start heading toward the shore off a private island.

"This is a good place to throw in," Austin said as he maneuvered the boat and dropped anchor.

"As much fish as you have all been bringing home, we're going to be eating it all year round," Kinsey said with a chuckle.

"Do you always do your own fishing?" Sage found it odd that a bunch of billionaires wouldn't just buy it from the store.

"No. But it's fun to take the boat out and do it ourselves on occasion," Kinsey replied. "Usually, it's just the guys who go, and personally, I think it's because they want a safe haven to drink and grumble about their wives."

"We would never grumble about you," Austin said gallantly.

"Sure, darling, sure," she said, giving him a quick kiss before getting out of the way so he could haul up his catch when his line tugged.

It wasn't long before they were pulling in the lines. Some of the catches were good, and some had to be thrown back. When they had several large fish in the cooler, Spence turned with a satisfied look as he patted Austin on the back.

"Dad will love this," Austin said, picking up his cell phone. Amazingly enough, it had reception and was answered quickly.

Sage sat back as he talked to his father, and from what she heard, they were going to have an early dinner before she and Spence flew back to Montana.

"It's all set. We're going to Joseph's dock to have a get-together," Austin announced, and he turned the controls over to Spence. "Let's open this up for a nice ride before we end our trip."

"Sounds good to me," Sage said. She found herself laughing as Spence picked up speed and the wind whipped through her hair. Yes, it was cold, but she didn't care. Spence, always the Boy Scout, had made sure a warm outfit was waiting for her at the hotel, so the only part of her that wouldn't be able to feel anything after their boat ride was her cheeks.

Spence slowed as he pulled up to the dock at the Anderson mansion, and now that the fog had dissipated, she could see the place well.

"I've never seen anything like it," Sage said.

They stepped onto a beautiful dock that was big enough to hold three or four large yachts.

"And you never will," Kinsey said. "It's a thing of beauty. Now come meet the family." She took Sage's arm and pulled her ahead of the men, who were busy securing the boat.

"Shouldn't we wait for the guys?" Sage didn't want to admit how nervous she was.

"They know the way." Kinsey wasn't going to let her go, so Sage had no choice but to follow along toward the mansion.

The men joined them before they stepped inside the marble entryway. The wide staircases to the left and right made her feel like a child—she wanted to run up them just so she could slide down the gleaming banisters.

"It's about time you came to visit, Spence," Joseph boomed as soon as he entered the room with his lovely wife, Katherine. He slapped Spence hard enough on the back to knock him over. She was surprised he was still on his feet.

"I was just here a couple months ago! And you were in Montana not long ago," Spence said with a laugh.

"Well, it sure feels like forever since you've

brought a beautiful lady to grace these halls. I'll forgive you for being away so long."

"Katherine, I'd like you to meet Sage. She's a first-year resident at our hospital and already outshining all the staff, including me," Spence said as he wrapped an arm around Sage, making her instantly blush. "Katherine Anderson, Sage Banks."

For Sage, it felt like school all over again, when she was the one person in the class who knew all the answers on the first day. She hated when all eyes were directed at her.

"It's nice to meet you, Sage," Katherine said as she reached for her hand.

"It's wonderful to meet you, too. You have a beautiful home," Sage said.

"What am I? A sack of potatoes? I'd like to be introduced to your girl, too," Joseph said with a glare at Spence.

Austin laughed. "How could anyone forget your presence, Uncle?"

"Underappreciated, that's what I am," Joseph grumbled. "It's a pleasure to meet you, young lady. We'll have a wonderful dinner with the family."

Sage found his hand surprisingly gentle for a man his size with such a loud voice. "Thank you for having me," she said, hoping that with the awkward introduction over with, the focus would now turn to someone else.

"Let's leave the men to boast about their catches

while we have a more civilized discussion in the sitting room," Katherine said, and Sage nearly sighed in relief.

"We'll join you soon," Joseph called after them when Kinsey took Sage's arm and they followed Katherine.

"Take your time," Katherine called back.

Sage walked quietly behind the regal woman as they went down a wide hallway with beautiful paintings and family portraits decorating the walls. This home was certainly a castle, but it was also a lived-in home, and *not* a museum. She was even more impressed now.

Stepping into the sitting room, she soon found her nerves calming and laughter coming easily. This family was a lot like the close-knit group in Sterling. Yes, they were wealthy, but they were pleasant and inclusive.

She knew that Spence bringing her here, sharing this part of his life with her, was a big step for him. Was she ready to move so quickly in this relationship, to become an actual couple? It seemed it didn't matter, because, ready or not, she was in a relationship now. She had zero doubt about it.

And the amazing thing was, she didn't want to change it.

32

"Have you proposed yet?"

Spence laughed as he took the glass of scotch Austin had just poured. "Wow, Joseph, you must not have wasted any time at all back in your day."

"Are you calling me an old man, son? I may have a few gray hairs now, but that only makes me more wise and mature." Actually all of his hair was white, but no one called him on that.

Spence held up his hand in surrender. "I would never call you old. You look as spry as a twenty-one-year-old."

"So answer my question," Joseph demanded.

"Oh, you're serious?" Spence said, then laughed again. "No. I haven't proposed. I will admit that I may just have to do that."

"Are you serious, Spence?" Austin asked in surprise.

"I know, I know. It's strange for me, too. I barely remember Sage from when I was a teen. I mean, she is eight years younger than I am, but since I met up with her again, I can't get her out of my mind." He moved to an easy chair and sat down. "When you know, you know."

"Yeah, that's how it happened with me. I knew almost from the moment I met Kinsey that she'd be my wife. There hasn't been a single day I've regretted chasing her so hard."

"Before you gloat, Joseph, I've already figured you and my dad out," Spence said with a mock glare Joseph's way.

"I have no idea what you're talking about," Joseph said, taking a long sip of his drink and looking down at the floor.

"I'll bet you don't. However, just because you threw us together and it worked out, that doesn't make it right. It could have gone in an entirely different direction and your messing with our lives could have brought disaster," Spence said.

"Well, it didn't go wrong at all, did it?" Joseph growled. "So I should be hearing a thank-you, not getting a lecture from a young buck."

"Thank you, Joseph," Spence said, surprising both Joseph and Austin.

"Well . . . um . . . you're welcome," Joseph said, an unexpected catch to his voice. He turned around and walked to the huge window in his den, and both Austin and Spence gave him a moment to compose himself.

"I think I just heard the door," Austin said, and sure enough the den door flew open a moment later and in piled several members of the Anderson and Storm families.

"Ah, I see my nephew Tanner is here," Joseph said as he strode over to slap him on the back.

"How are you, Uncle Joseph?" Tanner asked.

"I'm good, boy. You remember Spence?"

"Yes, of course. It's good to see you again, Spence." Tanner's dark hair lay straight against his head, and his trademark blue Anderson eyes sparkled with humor. Though he was technically Tanner Storm because his father had been stolen at birth, depriving him of growing up with his brothers, Joseph and George, his genes were all Anderson.

"What are you doing in Seattle?" Spence asked as he walked with Tanner over to the liquor cabinet.

"I'm working on remodeling a building in town. I don't see an end in sight, but my father says he has complete faith in me." Spence could see the man's tension—clearly he was under some stress—so despite his curiosity, he decided not to press him.

"And make the building shine you shall," Joseph boomed.

The young men both looked up and laughed, and the tension evaporated. Spence knew the story of the Storms, knew that Joseph and his twin, George, had lost a third brother at birth. It turned out their mother hadn't known she was carrying triplets, and the delivery had been a difficult one. When she came to, she'd been relieved to see that her twin boys were alive and healthy, never learning that she'd had a third son. Dr. Storm, her doctor, and his wife had decided to keep that boy for themselves.

Joseph and George had learned about their brother Richard in a Seattle newspaper article. They'd found him immediately, and now you couldn't tell that the brothers had ever been apart. Richard Storm's five children had been estranged and casting about for a while, but now they were getting back to the way they'd once been, and it seemed the Storms were falling as fast into matrimony as their cousins had.

Maybe Joseph really was a matchmaker. Things certainly happened when he teamed up with others, like his brothers or his best friend, Martin, Spence's father. People continued getting married after the men began their meddling.

After more members of the big family arrived, they enjoyed a wonderfully prepared meal that included the best and freshest fish. Then they all bundled up and headed down to the beach for a bonfire, the heat a welcome relief in the winter cold.

For the first time since arriving at the mansion, Spence found himself able to speak alone with Sage, and he didn't miss the opportunity to lure her away from the crowd. Taking her hand, he walked her to the water's edge, where they enjoyed the lights from the city as the fog rolled in, thick and heavy, obscuring their sight. Suddenly, an eerie sound filled the air, making Sage jump, then cling tightly to Spence and bury her head against him.

"What was that?" she asked in obvious alarm.

"It's all the souls of the past crying in the night," he said, and though he didn't think it possible, she burrowed even more tightly against him.

"Come on, Spence . . ."

"I'm just kidding, Sage. I've lived in Seattle a long time, and for those who don't know the sound, it does sound a bit like spirits wailing for something. But it's actually just a foghorn.

"There *are* legends of empty vessels floating in the ocean and still sending off the cry of a foghorn to drift across the waters, as if a lonely sailor were calling to anyone who would listen."

"Spence, you are horrible! Look, you're terrifying the poor girl." Sage turned to find Kinsey next to them.

"I was just filling her in on a bit of Seattle history."

"You were not," Kinsey said. "You were scaring her so she would hold you close. If you were a decent guy, she'd be clinging to you because she wanted you, not because she was frightened half to death."

Spence laughed and let Sage go, but gripped her fingers. She laughed when Kinsey began to lecture Spence as they turned and made their way back to the rest of the group.

It wasn't long until they had to say their good-byes, and Sage found it surprising that she was pulled into so many people's arms as they gave her a hug and told her she must come back for a visit soon.

Would she get to come back again sometime? Would she still be with Spence? He was infatuated, that was obvious, but would he grow bored now that he'd gotten what he'd been chasing after? She just didn't know.

By the time they boarded the jet, Sage was mesmerized as Spence began telling her the story of how he came to live with Martin, the rescue of his brother Michael, and the bond that had followed.

She'd fallen just a little more in love with him by the time the plane landed.

33

Sage stretched her arms, her eyes still gritty from lack of sleep over the last couple of days. As she recalled what Spence had told her the night before, her heart was still a little broken for him. So many years he'd lived in foster care, wondering if he'd ever have a permanent home. At least he'd had a happy ending. What a difference one person could make in the life of another.

She wondered where Spence, Camden, and Jackson would be today if it weren't for Martin—a man who had wanted no praise, a man who didn't need to talk about how he'd saved these young boys, but who simply accepted three new sons with no fanfare.

What fine men they'd turned out to be. Even losing his first child hadn't diminished Jackson, though he was obviously heartbroken. And though she didn't know Camden very well, she knew he did a lot for their community and all around the world. Martin had made sure to give his sons everything they needed, and their lives were living proof that he had succeeded as a father.

Then, of course, there was Spence. Without Martin, would he have become a doctor? She had a feeling it was rooted deep inside him, and no matter what, he was destined to be a healer. But medical school wasn't cheap, and without the direction from one who cared about him and his future, would he have known how to fulfill his destiny?

She couldn't answer that question. She was just grateful that Spence had made it, that he'd been given the opportunity to become the man he was today. And what a great man he was. He made everyone around him feel special, whether it was a patient, an employee, or the young or the old. He was intelligent and giving, and he made her feel like someone important. There was now no doubt that she loved him. She'd given him her body, and in the process given him her heart, her soul, and everything that was in her.

How could it not be terrifying to love another so much that you could no longer imagine what your life would be like without them in it?

"Good morning, sunshine."

Sage turned to find Grace in her bedroom doorway, holding up another shiny box.

"What's this?"

"Like you don't know. The princess gets another gift." Grace bounded into the room and landed on Sage's bed.

"This is an even bigger box than last time," Sage said. She ran her hand over the sparkling bow attached to the top.

"I know. Open it already. You are *killing* me," Grace said, reaching forward and threatening to take the box back and open it herself.

Sage laughed at her friend's dramatics. "I'm getting there." She undid the ribbon that held the box closed. Inside, under a lot of tissue paper, was a small wall mirror with words engraved on the bottom of the frame, right below the mirror proper. She lifted it and was surprised by how much it weighed.

"Wow. I think that's a real silver frame, Sage."

"You may be right," Sage replied, and examined the mirror closely.

"What does it say?" Grace was obviously growing impatient.

Her eyes filled as she looked up at her friend. "Believe," she whispered, and smiled.

"Oh," Grace said with a wobble in her voice. "I swear, if you don't marry this man, I will fight you for him." Grace leaned over and snagged the mirror. She looked at her image and smacked her lips in a pretend kiss.

"Don't you think this is all moving so fast, though, Grace?" Sage asked as she flopped back against her pillows.

"You've spent enough time with him to know whether you love him or not. He's the most creative, romantic guy I've ever heard of, he gets you gifts all the time, jets you off to another city for a date, takes you to meet the family, and, if I may hazard an educated guess, makes love like a god. So what's the problem in it moving fast?"

Leave it to Grace to make everything so very black-and-white.

"The problem is that he's too perfect. I keep waiting for the other shoe to drop and for the horns to sprout."

"Ah, honey, don't think that way. This isn't really a fairy tale. No dragon is going to attack, no poisoned apple is going to be placed in our kitchen, and no needles will put you to sleep. Don't be afraid of holding on to something that you already have. Don't fight it; just enjoy every moment of being together."

"I had a wonderful time on our last date," Sage said.

"I want to hear every single, sordid detail. I can't believe my meeting ran so late last night. I was planning on making popcorn and holding you hostage until you spilled all," Grace said. "But we have time now, and that hostage thing is coming into play if you're not careful."

Sage spent the next hour telling her all about their trip. "He was amazing. The sex was beyond anything I could have ever imagined. I mean, I'm a doctor, so I knew it would feel good. I know there are certain chemicals in the brain that fire off when your body gets excited. But I had no idea it would be so . . . so . . . just so."

"That's where you're wrong, Sage. Sex can really suck. Trust me, I know. If you aren't with a man who knows how to light you on fire, it's nothing, meaningless, and you're left feeling empty. Granted, it *seems* good sometimes. But it's not ultimately about what your body can do. It's about what your soul wants, what your heart is feeling—what you need most."

"Well, I don't have previous experience as a point of comparison, but I know I wouldn't mind doing that—with Spence, anyway—every single day for the next millennium."

Her body was still sore, but the soreness wasn't such a bad thing. Though she ached in places she'd never imagined aching, still, whenever she moved, it sent a naughty image straight to her brain, which in turn, heated her core and readied her for another hot night with her lover.

"Do you work tonight?"

"Yes. In a few hours, actually." Sage reluctantly threw off the covers and finally left the warmth of her bed.

"Is Dr. Hottie working with you?"

"Yes, I believe Spence is on the schedule." Sage grinned as she gathered her clothes and started making her way to their small bathroom. A shower would have her revved up to go.

Grace followed her. "Then totally shock him. Drag him into an on-call room and rock his world," she said, making Sage stop in her tracks.

"I couldn't do *that*."

"Why not? You have a pager, right? If any emergencies arise, the two of you can throw on your scrubs and be out there in seconds. It would certainly interrupt the mood, and if you haven't . . . you know . . . then he might go out there sporting some major wood. But, you might not be interrupted, and then you'll be so much more relaxed for the rest of the night. Besides, wouldn't the shock on his face be worth it? He won't know what to do with such a shameless hussy." Grace guffawed at the redness in Sage's cheeks. Little did Grace know that Spence had already suggested such a thing.

"I'll think about it," Sage said, now unable to rid her mind of the image of getting horizontal with Spence on a small on-call bed.

"Don't think about it. That's really the problem here, Sage. You're thinking too much. Just feel. Go with what your body wants and quit worrying or computing or analyzing or whatever else it is you do with that superhuman brain of yours."

Sage opened the bathroom door and looked back at Grace. "I need to shower," she said.

"Yeah, rub extra lotion in all the right places so you'll smell extra good for the doctor."

Sage could hear Grace's laughter even after shutting the door and turning on the shower tap. She couldn't get sex off her mind, and that was definitely not good. Walking into the hospital was going to be a feat, because the minute she saw Spence, she'd want to rip off his scrubs and do dirty things to him. Sex muddied things up, made a person think of nothing else. What if she was confusing sex and love? Well, she'd probably find out soon.

34

A hot cup of coffee and more sleep was all Sage could think about. Her trip three days ago had been wonderful, but she certainly hadn't slept much, and now being on her feet for endless hours was making her think that maybe she should have forgone the trip and stayed in bed.

"Sage, I don't know why you look tired, you've only been on call for twenty-six hours," Mo said while her fingers tapped against her hips. Sage could only tell it was a joke by the small upturn of Mo's mouth.

She loved Mo teaching her the stuff she *hadn't* learned about during medical school. Each shift she worked with the woman, she grew to love her even more.

"I've had more coffee than sleep lately, so please don't remind me."

"Well, you should have been a nurse then, because after twelve hours at this place I go home and sleep without another thought in my head except for which episode of *True Blood* I need to watch next." Mo was in midsentence when Sage saw her favorite nurse's eyes narrow.

Before Sage could even blink, Mo was already en

route to *discuss* why a second-year medical resident was attempting to put an IV in a patient in the wrong direction.

As Mo reamed the med student, Sage couldn't help but feel sorry for him. Then the thought dissipated as she downed her tenth cup of coffee for the night. They all had to learn, and part of that process was getting schooled by the nursing staff who knew what to do better than many of the doctors.

Since the heat was temporarily off her, Sage took a moment to sit down, resting her throbbing feet momentarily. The doctors' lounge was probably the cleanest room in the hospital since it was the least used. Closing her eyes for a blissful moment, the world felt right.

Not even five minutes passed when she heard chatter coming over the ER radio. Sitting up, she leaned in to listen and could hear bits and pieces of ". . . bus versus train, mass-casualty incident, en route code three."

Instantly she found herself on alert. Every cup of coffee she drank that night came back in full force and the sand in her eyes disappeared. Although her time in the emergency department had proven to be educational, nothing could prepare her for the unknown tragedies that had been unfolding before her since she'd begun her residency.

"This doesn't sound good." Turning, Sage spotted another resident throwing on a trauma gown as he rushed from one of the on-call rooms.

"No, it doesn't." Fear slithered through her, though she hoped it wasn't showing.

She scanned the ER, making a mental note of available rooms and resources as she locked eyes with Mo and they exchanged a look that spoke volumes. The previously quiet emergency room became a bustling hive of activity as everyone took their places like actors in a play.

As sirens sounded, and the first of the injured from the bus versus train came rolling through the emergency room doors, Sage began to doubt herself for the first time in a while. Nerves unsettled her stomach and she found herself clenching her hands into fists as she stuffed them into her pockets.

"Get him to bay three!"

"He's gone. I'll tell the family when they arrive."

"Put pressure on that wound now!"

Noise. Commands. Movement. It was synchronized chaos. Sage felt like she was watching from the outside and she began to panic, feeling as if she couldn't breathe.

And then she felt the warmth of strong hands on her back. "You've got this, Sage. Take a breath and close your eyes for two seconds and then dive in there," Spence whispered in her ear.

"I . . . I'm . . . I don't know what to do." The weakness in her voice frustrated her. Spence turned her toward him and looked into her eyes.

"Look, I've been watching you since the first day you

walked into this place, and I have no doubt that you will make a fine doctor. Don't think for one minute that not every single person in the medical field has felt at one point or another that they can't do it. It's tough work and we hold people's lives in our hands. But you will make it. You are strong and smart, and you know what you're doing. Have faith in yourself and your abilities."

"How can you be so sure?"

"Because I'm the best and I only work with the best." His confident smile empowered her. The knots in her stomach loosened and her shoulders straightened with determination. The ER doors burst open again with a whole new set of patients, and suddenly Sage knew what to do.

Within a half hour, every trauma room was filled with critically injured patients, as was the ER hallway. The noise of paramedics shouting out quick reports, doctors issuing orders, and family members sobbing was almost deafening.

Staff was using supplies faster than they could be restocked and the entire environment was looking more like a war zone than a hospital. Sage had little time as she moved from patient to patient, doing whatever she could.

"Sage, we need help over here!" Mo shouted as a young man was wheeled into a room that had barely been cleared out.

"He's spiraling quick," Sage said as she looked at the stats, her hands never stopping.

"Blood pressure seventy-two over forty-five and dropping, heart rate one fifty-two." Mo's voice was calm and sure.

"We need to get another IV in him right away. Open up that fluid and let's get two units of O-negative blood in here now. He's going into shock."

"I can't find a pulse," Mo said, looking at Sage as if she already knew the conclusion. Sage wasn't ready to give up on the man. He was too young.

"Start chest compressions, get the epinephrine ready." Sage directed the staff but was very aware that his bleeding was uncontrollable. After another fifteen minutes of resuscitation, Sage had to say out loud what everyone already knew. "Time of death, 10:40 p.m."

The fact that none of them had the time to mourn the loss of a young man's life was almost as disturbing as actually losing him. Before Sage and Mo could put on a new set of gloves, another patient was being wheeled in by paramedics who looked pale and exhausted.

"Twenty-three-year-old female, approximately eight months pregnant and in active labor. She's fully dilated. Vital signs stable, but she does have two superficial glass wounds to her right arm. Bleeding is controlled, but the baby is crowning and ready to come into this world."

The young woman was alternating between sobbing and screaming out in pain.

"Are you ready for this, Mo?" Sage said as she moved her onto the ER gurney.

Mo was prepared in less than a minute, with towels and tools needed to deliver a baby.

"I know you're scared right now"—Sage glanced at the chart—"Stacy, but your baby is ready to come out and meet you."

"It's too soon," Stacy wailed.

"You're eight months along. Your baby can make a healthy entrance, but you have to work with me, okay?" Sage looked the woman in the eye, knowing she had to calm her down or she would never be able to push, which would mean an emergency C-section.

"I can't do it. I hurt so much."

"Listen, Stacy, you either push this baby out, or you're going into surgery," Sage said forcefully, which startled the woman enough to quiet her as she stared at Sage in shock. "What are you having?" Sage asked.

"A girl." Stacy's lip trembled.

"Then let's bring your daughter into this world." Stacy nodded as she leaned back.

"We need a push now," Mo said, giving Sage a look that said it was getting more critical by the second. Sage barely had time to glance at the monitors before she felt another tightening of her own stomach.

"Push, Stacy!" Sage yelled, and much to her relief, the woman bore down and gave it all she could.

After a few tense moments and some strong pushes, Sage found herself delivering the too-still infant.

Before panic could set in, Mo was there, cleaning the baby's mouth out, and then a loud cry rent the air and could be heard above all of the chaos in the ER.

"Stacy, she's beautiful," Sage said in awe, amazed that in the midst of all this tragedy, a miracle had been placed in her arms. Sage looked at the messy, beautiful baby girl and gently laid her on her mother's chest.

"Thank you," Stacy quietly whispered as she took hold of her daughter while Mo and Sage then went to work on her other wounds.

Patient after patient came and went, and somehow the staff kept on going until finally the ER slowly calmed. When there were no new patients, Sage looked at the clock and realized she had just put in a thirty-six-hour day with a few short naps in between.

"It was a pleasure working next to you tonight, Sage."

Turning, Sage felt tears in her eyes. "Mo, there's no one I would rather work with," she said, knowing she was more emotional from pure exhaustion.

"I don't know about that. There's a certain doctor here I think you don't mind working with too much," Mo said with a taunting smile.

"Shh. I don't want people to hear you," Sage gasped as she looked around, grateful everyone else was just as exhausted as she was and wasn't bothering to listen.

"I just call it how I see it," Mo said before walking away.

"Well . . . quit calling it." Sage realized her comeback wasn't very good as soon as the words came out.

She gave up. Because right then, nothing sounded better than a long, hot shower. Somehow she made it to the locker room and gathered up her things, and then limped to the closest shower. Closing her eyes to push away the thoughts of the night, she threw her filthy scrubs into the hamper and stepped into the small shower bay.

The hot water was heaven on her sore muscles. Eyes closed and soaking in the water massage, she felt rather than saw his presence. A slow smile formed on her face as she felt his hard body press against hers.

"You did amazing, Sage," Spence said as his hands traveled up her stomach and cupped her breasts.

"I can't do this right now, Spence. I'm exhausted and there was so much trauma, more trauma than I ever expected to see here," she said, her eyes filling with tears.

Turning her around, Spence looked into her eyes, a gentle smile on his lips. "You are strong and capable and you saved lives tonight, Sage. Don't let the ones you weren't able to save take away the joy of the lives you gave back to terrified family members."

"But what about all of those people who didn't even get a chance to say good-bye?" she said, resting her head on his chest as the first tears fell.

"I don't know why or how some live and some don't. All I know is that we do our very best every single time. You are spectacular and there is so much ahead for you," he promised as his fingers massaged the back of her head.

"I am so glad I'm here with you, that I chose this hospital, that I get to learn from someone so great in the field."

"I'm glad you're here, too. Let me help you wash up, then I'm going to take you home, put you to bed with a hot cup of tea, and then sweep you off your feet tomorrow," he said, lifting her chin and giving her a light kiss.

"I think that's exactly what I need," she said, utterly drained, not even having the energy to lift her arms up around his neck.

Spence gently washed her body, then for once, helped her put clothing on before wrapping an arm around her and walking with her to his truck. She didn't get her cup of tea, because she fell asleep against his side within two minutes of leaving the hospital.

35

Waking up the next morning, Sage gasped to see it was almost noon. She had slept for a solid ten hours without waking once. That's when she noticed her phone was ringing.

"Hello." The sound of her groggy voice would certainly scare away a telemarketer if that was who had dared to wake her.

"Good morning, beautiful. You have exactly thirty minutes to dress and open your front door for me," Spence said, his voice pure sunshine.

"Thirty minutes will barely make me presentable," she warned.

"Baby, all you need is three minutes, just enough time to slip on shoes and a coat, because you wake up beautiful."

"Flattery will certainly get you whatever you want, Dr. Whitman," she said, feeling like giggling.

"Ah, then I must do it more often. You now have twenty-eight minutes," he warned.

"Then I better hang up."

Without waiting for a good-bye, Sage hung up the phone and rushed to her bathroom, where she showered and dressed in a flat ten minutes. She brushed on some mascara and lip gloss, threw her hair up into a ponytail, and bounced down the stairs. She made a cup of coffee, which she downed right before the doorbell rang.

Swinging the door open, Sage didn't even have a chance to speak before Spence lifted her in his arms, kissed her breathless, then carried her from the apartment and down the stairs and set her in his truck before running around to his side and climbing in.

"That's what I call a good morning," Sage said with a laugh.

"I told you I would be picking you up today. I hope you got enough rest," he replied, grabbing her hand and placing it on his thigh as he began driving.

"I slept like a rock. I feel more rested than I have in a while, and I desperately needed it after the week I've had."

"Being a resident is hard, but once you make it through, you will be so glad you did it."

"I am exhausted all the time, but I wouldn't trade it. I'm doing exactly what I love," she said.

"Being a doctor has to be in your blood. Some have it and some don't. You, Dr. Banks, certainly have it." She turned and kissed his cheek, overflowing with happiness.

"Where are you taking me this morning? Are we jetting off to another city? More jazz and sex?" Sage asked. For someone who liked order so much, she sure was a different person when with Spence, easily going with the flow.

"I'm kidnapping you. Isn't that obvious? And kidnap victims are never told where they're going."

"The weather is supposed to get worse today, Spence. We don't want to get caught out in it, and the ER will probably be busy because the roads are sure to get icy." The dark clouds were threatening to dump a lot of new snow onto the area.

"You worry too much," he said as they headed out of town. "Just let go and relax. Today will be fun."

"I can have fun, you know."

"Prove it, Sage. Tell me one reckless thing you have done in your life."

"Well, there was the time . . ." She had nothing. She dredged her memories desperately in hope of finding something—anything she'd done that didn't have a purpose.

"See, Sage? I'm right. As always."

"You're not always right, Spence," she snapped, her smile suddenly evaporating as she scooted over, no longer in the mood to snuggle. "And I demand to know where we're going."

So what if she liked to have her life organized? It wasn't a crime to be responsible. As a doctor, Spence should be a whole heck of a lot more worried about what he chose to do. He had a reputation to maintain. People had an expectation of the way doctors should act, and why shouldn't they? Wild and crazy guys weren't very reassuring.

"I'm ensuring that you keep a promise," he said, taking another turn and going up an old and winding logging road.

Big, fat snowflakes starting splatting against the windshield, and Sage watched while the road began to get a fresh layer of white atop its base of older snow.

"We should really turn around before we're stuck up here," she said. "Anyway, what promise?"

"We aren't leaving until we've reached our objective. As for the promise—you said you'd make sure I got the perfect Christmas tree. And that was weeks ago."

"We didn't need to come all the way up here for a tree. There are beautiful ones already cut and trimmed and ready to buy," she said as he pulled up to an old hunter's cabin and parked his truck.

"Yes, but those trees aren't fresh. They could easily die before Christmas, and become dry and dangerous. And you call yourself responsible! You don't want the lights to spark a fire and burn down my house, do you?"

"That's why you have to look at the base of the tree and make sure it's still moist. You just cut the last couple inches off the trunk so it can soak up water."

"There's nothing like cutting your own tree," he

told her as he stepped from the truck and walked around to her side.

"This is foolish. It's freezing out here and we're going to get stranded in a snowstorm." Sage refused to budge.

"Then we get stranded. The cabin's stocked for emergencies." Spence reached in and easily removed her from the truck, letting her body slide down his as he held her against him. "If we get too cold, I have ideas on how to warm us back up."

"What cabin?"

"This is my brother's hunting cabin. We come up here often." She looked at the snow-covered cabin, impressed. Then Spence leaned down and kissed her, making her forget all about the snow, the cabin, and her little fit, and heating her up while also leaving her trembling—not a bit from the cold.

"Fine, let's get your tree. I still say it's terrible to cut down a live one when there are so many that will go to waste. As a doctor, you should have more of a healthy respect for life." She gave him half a wink after her last remark.

"But the cutting down is the best part, Sage. And we try to make it all up to Mother Nature. For every Christmas tree we cut down, in the spring we get saplings we've been growing at home and plant two more here to replace the old one. It's been a Whitman tradition from our first Christmas together."

That stopped Sage. She walked beside him, turning her head to see if he was serious. That was a pretty great tradition. "Really? Can you point out any that you've planted?"

They moved through the trees of various heights. "I planted those four over there. Camden planted those three," he said, pointing to three huge pines. "And Michael planted that small group. The four over there, looking kinda frail, Jackson planted. I wanted that one Cam planted for our Christmas tree last year, but you would have thought I'd wanted to slay his firstborn. I don't think we've ever cut down any of the trees we've planted. We'd rather see how much they've grown each year."

The area was crowded with trees, and as Spence and Sage weaved their way through it all, she stopped to examine different ones. She'd exclaim that she'd found a perfect one, then find fault with it after circling it a few times. After an hour, Spence lifted her into his arms and kissed her again.

"What?" she asked when she was able to catch her breath.

"I never realized there was such science to picking out a Christmas tree. You do realize that I'll need you by my side each year from here on out so I don't make such a grievous error as to get an imperfect one."

"Are you making fun of me, Spence?" she asked in mock anger. She knew she could be a bit unbalanced in certain shaky situations. It was just who she was.

"Make fun of *you*? I'd never be so foolish as to do something like that."

As she flung her arms around his neck and rested her head against his chest, the snow coated their shoulders, and she didn't even notice. It was cold and wet, but all she could think about was how safe she felt. Even the stinging of her red nose and cheeks didn't bother her when she was in his arms.

Then she spotted it. They had to have passed it before, but she knew this was the tree. It stood about ten feet tall, which would be fine with the soaring ceilings in his living room. The branches were full and lush, with ample room for a whole lot of ornaments, and the tree was almost calling her name.

She pushed off against him and walked over to it, then circled it several times before stopping and nodding her head. "This is the one. It's a perfect tree," Sage said, a smile lighting up her face. This was the first time she'd ever come out to the woods to cut a tree, and though she'd been resistant the entire way, it now looked like Spence wasn't the only one addicted.

"Are you sure? I don't want to cut it down and then have you change your mind," he said as he picked up his ax.

"I'm positive. Swing away, Mountain Man."

"I knew I should have worn that red-checked flannel." Spence flexed his arm, walked over to the tree, and bent to clear the snow from the base so he could see what he was doing before standing back up.

"Now that's a fantasy I've never had," she said as she watched him lean back and then swing the ax forward. She was mesmerized by the rhythm, the accuracy of his body in motion. A slight sweat broke out on his brow and she found herself wanting to tackle him and have her way with him right there on the frozen ground. Just for cutting down a tree. Ridiculous.

"Timber," he called as the ax cut through the last of the base and the tree began to fall. The snow cushioned its fall, and a swirl of fresh white powder flew up into the air. He quickly removed a few of the bottom branches to give himself a bigger area to hold on to and then turned toward her. The snow was falling so thickly at this point that they had only about six feet of visibility in front of them.

"I think that storm has hit," he said as he grabbed the tree with one hand and took her gloved fingers with the other.

"Yes, it's really coming down. I hope you know your way back to the truck."

There was a rustling in the bushes to Sage's left, and she stopped. "What was that?" she whispered, knowing they should probably move, but her legs were frozen solid.

"It's just a deer."

"Are you sure?" Her knees finally unlocked, and she started walking beside him again.

"Positive. We need to hurry, though. I want to get

down the hill before this turns into a full-blown blizzard."

His pace was making her breathe heavily. She was used to being on her feet all night long, but she wasn't used to hiking through snowy woods. When his truck came into view, she breathed a sigh of relief, then attempted to help when he lugged the tree onto the bed of his truck. When he opened the passenger door for her, she heard rustling again and whirled around toward it.

"Oh, Spence!"

He turned in the direction she was looking, and before them, practically close enough to touch, were several huge stags, their antlers reaching toward the sky.

"They're gorgeous, and must be having a hard time finding food if they're getting this close," he said, wrapping an arm around her.

"Do you think they'd let me pet them?" She was surprised by how much she wanted to. She'd normally be thinking of the diseases they could be carrying, or the bugs in their fur.

"Not a great idea. They might get a bit upset when they find out you don't have anything to offer them."

Sage reached out to the deer anyway, but the one in the lead got spooked and ran off. The others followed.

"We need to go," Spence told her. He lifted her inside the truck, then quickly moved around to the driver's side.

Once he started the engine and the heater kicked in, Sage began shivering. She hadn't realized how cold she'd become. Though she'd layered up, brutal temperatures like these really seeped in.

"Now we need to get into town and pick up ornaments," he announced.

"You don't have any? Everyone has ornaments."

"No. This will be my first tree at my own place. We've always had one at Dad's, after all. There wasn't room for one while I was in school, and I just didn't bother when I was in Seattle. What was the point? I was there on my own," he said with a shrug.

"That's . . . sad," she said. "Even when I was in my small dorm room, I'd get one of those little trees they have in pots. It wasn't much, but I put tiny lights and decorations on it. It made me smile. When I left for home for the break, I would take the tree to a shelter nearby and they loved it. It's not Christmas without a tree."

"Agreed. But I always came home for Christmas—when I didn't have to work, at least. I just never felt the need to decorate. You'll have to come to the ranch, though. Dad goes all out."

"So does my grandma. I've been so busy with work, and then it seems I'm with you during all my free time. I really should get over there. She's probably been sad that I'm so close to town now, but not bothering to visit."

"Ha. You don't know your grandmother that well,

then," Spence said. "She and Eileen and Maggie seem to have events planned for every night of the week. They play poker, have a dance class, and run the local toy drive. This is a busy time of year for them."

"They play poker? How would you even know that?" Sage couldn't picture her grandmother, Maggie Winchester, and the very petite Eileen Gagnon playing poker. In her imagination, only burly old guys smoking cigars and guzzling whiskey did such a thing.

Spence chuckled. "I know a few people who have complained about the girls being sharks and wiping them out."

"I just can't believe it. I wonder what else I've missed out on while I was in med school."

"Don't worry. If there's anything you've missed out on, you *will* hear about it. There are no secrets in Sterling, I'm afraid."

"That's something I've always hated about this place, Spence. Absolutely no privacy."

"On a positive note, there's little crime because no one can get away with anything."

"Except for Grace," she grumbled.

"You clearly need a partner in crime—a top-rate detective—to help you find some answers."

"And you're telling me that you're that detective?" She couldn't hide her skepticism. Still, Camden *was* his brother.

"I'm a man of many skills, Sage."

She agreed with *that* statement 100 percent.

They somehow managed to make it down the mountain, then pulled up in front of the only store in Sterling that carried tree ornaments. Spence practically cleaned the place out of supplies, making the shop owner a happy man. Christmas was only a week away, and the fellow had most likely been thinking he'd have to unload it all at clearance prices. On the other hand, the dust Sage found on some of the packages suggested that the man just stored unsold holiday stuff and brought it out again the next year.

She wasn't entirely happy with their purchases, and not because of the dust. "None of this matches," she complained as she walked with him to the truck.

"That will be the beauty of my tree. Its seeming lack of organization will make it look even more cheerful."

Those were hardly words to convince a woman like Sage. Still, she'd do her best to make it look as beautiful as possible. She was incapable of doing anything less.

36

"No, no, no!" Sage guarded the tree with her feet spaced apart and her hands on her hips. He was slaughtering this decorating party. She'd tried to be patient, tried to stand back and let him do what he wanted. It was *his* tree, after all. But she just couldn't take it anymore.

Was he doing it on purpose to get a reaction from her? If he was, he'd win hands down, because, after suffering so long in silence, she simply had to intervene.

"What? I think it looks great," he said, eyeing the mishmash of ornaments in many colors and shapes that were placed at random on the noble tree. Some were pushed deeper inside their branches, and some clung for dear life right on the edge. Some were jumbled up together and others were miles apart.

This was a disaster. Her side looked perfect—okay, as perfect as it could look with the ornaments she'd been given. But Spence's side looked terrible.

"You're kidding. You *have* to be kidding," she said, pushing him back when he tried to hang another ornament. She held out her hand and glared, daring him not to give it to her.

"Is this what you want?" he asked, dangling the bright red sphere on his finger.

"Yes, hand it over," she said, her foot beginning to tap.

"But I have the perfect place for it, Sage." He moved toward the tree.

She held out her hand. "No." This had to be the most stupid fight she'd ever had with another person, but she was putting her foot down. He'd asked for her help on the tree and he was doing a grave injustice to the lush foliage by making it look so all-fired ugly.

"Did you just tell me no?"

"Yes, I told you no. Now surrender the ornament and go . . . go make us hot chocolate or something." She ran one hand through her hair but left the other hand out and open as she waited for him to comply.

"Ah. I like an aggressive woman," he said, now taking a step in her direction. The ball was in serious danger of being dropped.

"Good. You've got one." She wasn't backing down. He was handing over that ornament—one way or another.

"Perfect," he said, and she was horrified when he tossed the ornament behind him, not caring whether it shattered somewhere in the distance. Before she could react, his arms snaked out around her waist and he pulled her tightly against him. "You realize I get all worked up when you're so cute and bossy, don't you?"

Spence didn't give her time to answer; instead, he leaned down and attacked her lips hungrily, taking over and showing her he was certainly in charge right now. She forgot all about the tree when his hands slid down and grasped her behind.

He stopped kissing her for only two seconds in order to growl, "You make me burn," and then he was plundering her mouth again.

When his lips moved down her throat, she desperately sucked in air, her chest heaving as he gripped the bottom of her shirt and tore it from her. He slid his hands back up and circled her breasts.

"Yes," she moaned, grinding against him as his fingers pinched her nipples through the lacy fabric of her bra.

He now licked the swells of her breasts, nipped her skin, then proceeded to unclasp the offending garment, leaving her naked from the waist up. He didn't slow his movements; his mouth rounded the curve of her breasts and his lips clamped down around her peaked nipple, making her cry out.

As he suckled her, he dealt with her slacks and panties, leaving her naked in his arms and feeling vulnerable but too turned on to care.

She reached for him, wanting his flesh bared to her, needing to touch him the way he was touching her. Finding the top button of his jeans, she tugged, freeing it, and then gave a hard yank so the rest of the buttons came lose. Her hands slipped inside the back of his waistband and pushed downward. Grabbing the solid flesh of his behind, she squeezed, and gloried in his hot skin, his flexing muscles.

"Yes, Sage, touch me," he ordered her as his mouth continued devouring her aching peaks.

"With pleasure," she sighed, grasping for the buttons of his shirt, pushing it from his shoulders.

Sage pulled back from him, then ran her tongue along the salty flesh of his neck while her hands roamed over his back. Moving to his muscled chest, she mimicked what he'd done just before, tasting him, devouring him, loving him.

Her teeth scraped over his nipples, sending a shiver through him, before she dropped to her knees and let her tongue swirl around the hard planes of his stomach.

"Sage," he groaned when she lifted a hand, grasped his manhood, and stroked the searing flesh.

She now ran her tongue over the tip of his erection, surprised by his taste, turned on by his growl. Sucking him into her mouth, she reacted to the cries he made, moving along his flesh now faster, then more slowly.

"Enough," he cried, pulling free from her, making her whimper at the loss before he dropped to his knees and grabbed her into his arms, quickly rolling her onto her back and pausing as he looked into her eyes.

"Spence?" she questioned when he was still for several excruciating moments.

"Shh. I'm mesmerized by you. I just want to look at you—always look at you," he whispered before bending and kissing her so tenderly she felt emotion clog her throat.

Their eyes connected and their mouths barely brushing, he slid his arousal inside her, slowly, inch by beautiful inch, until she was full—until she was quivering around him.

What had started as pure hunger was morphing into pure love. He never stopped looking into her eyes, never stopped gently nipping at her lips, his tongue soothing the tender flesh while his body slowly moved within her.

Minutes or hours could have passed—she didn't know, didn't care. Heat built, slow and steady, strong, so strong, until her eyes widened and she gasped, her body gripping him in a shattering moment of pleasure that he drew out with his smooth and stirring thrusts.

As she began floating back to earth, he cried out, his erection pumping against the swollen flesh of her core and releasing inside her. After he collapsed on top of her, she gazed up as he nuzzled her neck. When she looked now at their tree—their first tree together—she decided it was absolutely perfect.

37

"I'm getting it!" Excitement bounced off her in waves as Sage slowly made her way down the slope at the Red Lodge Mountain. They'd been at the large ski resort for the past six hours, and after a couple of hours of instruction, and much patience on Spence's side, she was finally coming down the mountain on her own.

"You're learning much faster than most," Spence said with a blinding smile.

"That's because I have an incredible teacher," she said with a wink.

When they came to a stop at the bottom of the hill, Spence slid his skis between her legs and pulled her to him, giving her a chaste kiss before leaning back.

The more she was with this man, the more she wanted to be with him. Work was all consuming, but every single minute of free time was now a new adventure with Spence, whether it was a romantic dinner at his place, a quick jet ride to somewhere she'd never been before, Christmas tree shopping, or just finding a dark corner where they could make out. It didn't matter. All that mattered was being with him.

"Are you ready for a break, Sage? Maybe a snack and a drink?"

"More than ready. Though it's cold outside, this thick coat is making me sweat, and my thighs have received more of a workout than they're used to."

"I thought I'd been giving you plenty of exercise," he said as he let her go and gave her a salacious smile.

"Mmm, your workouts are the best ones, Spence."

"Always nice to hear," he said.

After removing his skis, he helped her off with hers and stacked them in a holding area. They walked inside the large lodge, where a fire was burning bright and hot and small tables placed about allowed guests to relax for a while before getting back on the slopes.

Sitting there with Spence, Sage found herself looking at him and wondering whether she had the courage to tell him what was on her mind. She loved him. She wanted him to know that. But was it too soon? Would she frighten him away?

What if the two of them were rushing into this way too fast? It had all seemed like a fairy-tale romance, almost from the beginning. What if it all wasn't real when the magic settled down and regular life intruded?

"What has you looking so intense?" Spence asked, reaching for her hand.

"I love the way you hold my hand," she said, and he looked a bit startled.

"Are there different ways to hold hands?" he said.

"Well, not that I have a heck of a lot of experience in the hand-holding department, but I have been watching couples lately, and before you can tell me that's strange, I know it is, but most people just clasp their fingers together. I love how you hold my hand so softly, and how you rub your thumb along my knuckles." When he chuckled, she felt her cheeks flush. Had that been a stupid thing to say?

"I don't even realize I'm doing it. I just love touching you, love the little shudders that pass through your body when I hit a place that feels good to you. I can't seem to ever get close enough to you," he said as he flipped her hand over and began tracing the lines on her palm, sending those shudders he'd just been speaking about right through her.

"I feel the same way, Spence," she said, thinking now was a good time to admit her love.

Before she was able to say another word, the two of them were interrupted. "Spence? Spence Whitman, is that you?"

Sage turned to see a brunette wearing a perfect white outfit and a red-lipsticked smile rush over to their table. No alarms bells were ringing, but when she turned back to Spence and saw a big smile light his face, she felt the tiniest stirring of jealousy. Knowing she was being ridiculous, she repressed it and waited for Spence to introduce her to his friend.

"Becky! I haven't seen you in ages. What are you doing up here?"

He dropped Sage's hand and stood up just in time for the woman to fling herself into his arms. When the hug lasted just a bit too long to make Sage ever be able to like this woman, she squirmed in her seat.

"I'm here with my parents. They were going on about being homesick, so we flew in a couple of days ago. Had I known you were down in Sterling, I would have called you," Becky said.

"How long are you here?"

"We're leaving tonight, darn it. But there's certainly time for a few drinks before I go," she said, with her hand clinging firmly to his arm.

Sage was now fuming. Spence seemed to have forgotten that she was even there, and he wasn't in much of a hurry to introduce her to this woman, who wouldn't even look in Sage's direction. When the woman maneuvered Spence to push Sage out even further, Sage thought seriously about simply standing up and walking out.

"Oh, I'm so sorry," Spence said as he turned back toward Sage. "Becky, this is my . . . friend, Sage Banks. Sage, this is Becky Marshal. We went to college together and then discovered she grew up only about fifty miles from me. We've been close friends ever since."

Sage didn't know what to think about his "friend" comment, so with as much dignity as she could muster, she stood up and held out her hand. "It's nice to meet you, Becky."

Becky took her time but finally gave Sage her hand for all of one second before saying a quick hello and then directing her attention right back at Spence.

"So, drinks?" she said, and it was clear the invitation was for Spence only. "My parents are over at the restaurant. You must join us."

"I would love to, but Sage works tonight, so after we warm up, we're leaving," he said. There was clear disappointment in his tone.

"Are you working?" she asked.

"Not tonight, but I need to take Sage in."

"Our driver can take her," Becky said quickly. "I insist that you join us. I want to hear all about what you've been up to lately—it's been months since we spoke last. I'm sure Sage wouldn't mind." She turned and gave a look that suggested that Sage would be an awful person if she protested.

Though steam was practically coming out of Sage's ears at this point, she pasted on the brightest smile she could manage before responding. "Of course you should join your friend, Spence. I should head back now so I can shower before going to work."

"I don't know," Spence said, but Sage could clearly see he would like to visit with his old friend.

"As long as I have a ride home, I'm all good," Sage told him.

"Great! Then it's all settled," Becky said, and slid her arm through Spence's. "I'll let Daddy know. He's going to be so excited."

Sage walked beside the two of them as Becky chatted away, making Spence laugh at some of her stories. Sage was clearly the odd man out and was more than relieved when they stepped outside and Becky took them to her car.

"I'll stop by tonight," Spence told her before bending down and giving her a quick kiss on the mouth.

"It was great to meet you, Page," Becky said, and Sage had no doubt the woman had gotten her name wrong on purpose. She didn't bother correcting her.

"You too, Becky."

Sage stepped into the car and soon was traveling away from the ski resort. Tears filled her eyes, but she refused to let them fall. What had begun as a flawless day had not ended the same way.

She really didn't even know what had just happened. Had Spence been ashamed of her? Did she not stack up to his more worldly friends? Was Becky an ex-girlfriend?

When she got to work and began her shift, the hospital too quiet, Sage had plenty of time to think about their day. She was grateful she hadn't told him how she'd been feeling, because right now she was thoroughly confused.

When the night went on and Spence didn't stop by as promised, her mood turned even more sour. Was their euphoric time together already coming to an end? By the time her shift ended and she managed to drag herself home and into bed, she had no answers. She'd just have to wait and see what Spence would do next.

38

"Move in with me."

Spence was standing outside her open front door, letting the cold in with her wearing nothing but a nightshirt. Mouth open, Sage stared at him and tried to clear her head. The night before he'd taken off with another woman, hadn't stopped in to see her, though he'd said he would, and then he just shows up at her door and those are the first words out of his mouth?

"What?" Maybe she'd just heard him wrong. She had to have heard him wrong.

"I said move in with me."

Sage wanted to throw something at him. She hadn't slept well even after a long day's skiing and a longer night shift at the hospital, was less than pleased with him right now, and he was asking her to live with him. They hadn't even spoken of the future. They hadn't even said anything about love. Yes, she'd spent a lot of nights at his place over the past couple of weeks, but she also knew she could come back home at any time. She couldn't just move in with him. Her grandmother would be disappointed in her. *She'd* be disappointed in herself.

"This is not a wake-up kind of conversation," she said, her forehead creased with a frown.

He stepped inside her door, shut it, and then wrapped his arms around her and nuzzled her neck. "You're never very talkative when you wake up, are you?" He was acting as if everything was perfectly all right. Maybe in his mind it was.

"No," was all she replied. She was busy trying to gather her thoughts, to figure out what she wanted to say. She pulled away and tugged her fingers through the tangled mess that was her hair.

"Are you hungry, Sage?" he asked, gripping her hand as he moved toward the couch and sat, pulling her into his lap. As he continued nuzzling her neck, she wanted to forget the unpleasantness of the entire day before and just fall into the lovemaking part of their relationship. When his hand climbed up her thigh, and then a finger found her heat, she did forget—she forgot about everything but wanting him.

It was another hour before Sage was able to speak again. If only she could forget her concerns, forget her worries. Then there would be no arguments, no decisions, no heartbreak. She suspected she was in for some real heartbreak with Spence.

"I hope you're feeling less . . . feisty now," Spence said as she leaned against him, her breathing still a bit erratic.

"Really? I thought you liked me feisty," she said,

struggling just enough on his lap to feel his arousal beginning to rise again.

"Mmm. Scratch that. You're right, I do like you feisty."

"I'm always right—I'm a woman."

"Are you going to answer my question? We're together practically every minute, so it wouldn't be difficult for you to move in. It would be just a matter of shifting a few boxes to my place."

Taking a deep breath, she pushed away from him. "I need to get up."

"Not yet, darling. I'm ready for round two."

Somehow she managed to pull away and then walked to the bathroom, where she stared at herself in the mirror for several moments before turning on the water and cupping it in her hands, splashing the coolness against her face.

After becoming more herself, she climbed into the shower and hoped the pulsing spray would clear the cobwebs from her brain. When that didn't help, she stood in front of the mirror again, taking her time combing her hair. She still didn't know exactly what she was going to say to him when she came out, but she felt a little more prepared now that she'd had a few minutes alone.

Walking out into the kitchen, she thanked him when he handed her a hot cup of coffee. And then she sat at the table, still unsure what to say. Why did everything have to seem so uncomfortable when, just twenty-four hours earlier, it had been perfect?

"I love the smell of your shampoo," he said, leaning down and kissing her before sitting down.

"I love that you love it," she replied with her first smile since he'd shown up at her door.

"That's much better. I love your smile, Sage, love how it brightens your face." Spence leaned back and assessed her mood. "I've scared you, haven't I? I'm moving too fast."

"A little," she said, though it wasn't that he was moving too fast; it was that she had no idea where they stood after the day before. "Did you have a pleasant night? I thought you were going to stop by." She wanted to kick herself for letting that out.

"I'm sorry, Sage. I should have called, but Becky's father wanted some medical advice, and we ended up staying until he had to catch a plane out."

"So, were you and Becky a thing?" She refused to look at him while asking.

Spence laughed, making her look up. "Not ever," he assured her. Then his smile vanished and he stood up. "Were you worried?" He knelt down in front of her and clasped her chin.

"No," she lied, but the blush in her cheeks gave her away.

"I'm sorry, Sage. I wasn't even thinking. I haven't seen Becky or her family in a while. I assure you that I don't want her, and I never have."

The sincerity in his voice proved he was telling

the truth. "I'm sorry, Spence. I think I overreacted," she said, feeling stupid now. Of course, the idea of moving in together was still on the table and she really didn't know what to say about that.

"How about we revisit my suggestion of living together later. Are you hungry?" Though he was trying to make his tone light, she could hear the tension in his voice.

"You don't get told no very often, do you, Spence?"

When his shoulders relaxed and he looked at her as if deciding how to answer, then laughed, she was shocked. This wasn't the way she was expecting this conversation to go. One minute he was upset, the next laughing. She couldn't figure him out.

"No. I can't recall the last time I was told no by someone other than you. It's not a pleasant feeling."

"I didn't say no, exactly. I just—" She stopped, not knowing what she wanted to say.

"Well, to prove that I can be a bigger man, I have something for you." With that, he walked from the apartment, then reentered a few minutes later carrying a package.

"You can't keep buying me gifts, Spence. This is getting out of hand."

"I like getting you gifts, because in a couple of days we'll be sharing our first Christmas together, and I want you to know that not a single day goes by without me thinking about you. Who needs twelve days of Christmas when there can be twenty-five?"

"Still . . ." she said. With all her so-called intelligence, why didn't she have another excuse up her sleeve?

Giving up and giving in, she undid the ribbon and took off the lid, then had to fight silly tears. This man was making her crazy. Inside the box was a delicate bracelet. She lifted it and looked at the sparkling jewels. She'd never received jewelry before, and though she shouldn't accept what looked like an expensive present, she couldn't seem to keep herself from holding it tight.

"Thank you, Spence. It's beautiful," she said, and he took it from her and clasped it on her wrist. It was a perfect fit.

"That's only part one of the gift. Tomorrow, we're flying to Vegas for a show," he said as he lifted her up, then sat and pulled her down into his lap.

"I can't go to Las Vegas, Spence."

"Why not?"

"It's almost Christmas, and I have to work . . ."

"You don't work tomorrow night, and we won't stay. We'll just see the show and come right back. If you have any last-minute gifts to buy, it's the perfect place."

"You are ruining me for all other men, Spence Whitman. Who jets off to Vegas just for a date?"

His eyes narrowed, but she couldn't miss their dangerous gleam. "There will be no other men, Sage." He pulled her close and kissed her soundly, showing her exactly whom she belonged with.

When she was able to come up for air, she pulled back and looked into his eyes. "I can't think when you touch me. I can't make a single decision. I don't like that—I don't like feeling so out of control. I *always* know what I'm doing. I always have a plan. Why do I feel this way with you?"

She wasn't really asking him the question, just expressing her thoughts aloud. She needed to find the answers, and she needed to find them fast. The last thing she wanted was to lose herself, to be consumed by this fire between them.

"You do realize that both of our families are already planning the wedding, so maybe we should just give in and elope while we're in Vegas."

Sage stiffened in his arms. "What?" Her brain tried to compute what he was saying.

"Let me get you some food. We've burned off a lot of calories," he said, removing her from his lap, jumping up, and moving to the fridge.

She followed him. "You can't make a statement like that, Spence, and not clarify it. I'm not going to be sidetracked this time."

"It was just a comment, Sage."

"Have you talked to my grandmother about me?" She wasn't that upset; she just wanted him to be truthful. Why would he go to her grandma and talk marriage before talking to her?

"No, not exactly," he said, and she knew he was lying. Like her, he wasn't very good at it.

"I wasn't upset, Spence, but I'm fixing to get there. You need to explain," she told him as he broke several eggs into a bowl and began stirring them so hard that they slopped over the side.

"It was just something my dad and your grandma said about . . . us. They . . . well . . . they sort of threw us together. I didn't think it was anything to get upset about," he said, finally putting the whisk down and giving up on his attempt to distract her through cooking.

Sage stared at him, trying to process what he'd just said. "How did they throw us together? I don't understand this."

"You'd really have to talk to them, Sage."

"I want to hear it from you." But she didn't need for him to tell her. The pieces were falling together. The reason she'd had to accept the offer for residency in Sterling, the reason Spence, only a few months later, accepted an offer that would put him in charge of her training. The party. The meetings her grandmother had been having with Martin Whitman.

They'd all thought she was so pathetic that she wouldn't be able to find her own husband, so they'd rigged the game, placed her and Spence in each other's path and lit a fuse, hoping there would be one hell of an explosion. Well, they just might get to see a show that would put the Fourth of July to shame.

"How long have you known about this?"

He looked lost as he searched for the right thing

to say. "A couple of weeks," he admitted, and the rockets' red glare had nothing on her.

"Did you find it amusing? Was it all a game? Let's get the poor little virgin a boyfriend. She can't possibly attract one on her own. She was in love with Spence when she was a child, so throw a little gasoline, light a match, and watch her go up in smoke. Did you have some bets going on? Was any of this real?"

They'd all deceived her, all treated her like their personal puppet on strings. She'd been great in that role, doing exactly what was expected of her.

"I didn't have a plan!" he exploded, throwing his hands in the air. "I'm in love with you—stupidly, ridiculously, till-death-do-us-part in love!"

Her entire body froze as their heated gazes locked. She didn't know what to say, didn't know what to think.

Spence now spoke more calmly. "That didn't come out the way it should have." He began to take a step toward her, but she held out her palm to ward him off. This was too much; too many emotions were being thrown at her in such a short time. She was on overload and she had to get away.

"I need to go," she said. She dashed to her room and grabbed clothes. She had to get out of there right now.

"Sage, don't do this. Let's talk," he said through the door as she yanked her clothes on in record time.

"I don't want to talk," she said, flinging open the door and storming past him.

To his credit, he didn't try to grab her. "Do you love me, Sage?"

That stopped her. She turned toward him, her purse in her hand. "I don't know how I feel, Spence. You move at the speed of lightning. One minute you're telling me you want to move in together, and then before I can even process that, you're telling me that our families feel we're meant to be together. And then you tell me you love me and suggest that you want to get married. I can't do this. I can't . . ." And it was true. She just couldn't.

"It's simple, Sage. You either love me or you don't," he said, moving closer but still respecting her very electrically charged personal space.

"I don't know!" she said, her eyes burning. "I don't know," she said again more quietly. Panic was starting to rise. "Nothing is simple."

"Just because someone else may have made plans for us, that doesn't make what we feel toward each other any less real. I know how I feel, and I know that I will always want you. Once I make a decision, I don't back down. I'm strong enough to tell you how I feel. Are you strong enough to accept what I'm offering?"

"No. I can't do this," she said, and practically ran to the door. She glanced back to find his eyes not angry but determined as he watched her leave. It wasn't rational, but she was overwhelmed. Her once orderly life had just been thrown in total chaos and she needed to escape, to regroup.

"I'm not giving up." Those words followed her out the door and to her car. She realized she'd left him in her apartment, but she didn't care. Getting away was her only thought.

She took pride in the fact that she was organized, that she made her own choices, that even if she made mistakes, they were her mistakes. To find out that her grandmother had stooped to games to find her a man was humiliating. It also made her wonder if any of it was real.

39

Sage tripped as she walked up the steps to her apartment, and her short heel snapped, making her fall to her knee. The impact cut into her slacks and gave her a deep scratch.

"Son of a—" Managing to stop the swear word from coming out, she gritted her teeth and stood up. This wasn't her day—not even close. Seriously grumpy after enduring a fifteen-hour shift and missing the last two meals, she finally managed to get the key in the door and open it.

She refused to admit to herself that her mood had been bad from the beginning, its gloom and savagery only escalating when Spence hadn't been at work for the second day in a row. Christmas was only a couple of days away and she hadn't seen him since she stormed off after their confrontation.

That's what she'd wanted, to get away from him. She wasn't going to be controlled. He was giving her the space she'd requested, and that was just fine by her. It certainly wasn't the case that any action of his, or any inaction, was making her insides twist in two. So what if he was moving on? So what if he was back in Seattle? She hoped he stayed there. The prickling in her eyes had nothing to do with the fact that he might not come back.

Sage had always thought logically, had always been the one to laugh at those silly girls who wrapped their worlds around whomever they were dating. She wouldn't be such a fool as to join their shallow ranks.

It was just the long shift, the fact that she was starving, and that she'd just broken the heel on one of her favorite pairs of shoes. It had been a silly, impulsive thing to wear them in the first place. After a fifteen-hour shift, the last thing she had wanted to do was put on heels, even if they were only two inches tall. It had nothing to do with the fact that she'd wanted to look pretty just in case a certain doctor had decided to show up at work.

When Sage saw the blinking light on the answering machine, she turned away. She had no curiosity at all to see who'd called. She deserved a trophy for not calling her grandmother and berating her for her unconscionable actions. Not that Sage would be able to do that. It was just best not to talk to the woman until she could say something nice.

"Meddling old people thinking they know best," she mumbled as she kicked off her shoes, not caring that they were flying beneath her perfectly decorated Christmas tree.

Looking at the tree only reminded her of her trip with Spence to the mountains, of the fun they'd had picking out his tree, of decorating it, of the absolute euphoria that had come afterward.

Turning her back on the tree, which she now wanted to throw outside as yard waste, she walked slowly toward the kitchen. Although the thought of food repelled her right then, she had to get something into her stomach, and then climb into her bed.

Sleep. That's all she needed. A great night's sleep, and then a beautiful Christmas Eve and Christmas Day with her grandmother. Of course she wouldn't hold a grudge against the woman who'd raised her— she loved her grandma, and she could see how the woman had been trying to help, according to her old-fashioned ideas. If only it hadn't meant that Sage was more miserable now than she could ever remember.

Still, the apartment was too quiet, bitterly quiet. Sage really wished her best friend were there. She and Grace had been missing each other too much. Both she and Grace worked erratic hours, making it near impossible to see each other. Sage didn't want to admit any form of weakness, but she could really use a friend right now.

"No. I'm fine. Women survive breakups all the time. One little fight won't turn me into a blithering idiot. I will eat some dinner, and then I will sleep. When I wake up, I'll be back to myself, putting this whole Spence situation far behind me." There. If that little speech didn't turn her around, she didn't know what would.

She halted when she reached the kitchen. There on the table sat a wrapped package. At first her heart fluttered, and then she forced it to calm down.

"No. This will not make me sappy. This will not change my mind. It's ridiculous. I'm not even going to open you up," she said, before realizing that she was speaking to an inanimate object. Was this what it was like to lose your mind? She wouldn't be a bit surprised.

She went over to the fridge and reached inside, grabbing the orange juice and a couple of sticks of string cheese. Just to show how strong she was, she sat at the kitchen table and carefully pulled back the plastic on the cheese, then began peeling it apart and taking tiny bites on each strand, while sipping on the orange juice to lengthen the "meal."

"I don't care what the package is. As a matter of fact, I think I'll just throw it in the garbage. It's probably something stupid anyway," she muttered. She finished the first stick of cheese and slowly unwrapped the second one.

The box was screaming at her to open it. No. Sage was much stronger than her curiosity. It wouldn't matter if the box was filled with twenty-four-karat-gold bars. She didn't want to know.

Her brain mocked her. *Yes, you do.*

"No, I don't."

Sage's mouth dropped open when she said those words out loud. That was it—she was officially going crazy. If she was going to argue out loud with herself, she was in serious trouble.

"I'm a doctor, for crying out loud. I've been through undergraduate school, medical school, many sleepless nights. I don't need to get this upset over a man, and I don't need to argue with myself over whether or not to open a stupid box."

She wished again that Grace was home. Then, at least, she'd be speaking to another human being and not a package or the wall or, even worse, herself.

Sage finished her cheese and orange juice, then turned and walked deliberately from the kitchen, not allowing herself to turn back around. She made it halfway down the hallway before she stopped and glanced over her shoulder. Unable to see the kitchen or the table from this vantage point, she gripped the walls.

"No, no, no."

She wouldn't do it. She wouldn't cave in to such a weakness as curiosity. "Curiosity does kill the cat," she reminded herself. But she still turned and began walking back toward the kitchen.

"What if it's something that's alive?" How could she not open that package? "I mean, it would be wrong if something died because I didn't care enough to take off a lid. It's not that I really care what Spence has sent over." Sure, she told herself, there were no airholes, but you never knew . . .

She stood there at the kitchen table, gazing at

the bright silver box and sparkling blue bow, and she waited. Running her finger over the bow, she looked for a card. Nothing. There was always a card attached, usually only a few words, but there was always a card.

Why not this time? Maybe because he'd given up caring about her, but he wanted to finish this silly game he'd begun. Okay, if he wanted closure, she'd give him his stupid closure. Anyway, she couldn't stand the suspense anymore, so she lifted the lid and found tissue paper on top. Almost fearful, she removed the paper and then sank down into the chair.

"It doesn't matter," she whispered as the stinging in her eyes increased, turning her vision into a blur before the tears finally spilled over.

She was done for. She was in love with a man she shouldn't be in love with—a man who hadn't even found her himself. She was being a good little puppet in a game set up by people she loved because they thought she wasn't capable of doing something on her own.

Though she was twenty-six, she would forever be a frightened ten-year-old child who had lost her parents too soon, who was afraid to love because love was so easily snatched away. Who always put work first. Who had goals and aspirations in life.

And she couldn't be in love with Spence—she couldn't. It was just her hormones thinking she was in love because she'd given him her body, not because she couldn't imagine a life without him. She reached into the box and picked up a wand; a note lay next to it.

Make a wish, and I will make it come true.

This wasn't just any wand, some toy from a store. It was a scepter. Sage knew her history, and this was the real thing. At one time, royalty had held this, not to wield some magical force, but as a symbol of their importance.

Did this mean he'd returned to town? She hated that her heart thundered at the thought. Was he telling her that he hadn't given up? She didn't know what to do. They'd been manipulated into dating, and then he'd found out and hadn't told her. Didn't that mean she couldn't trust him, couldn't trust anyone? Maybe it was herself she couldn't trust.

40

Spence gazed out his window and watched as the neighbor children built another snowman. Three snowmen now stood in their yard, each with a carrot nose, rocks for eyes, and something he couldn't quite figure out for mouths. Each had sticks in its sides for arms, and he couldn't help suspecting that the little tyrants had purposely chosen one of those branches because it had what looked like a hand making a gesture particularly inappropriate during the holidays.

Chuckling, he watched as a snowball fight happened down the street, and his neighbor three doors down hollered at Jimmy to come back inside. On the other side of the street a father was pulling his daughter on a sled, and she laughed with glee when he slipped and landed on his behind.

"It's almost as if I'm living in the middle of suburbia," he said aloud. "Except that Sterling isn't urban enough to have any suburbs." Why he'd chosen to live here instead of buying a nice estate nearby, he didn't know. When he'd found this place, he hadn't hesitated. The Realtor was pleased. A little too pleased at first. When he'd shown no interest in her personally, she'd finally stopped calling—two months later.

She probably figured he'd be looking for a wife to fill the five bedrooms, three bathrooms, and bonus rooms. She was right. He *was* looking for a wife—it just wasn't her. And when he bought the house, he'd had no thought of marriage, but after one day in Sage's presence, he'd known she would be his.

Maybe he hadn't *known*, exactly, but deep inside, he must have. All he had to do now was convince the woman. It wasn't going to be easy, though. It had been four days since he'd seen her, and Christmas was only two days away. If his plans for Christmas Eve didn't work, there was no hope.

But of course his plans would work. He was a closer—he didn't ever lose. It just wasn't in him to give up until he got what he wanted. And right now he wanted Sage Banks to become Sage Whitman.

When he knew something was right, he went for it, and he had no doubt that the two of them were meant to be together. It didn't matter how their relationship had started. The bet, the meddling, none of it mattered. The point was that it *had* started, and now he couldn't seem to focus on anything but her.

It really didn't help that he'd been called twice to Seattle this month for emergencies. It seemed the holidays were causing a lot of heart conditions. Maybe people should lay off on the eggnog and fudge. He normally lived to do surgery, and he'd done his job perfectly, but the second he'd finished with it, all he wanted to do was fall into Sage's arms.

Being away from her just wasn't an option any-more. The sooner she came to the same conclusion, the happier they both would be. Running his fingers through his hair in frustration, he paced his large living room. Though he was normally a smart man, he'd still pushed her, still expected a different reaction from the one he should have known he'd get.

Maybe love really did make a person blind—make them do things that were out of character. Though he didn't analyze everything like Sage did, he generally used his brain a bit more than he had been since meeting up with her again. She was probably wondering how he'd managed to get through medical school.

He was wondering the same thing. When he realized he'd crossed his living room for the hundredth time, still with no answers, he decided enough was enough. With a determined step, he grabbed his coat and keys and walked out the front door.

He was careful when he pulled out of his driveway and drove off—the neighborhood was full of playing children. But when he hit the main road, he picked up speed. He was on a mission, and the sooner he got to Sage's place, the better.

After pulling up at the apartment, he let out a deep breath and gazed up at her window. The string of lights circling it were inviting and warm, just like the woman he loved. Stepping from the truck, he moved slowly up the steps, his heart pounding and his hurry all but forgotten. It was ridiculous to be nervous. He knew she loved him. She was just frightened.

He knocked on the door and tensed when he finally heard the sound of footsteps nearing and then the sound of the lock as it clicked open. Sage was now standing there, her eyes widening at the sight of him. Maybe he should have cleaned up first. That he hadn't shaved for two days, or brushed his hair this morning, and probably looked slightly crazy— he'd gotten a ridiculously little amount of sleep— wouldn't inspire confidence.

"Good morning," he said, thinking maybe he should have stopped for doughnuts. She loved the cream-filled ones with glaze on top. Maybe he should turn around and go back for some. Maybe not. She wasn't likely to open the door again if he just left without saying anything else.

It took her several seconds to respond, and all she could manage was, "Um, hi."

"Are you going to invite me in?" Boldness seemed to work best. Before she could say yes or no, he pushed forward, giving her two choices: to get run over or step aside. She moved, her hand still on the doorknob as he made his way inside.

"What are you doing here, Spence? Studying for a future in door-to-door sales?" she asked as she finally shut the front door and wrapped her pink robe more tightly around her.

"I wanted to see you. I missed you." He led her to the kitchen.

After another pause, she reached a height of eloquence, at least to judge by what they'd been saying to each other this morning. "Would you like a cup of coffee?"

"Would love some." That would give him at least fifteen minutes with her.

"You look tired. Did you have a hard case in Seattle?" She sounded more like herself as she poured their coffee and sat down with him at the table.

"Yes, father of three, only forty-two. Had a massive heart attack and needed an immediate bypass. I think he'll make it, but he needs to either quit his job or hire some help. He's obviously dealing with too much stress."

"It's just too bad when it takes a major surgery for someone to slow down," she said with a shake of her head.

"Yeah, I see it all the time." It was almost strange how polite they were being to each other, how they were both skating around what they really wanted to say. He'd pushed for her to be his wife—she'd said she needed time. Wasn't four days plenty of time?

"You know you need to stop sending gifts, right? I love them, each one, but it's too much, Spence. You weren't even here, but you somehow managed to have another one delivered," she said.

"You didn't like the last one?"

"I loved it. That's not the point. You don't have to buy me. In fact, you can't."

"That was never my intention. Like I told you before, I enjoy getting you things. I enjoy the sparkle in your eyes when you talk about it. I don't think you've been nearly spoiled enough and I plan on doing it for a very long time—the rest of my life, actually."

There. He'd said it. She could either step up and face this with him, or run and hide. He was through hiding. He'd done it most of his life, always protecting his heart, worried about being rejected, abandoned. Well, that wouldn't happen with her.

"It's almost Christmas, Spence. I . . . I still don't know what I think about all this. I want to be with you—I do. But, I just need time. I need for everything not to move so quickly."

He didn't know what to do. Should he let her retreat, build up walls that were unnecessary? Or should he push her, make her accept what they both knew to be true?

"We just need to be logical, to think about this," she continued. "We don't want to rush into anything, and we certainly don't want our family members to be the ones pulling the strings. I'm not a puppet."

"I have never thought you were a follower, Sage. Far from it," he said, temper creeping into his voice.

Yes, he was angry—thoroughly pissed off, in fact. He'd been walking on eggshells in fear of offending her. But was she giving him the same consideration?

Did she care that he'd laid his heart out there for her? No. Did that mean he was giving up? No. But it would certainly feel good to shout.

"Love isn't logical, Sage. It isn't something you can put in a box, take out when you want to play with it, and then put it back away when it frightens you. It's imperfect, comes with fits of emotions, and makes your insides flip out. There's no reason to it, and if it doesn't scare the hell out of you, you aren't feeling it strongly enough. Love is scary because when we love someone, we fear losing them. But without love, what's the purpose of life? If we give ourselves over to love, we win—we always will win."

"That doesn't make sense," she snapped, shooting up from the table. "Why would anyone want to feel an emotion that turns them inside out? I'm not afraid. I just like to make smart choices. That doesn't make me a bad guy."

"It's not supposed to make sense!"

"Do you think bullying me will make me tell you what you want to hear?"

In less than a heartbeat, he moved to her, trapping her against the counter, pressing his body close. Without a word, he bent down, captured her lips, and drank in her flavor, groaning into her mouth when she opened for him, when her hands came up and gripped his hair.

Pulling back, he looked deep in her eyes. "Now

tell me to go away. Tell me you don't love me, never want to see me again," he said before kissing her again.

"I . . . I . . . I can't concentrate . . . can't think," she cried, her fingers gripping him tight.

He lifted her onto the counter and pulled her against him. Her robe had parted, allowing her to feel how much she stirred him. With his fingers in her hair, he kissed her again before drawing back.

"You don't need to think. You just need to feel. What do you feel, Sage? What do you want?"

It took all his restraint to keep from undoing his jeans and plunging inside her. He could take her right now, light her on fire. But he didn't want just her body—he wanted her heart.

She breathed heavily as he pressed against her, but her lips stayed sealed. "I don't understand how you can do nothing but look at me. I'm trying to give you everything," he said, frustration pushing him to act almost irrationally. When she still said nothing, he lost what little cool he had left.

"This was a mistake," he told her. "I shouldn't have come over." He turned, upset with himself for caving in to his urges. He shouldn't have kissed her. He already knew they had no trouble in the sex department. He'd proven nothing by doing it.

"I'm just confused, Spence. I'm so confused," she cried out as he reached the door, making him turn. He said nothing as he waited for her to continue.

"I don't like this. I don't like to feel out of control. I don't like not knowing what will happen next. I've never felt this way before. It's not me. It's not pleasant. I . . . please understand."

Love shone in her eyes, but fear was its companion. She wasn't afraid of him—it was herself she feared.

"Then I'll give you time." But maybe it wouldn't work out after all. Maybe she wouldn't be able to love him as much as he loved her. The very thought sent sharp pains through him, body and soul. He left the apartment not knowing what the future would hold.

He was at the bottom of the stairs when her door opened and he heard his name. He looked up to see Sage standing there.

"I love you, Spence, but . . . but it's just not enough."

The door shut, the click of the lock echoing down the stairs.

Spence bounded to the top of the stairs before he halted in his tracks. Even if he pounded on the door, woke all the neighbors, and demanded she come out, he knew she wouldn't open it again. But she'd called after him. She hadn't let him just leave.

She'd given him . . . hope. She loved him. Joy coursed through him at the realization. Yes, it was enough; yes, she would be his. His plans were back on, and he had no doubt that the future Mrs. Whitman was going to be his forever. Running a hand over the stubble on his jaw, he laughed aloud as he descended the stairs and got into his truck.

Ravenously hungry for the first time since their fight a few days ago, he headed to the local diner. A hearty breakfast followed by some phone calls and everything would be back to normal. Picking up his phone, he pressed in the familiar numbers.

"Dad, I need your help."

41

"You said *what* to him?"

Her grandmother was staring at her as if she'd grown three heads and was spitting fire. Sage felt ashamed and didn't understand why. It wasn't her grandmother who had the right to be upset; it was *her*.

"You were meddling in my life in a way that really wasn't okay, Grandma. I'm all confused now, and I don't know what is happening. I did what I had to do." Sage clutched her cup of hot chocolate so hard she was surprised the cup didn't shatter. It would almost be a good thing if that were to happen. At least then her hand would hurt instead of her heart.

"He's perfect for you. And he wants to marry you. Instead of running away, you should embrace him, give him your heart."

"I won't even bother to discuss what you did to my career—and, perhaps, to his. The point here is that it's my heart to give or keep, Grandma. It's not right for people to interfere," she said more sternly than she'd ever spoken to her grandma before. When Bethel winced, Sage felt about two inches tall. "I'm sorry," she said. This had been a bad idea.

Bethel sniffled. "I just want you to be happy."

"I know. I'm sorry," Sage repeated.

"What is wrong with him? Did he hurt you? Was he rude? Should I have his father take him out to the woodshed? A boy is never too old for that."

"No, Grandma," Sage gasped in horror. "He's been a perfect gentleman. And the Whitmans don't even own a woodshed."

"Well, then, what's the problem? If he loves you and you love him, why be confused?" she asked, her eyes gleaming, making Sage suspect her shattered look had been nothing but an act.

If Sage had been sure about that, she might have called her grandma out. But if the woman was truly upset, Sage didn't want to make it worse.

"I know it was hard for you when you lost your parents," Bethel said. "It was hard for me, too, darling. I raised your father, loved him more than anyone in this world. You know I wasn't blessed with another child. And then, when he married your mother, I got a daughter. Losing them tore me apart. The only reason I kept on standing was because I had you to look after. Situations in life happen for a reason—I'm sure of that. Being afraid doesn't help. Don't be so fearful that you miss out on something great." Bethel placed her warm hand gently over Sage's clenched fingers, giving the young woman no choice but to unclench them.

"I just don't like being pushed. I don't like someone else deciding my fate. I'm an adult now, and maybe I'm just not ready to get married—to commit myself to one person for the rest of my life." Sage needed her grandma to understand it was her decision, and hers alone.

"Oh, bah humbug. That's a bunch of fancy words. What does it matter how the two of you met? What matters is how you *feel* about him."

"Grandma!"

"Don't you *grandma* me. I've been around a lot more years than you have. Sometimes you just have to accept that Grandma knows best." Bethel rose from the table and poured more coffee before reaching into the cupboard, grabbing her secret bottle of Jack, and adding a dollop to her cup.

"Who are you?" Sage gasped.

"I'm the woman who raised you and deserves respect," Bethel replied before taking a sip of her spiked coffee and sighing. "I don't have a drink too often, but dealing with a grown woman who's acting like a child requires some extra strength."

Sage sat there with her mouth open. She'd never seen her grandma behave so . . . so . . . well, so human.

"I'm . . ." Sage didn't know what she was or how she should finish that sentence.

"You're acting like a fool. That boy has romanced you, spoiled you, declared his love for you. Now, if you tell me that you can't stand the sight of him, that he makes your skin crawl and you'd rather live in the swamps than be in his presence, I'll understand and support you. But if you're telling me that you *love* him and are too scared to be with him, I'll have to get out my broom and smack you on the behind."

"Yes, I love him, I just . . . oh, I don't know." She realized she wasn't making the least bit of sense. Why did she have to overanalyze this?

"Well, in my time, if you loved someone, you just did. There wasn't all this game playing. There wasn't a competition to see who told who their feelings first. It was simple. Boy meets girl, girl likes boy, boy proposes, and then everyone lives happily ever after."

It didn't get any more black-and-white than that.

"And no one from your generation ever woke up one morning and realized they'd made a huge mistake?"

"Well of course they did. Love isn't perfect. It doesn't come with a guidebook—though you can get a book on just about anything these days—and it doesn't come with guarantees. But if two people love each other, they work through those hardships. They don't dwell on a problem, they face it head-on, together. They decide the person they love is worth the fight."

"I'm a pain. I know I am. I do things sometimes that drive even *me* crazy. How long would it be before he just gives up, before he decides I'm not worth the hassle anymore?" Sage asked, her throat clogging up.

"Oh, baby. You aren't a pain. I know this—I've been with you since the day you were born. You are an intelligent, spirited, beautiful woman any man would be proud to have," Bethel scooted her chair next to Sage's and drew her into her arms.

"You have to say that because you're my grandma," Sage said with a hiccup. "But why is this so hard? Why hasn't anyone else wanted to be with me?"

"Because you are brave and strong. Sadly, there are many men out there who feel better about themselves when they get to be the big, strong protector. I'm not saying there's anything wrong with a man protecting his castle, but there's also nothing wrong with a woman defending her home. Has Spence ever asked you to be anything other than who you are?"

Sage paused as she thought over the last several months with Spence. He'd challenged her, forced her from her comfort zone, and given her more than any other person ever had, but had he asked her to change? Had he asked her to be something she wasn't?

"He asked me to marry him after he asked me to move in with him and I freaked out."

"Baby girl, that's not asking you to change. That's asking you to merge your life with his."

"I don't know . . ." Sage was wavering, and that wasn't the way this conversation was supposed to go. She was supposed to have a talk with her grandmother, make sure the woman knew never to interfere in her life again, and then get this miserable Christmas over with. She wasn't supposed to be having a soul-shattering moment.

"Do you love him, Sage?"

"Why do you keep asking that?"

"Because that's all that really matters in the end. It comes down to whether you love him. If you do, the rest will work itself out."

"Love isn't the point, Grandma."

"Love is always the point, darling."

"I don't need a man to be whole."

"You are quite right. You don't need anyone to make you whole. But take this from me—it's mighty lonely at night to be whole by yourself."

"I'm sorry that you gave up a chance to find another man because you were raising me, Grandma." Sage had never thought before of the sacrifices her grandmother had made so that she could grow up feeling loved.

"I didn't give up on love because I had you. I lost my husband and I grieved him for many years. Then when my sorrow grew a little less, I just wasn't interested in finding love again. The love your grandfather and I had was beautiful and kind. If I truly thought I could have that again, I wouldn't hesitate and he wouldn't want me to. The truth of it is that I just never felt that way about another man." The blush on her cheeks led Sage to believe there may be someone now.

"Would you marry again if you did feel that way?"

"In an instant."

"Then maybe I should do some matchmaking of my own—a little payback,"

"If you can play Cupid, bring it on, sweetheart. But enough about me. Why don't you quit worrying about emotion and tell me about Spence."

"You already know him, Grandma, probably better than I do."

"Let's just pretend I've lost my memory. I want to hear what you think about him, who you think he is."

Sage leaned back in her chair and thought about it. Who was Spence?

"He's . . . well, he's kind and brilliant. The most talented doctor I've ever worked with. He's funny, and knows his job so well. He knows when to be serious and when to laugh. Everyone we meet loves him. We can't go anywhere without getting stopped. People just want to chat with him. He has this smile—oh, his smile—it's so bright, so infectious. He's spontaneous, and likes to jump right in with both feet, but he also knows when something needs careful planning. And the way he looks at me . . . it . . . it just makes me feel like I'm the only person on the planet."

Bethel didn't say anything, and Sage realized she'd been going on and on. She closed her eyes and pictured the Christmas tree, the tree she and Spence had found together and how it had become perfect because he had been perfect. She thought of fishing in Seattle, of the intimate club, of the laughter on the ski slope. She thought of those moments in the hospital when he'd cornered her in a dark room and left her breathless.

Every memory with him made her smile. She never knew what to expect when he showed up, but she wasn't frightened by that uncertainty. She knew whatever he had planned would make her smile, would be a new adventure.

"I do love him—*really* love him. But what if it's because it's new? What if it does fade?"

"Then you'll survive and you'll learn ways to keep it fresh," Bethel said.

"Just like that?"

"Yes, just like that. Haven't you survived the most tragic of circumstances?"

"Yes. I still open my eyes sometimes in the morning and expect Mom to be right there." Even if she did accept what was right in front of her, and then somehow lost it, she would survive that, too. Nothing could be as bad as losing her parents, not even losing the man who was already wedged tightly into her heart.

"It doesn't matter, does it?" Sage asked.

"What doesn't matter?" Now it was Bethel's turn to be confused.

"I'm already invested. I've been dwelling on this for days, trying to rationalize it, trying to figure out how to make this black-and-white, how to outline it and tuck all my emotions into nice little corners. But the bottom line is that I love him. Whether I lose him now or in ten years or in sixty, it doesn't matter. It will hurt no matter what. I can't go back now."

"No, no, you can't," Bethel said with a grin.

"Well, being in love stinks." Now, her grandma could call her a child all she wanted. Sage stood up, then leaned down and kissed Bethel's cheek. "I love you," she said, then she moved through the house and went upstairs.

She didn't even have the energy to go home. Being at her grandmother's would always be home, though. Falling into her old bed, she drifted to sleep, her only solace.

42

Grace was expressionless as she faced Camden. Why did he have to keep pushing her? Why wouldn't he just let this go?

"Do you really think this will all just fade away, that you can keep lying to your friends, the people who care about you?"

"I don't have friends," she said, putting an emphasis on the *S* at the end of the word *friends*.

"Come on, Grace. I've known you since you were a kid," Camden said, blowing out his breath as he paced her small apartment.

"You're certainly not my friend, Camden. Please don't insult my intelligence by pretending you are," she snapped, going to her fridge and pulling out a bottle of water.

"There was a time when we were more than friends, Grace." She turned to find him right behind her, way too close for her comfort. "You know I would never purposely hurt you."

"Ha. That's amusing, Camden. It's amazing how you can twist our history. The only friend I have is Sage, and I don't want to pull her into this. I'm going to live my life, and if everything goes to hell, I guess that will just happen."

There was no possible way that she was giving this man ground—*or* anything else. He'd already taken her heart eight years before. Then he'd smashed it into tiny little pieces and he'd never looked back.

"I'm offended that you think so little of me, Grace."

"I have a feeling you'll get over it. Just put an ad on Facebook telling all the lonely singles that you need some consoling."

"Why are you such a pain?" he practically shouted.

"Maybe because that's how I survive. You can either deal with it or you can stay the hell away from me. I've already told you I have nothing to say and I've been more than clear that I don't want your help. I don't care what anyone does or says, I will not cower in a corner."

"I'm not asking you to cower in the corner, but you don't need to put out flashing neon lights saying *Look at Me*."

She knew he wasn't dealing well with the situation. They'd already had this conversation a million times now, ever since he'd received that blasted file, ever since her father—not that he deserved the title—had royally screwed her over.

"Maybe I'm a girl who likes to play games— dangerous games, Camden. Maybe I've decided my life has been boring so far. Maybe, just maybe, I'm the perfect protégée for my parents," she said, sending him a wink and shrug.

"I don't know what you're trying to prove, but you're doing an excellent job of acting like a spoiled brat. If you want to roll over and play dead, I should let you, but I know somewhere, maybe locked deep down inside, is the smiling girl I used to know. Where is she, Grace?"

"How dare you! You have no right to psychoanalyze me. You have no right to step into this apartment. Where in the hell were you when I needed you most? Was that your week with bimbo one or bimbo two?"

"What happened in the past is in the past. You need to let it go."

"Please go away, Camden. I'm too tired to deal with you anymore today." The fight had been drained from her. She needed to put on her happy face and pretend everything was copacetic.

"This isn't over, Grace," he warned as he moved toward the door.

"It never is, is it, Camden?" She sighed as he turned toward her, fire burning in his eyes. Yes, she knew there was still hunger there, but more than that, there was rage. Right now they both felt it in spades, each at the other.

"I'll leave for now, but don't think for a minute that I'm going to just roll over and watch you ruin your life," he said as she yanked open the door to push him out if she had to.

"Trust me, Cam, I would never think you were the type to ever roll over," she said, trying unsuccessfully to smile.

Cam said nothing else as he left her apartment.

Grace sagged against the door, allowing herself a moment of pity. Then, blowing out a breath, she pushed her worries from her mind. It was Christmas Eve and she was going to spend it with her best friend. She'd had enough anger and sadness to last her a lifetime. She was going to bury all of that for at least the next few days.

43

"Sage, wake up right this minute!"

Sage sat up, disoriented and rubbing her eyes. "What time is it? What's the problem? Is everyone okay?" she blurted out, still half asleep.

She'd taken naps at the hospital before, and she knew how to wake up quickly and be prepared for an emergency, but with her recent insomnia due to high emotions, she was struggling to clear the fog from her brain.

"Nothing's wrong," Grace told her. "You just have to come with me right now."

"What are you doing at my grandmother's? I thought you were flying out tonight."

"I was, but I got stuck behind a major pileup on the freeway, and I had no choice but to turn around."

"Well, I for one am glad. Spending Christmas in Hawaii was a dumb idea, Grace."

"With all of this snow, I thought it would be a nice change."

"Of course lying on the beach and soaking in the sun is always nice. But Christmas is time for family, and since you're basically my sister, I call it abandonment when you leave me like that."

"Well, I'm here now, and very grateful to be with you. Now get your butt out of bed and come with me. I can't believe you're sleeping at 6 p.m. on Christmas Eve. I've gone to bed early before so I can wake up in the morning, but never that early." Grace tugged on Sage's hand until she was standing, and then handed her a thick sweatshirt.

"Are we going somewhere?" Sage asked.

"You'll see. Come on." Grace shimmied Sage over to her UGG boots and stood there while she slipped them on, then dragged her down the stairs.

It sounded like music was playing, but that wasn't a surprise. Her grandma always played Christmas carols when she was baking, and she always baked the night before Christmas. Actually, she baked the entire week before Christmas. Her pies had become quite famous in their little town.

Lots of people usually stopped by Bethel's house during the entire month of December. All the neighbors wanted the woman to see their faces, a reminder they were still there so they could have some of her goodies. Then they acted all surprised when Sage and Grace handed out sugary confections. And Sage loved doing that. It was always a pleasure to see how much joy her grandmother brought to others.

As they reached the bottom of the stairs, Sage realized that the music was coming from outside the house. The entire downstairs smelled like gingerbread, and Sage's stomach rumbled as they passed the kitchen.

"What is that?" Sage asked as they reached the front door.

"Come and find out," Grace told her. She stood next to the door but didn't open it.

Sage was suddenly afraid. The light in Grace's eyes told her that this was something big, something special. Was she ready to see?

"It's Spence, isn't it?" she said, hope and fear dueling inside her.

"I guess you'll have to open the door if you want to know," Grace replied, a grin splitting her face.

"A true best friend would tell me what's on the other side of that door. A true best friend wouldn't leave me hanging like this."

Sage didn't do well with surprises. Or at least she hadn't until she'd met Spence. Now, it seemed, she was more used to them, and even anticipated them. Her fear was dwindling as she stood there. In its place a calm acceptance was rising up—a feeling of security and warmth.

"A true best friend would be green with envy and planning on heading to the nearest voodoo shop to get a doll and stick pins in it whenever she thought about how sickeningly romantic your future husband is."

"What's he done now?" Worth a try to ask again.

"I'm still not telling you what's on the other side of this door, Sage."

They knew each other well—heck, they each knew what the other was going to say before she said it.

"Fine!" Sage couldn't stand it a second longer. She moved to the door, yanked it open, then stood for all to see with her hair a wild mess, no makeup, and wearing a thick, baggy sweatshirt, unflattering sweatpants, and sheepskin boots. And she didn't care—not even a smidgen.

"I just want to say that I am the most jealous best friend in the world. If you don't run to him right this minute, I'm going to push you down the porch steps and use your body as my own personal red carpet so I can take him myself."

"Then I guess I'd have to get Camden to console me," Sage said slyly.

"I would scratch your eyes out," Grace said before her eyes opened wide and she covered her mouth. "I mean . . ."

"I *will* find out exactly what you mean, Grace, but later. Right now I'm going to push you out of the way and run out there into the arms of the man I love."

At least a hundred of their neighbors were standing in front of Bethel's house, and more were showing up by the minute. They were all singing Christmas carols and holding paper sky lanterns with candles glowing inside them. Spence was in front of them all, down on one knee, a lantern in one hand, a box in the other.

"Sage Banks, I love you," he said as she moved toward him, her legs trembling, her heart thudding. It was simple, and it was sweet. He was opening his heart to her in front of people they'd known their entire lives. He was telling the world that she was worth the risk. He was telling her this was forever.

She dropped to her knees in front of him, and she didn't even feel her sweatpants get soggy in the snow. "Spence Whitman, I love you," she replied, then took the initiative and leaned forward, kissing him and clinging to him for all she was worth. She was through analyzing this, through thinking it over. Sometimes, as her grandmother said, you have to take a leap of faith.

Their friends and family continued singing as he returned her kiss. Her heart was so full now it seemed almost unfair to all the people who didn't have someone to love.

"Marry me, Sage. That's all I want for Christmas. I just want you to be my wife."

"Then it looks like you've been a good boy, Spence." His eyebrows furrowed in confusion, so she continued. "Santa is giving you exactly what you want."

Spence grinned as he drew back, took an exquisite diamond ring from a black velvet box, and slid it onto her finger. "She said yes!" he called out, and their neighbors, in sync, released the sky lanterns, the hot candles helping them to soar.

Spence stood, pulling her up with him. He lifted his arm and released his lantern, and together they watched them all float into the sky.

"Your last gift, Sage. All our prayers and wishes have just floated upward. I plan on making every dream you've ever had come true."

"You gave me the dream I didn't know I wanted, Spence. You love me—my faults and all. And I love you—your faults and all."

"I will forever be grateful to our meddling family members, but let's not tell them—ever," he said with a chuckle. The two of them turned to find Martin standing nearby with his partners in crime: Bethel, Maggie, and Eileen.

"I agree. We'll make them suffer. It looks like the meddlers are only missing one member of their scheming group."

"Ah yes, Joseph Anderson. We both know he's the one who got them all started," Spence said.

"Should we feel sorry for your brothers, or happy for them? Because right now I know I should still be angry at the meddlers, but I'm so happy I can't find room for any other emotions to fit inside."

"I say we step up and help them out," Spence said.

"You are a terrible man—and I say . . . I agree."

Then the two of them forgot all about talking as Spence took her into his arms and kissed her, showing her exactly what she meant to him. Their neighbors and family faded away as he lifted her and carried her inside.

EPILOGUE

"What a beautiful wedding that was," Joseph said to Martin, Bethel, Maggie, and Eileen.

"That horse-drawn carriage looked like it came right out of the pages of *Cinderella*," Bethel said with a sigh as she looked across the room at her granddaughter dancing in her husband's arms.

"Yes, Spence really went all out to make her dreams come true. I'm mighty proud of my boy," Martin said, his heart glowing.

The words brought tears to Bethel's eyes. "And I'm so happy that Sage has found a man strong enough to hold her heart."

"And I have another daughter to warm our home," Martin observed. "This matchmaking stuff is pretty wonderful."

"I was a little worried there for a while. Those two just weren't cooperating," Eileen said. She was glad it had worked out, but a bit bored now, though she didn't want to admit it. She and her friends hadn't been doing anything to move things along with the other two victims—er, bachelors—in the Whitman family.

"Yes, your kids are certainly as stubborn as my own brood," Joseph replied with a laugh.

Martin joined in the laughter and said, "Oh, look at that. Spence is scowling."

The little group turned to see Austin tugging Sage into his arms for a dance. Before Spence could claim her back, Austin's wife, Kinsey, tapped his shoulder. He smiled at her and then offered his arm.

"He doesn't want to let go of Sage for even three minutes," Eileen said. "That boy is head over heels in love." The woman directed a shy glance at Martin.

"Yes, love is certainly in the air. Just look over there in the corner," Martin said.

The group turned as one and spotted Camden and Grace, who seemed to be having a heated debate.

"That boy's eyes just about popped out of his head when Grace walked into the room," Maggie remarked. "Her name is quite fitting, because she sure has a lot of class."

"I'd given up hope on the two of them ever reconnecting, but from the look of things, the sparks we've set are starting to catch fire," Martin replied.

"Camden has no idea that we're the ones who put that file on his desk?" Joseph asked.

"Not a clue. He thinks it was her parents—those worthless people," Martin grumbled.

"And has Camden stepped up like you thought he would?" Joseph asked. He hadn't managed to make it back to Sterling in the last few months, not with so much going on in Seattle.

"Of course he has. Not only will he save the girl,

but I'm hoping for another wedding. I'm thinking around Christmastime would be quite pleasant."

Bethel's eyes lit up. "Well, since it's only June now, maybe we'll get lucky and swing that wedding, and then a Christmas baby for the next year."

"That would indeed make a mighty fine Christmas," Eileen said with a sigh.

When Spence took Sage back into his arms, both their faces shone with the pure love that they shared. They might not have been thanking the five people who'd plotted their union, but their radiant joy was thanks enough.

"To love," Joseph said, and the four friends joined the toast. They hadn't had a single miss yet.

Turn the page for a sneak peek of
the next heartwarming novel in the
Unexpected Heroes series

HER FOREVER HERO

Coming in spring 2016 from Pocket Books

Some welcome home. The railing and eaves of the porch were decorated thickly with spiderwebs, and weeds were doing their bit, too, creeping up between the now rickety boards to act almost like potted plants. Mother Nature had pulled out all the stops in her honor.

Grace picked up a dull gray stone, tossed it upward, then felt its expected weight as it landed back in the palm of her hand. She tossed it over and over, her mind adrift and haunted.

Why was she here? Why torment herself?

Because she had nowhere else to go. Her life had been in shambles for the past ten years, ever since she'd left Sterling. She could fix up her childhood house—a house, never a home. The spacious rooms could be cleaned, the rotten boards replaced, the cobwebs torn down. But she didn't have any desire to live in a house with no pleasant memories to be found inside its walls.

Her happiest times in Sterling had been outside this mausoleum that had been her mother's pride and joy. They might not have been the wealthiest family in the small Montana town, but they'd had a lot, and Mrs. Sinclair felt true love for her possessions, including the six-thousand-square-foot home now standing nearly empty before her daughter.

Grace's journey down memory lane—tiptoeing through the funeral tulips—wasn't finished yet, though. Letting the rock drop to the ground, she walked up the rickety steps, cautiously avoiding the sticky cobwebs. She tested the door handle, only to find it was locked. She hoped the key still worked.

It took several tries, but twisting the key a little this way and that, she finally managed to get the lock to free itself, and then, with the help of a strong push, the door was swinging open. Sunlight filtered through the dust-coated windows, showing years' worth of grime covering the floors, counters, and odd pieces of furniture that had been left behind.

"Somebody call *Better Homes and Gardens*!" she said out loud to break through the gloom. Too bad it didn't work.

Her father had told her he wouldn't sell the home, that someday she might want to return to it. This property had once belonged to her grandfather, and to her grandfather's grandfather before that. Her ancestors had moved to the area in the eighteen hundreds and had made a beautiful settlement for themselves.

Her mother had wanted to tear down the original homestead, a quaint one-room cabin with a woodstove and loft. Her father had refused, and restored it instead. That was where Grace had some of her best memories, because they had been outside the walls of her jail—the Big House. She and Sage had spent many nights sleeping in that small cabin, telling each other their dreams.

Never had she thought back then that her life would turn out the way it had. Never had she thought she would become this bitter, broken woman. *No.* She wasn't broken. She was too strong for that. As soon as she had time to heal, she would once again show the world that Grace Sinclair was a fighter.

The old piano she had spent so many hours playing sat forlornly in the corner of the family room. Sheesh. Even thinking the word *family* made a bitter laugh escape Grace's lips. Her father had once tried to be a good man, but he was so focused on making the next dollar and on making her mother happy that he wasn't capable of real love, and her mother—well, her mother was the proverbial . . . okay, the Total Bitch of the West. Grace had tried to escape them every chance she got, after she'd learned that, on the outside, away from this house, real families existed. But her parents always managed to get their chains back around her, making sure she knew exactly where she came from and the limits of her freedom.

Though her father had wanted a son—all men were like that, weren't they?—she'd ended up being his only heir, so once every few years he would try to do something fatherly, such as give her the title to the land and house that he knew he'd never return to. Love from her parents always involved money. Hugs were unheard-of in her family, and real emotion was to be held inside. They had a reputation to maintain, after all.

Drawn to the piano, Grace trailed her fingers absently along the top, smearing them with dust along the way. She lifted the curved wooden cover of the ebony and ivory keys only to discover more filth. The instrument was out of tune, but it, at least, brought up good memories. She'd taken lessons her entire childhood, and though she was certainly not a master pianist, she still enjoyed the soothing music a piano could create.

Sitting down on the bench, she hung her head. "It's time for a new start. First of all, this house needs to go, though I think I'll keep the piano," she said aloud, her eyes closed as she fought emotion. There would never be a day she could live within these walls again. She'd rather live in the tiny cabin tucked in the trees behind this monstrous home.

"I remember when you used to play for me."

Grace didn't need to turn around to see who had walked in uninvited. That voice had lived only in her dreams since the day he had so coldly walked out of her life—Camden Whitman, her first, and probably only, true love.

She stared at the dusty keys of the piano, unwilling to face him. "What are you doing here, Cam?"

"My dad told me you were coming back to town. Then Maggie said she spotted your car heading out this way."

She turned slowly and saw him still standing in the doorway as if he was waiting for an invitation.

"I forgot what it was like to live in a small town. There's no such thing as privacy," she said acerbically.

And then their eyes met and something shifted deep within her. Only one person had ever made her feel the unquenchable love that consumed the entire heart, and what a fool she'd been to think that time and distance would make that feeling go away. Not even taking another lover had weakened it.

What was even worse was knowing that, although his features might appear composed to anyone else, she once had known his soul, and for one unguarded fraction of a second, she saw surprise leap into his expression before he snapped the shutters closed and gave her a cool, nearly mocking expression.

The moment was so brief that she wondered if maybe her heart was asking her to see something that really wasn't there.

Instead of showing him pain, she allowed her all-too-familiar anger to carry her. How many times and in how many ways had she tried to forget this man? And in a single millisecond all of that hard work almost came to naught when she misread something in Cam's eyes.

Though she'd called him a liar, a cheater, a heart-breaker, it was really she who deserved to be scolded, because she'd told herself those lies for years, so long that she'd almost started believing them.

The velvety sound of his voice brought her back from her grim thoughts. "That's certainly true. You can't do anything here without it being broadcast at full volume into everyone's ears by morning light." His tone was light, careless. That was Cam—the life of the party and everyone's best friend.

The guy who'd decided she just wasn't good enough for him.

"It's good to see you, Grace. I've missed you."

She stared at him incredulously for a few heart-beats before her lips curled in a sneer. The lyrics of an old Rihanna hit, "Take a Bow," came to mind. He certainly was good at putting on a show, but she wouldn't be fooled by him ever again.

"Well, now that you've seen me, you can go," she replied with syrupy-sweet sarcasm in her voice.

"Have you spoken to anyone since you've been back?"

"Do you listen when I speak?" she countered.

"You haven't spoken to me in nearly ten years, so I guess we'll find out." He leaned against the doorframe and smiled, the smile that had haunted her for so long.

"I haven't spoken to anyone because I haven't been ready to announce my return."

"Are you staying?"

"That's really none of your business," she said.

Ignoring her clear dismissal, he told her, "I'm meeting a client at the offices in an hour, but I should be out of there by five. Why don't I pick you up and bring you to my dad's so you can visit with everyone? I'm sure they'll be more than thrilled to see you."

"Not gonna happen," she responded flatly without skipping a beat.

He stared at her quizzically for a few seconds before speaking. "Come on, Grace. You've been gone a long time. The prom queen is back, and you know your court will want to hold a ball."

"It's funny you should mention that particular event, considering you promised to come back and take me to the dance. But your new girlfriend most certainly wouldn't have approved of that. No, you had become a college stud by that point." The bitterness in her tone gave away far more than she wanted, but she couldn't rein in her feelings. Her heart thudded like a galloping Thoroughbred at the chance to say what she'd bottled up all these years.

"That was a long time ago, Grace. I think we're both mature enough to let bygones be bygones."

"I don't forget anything, Cam."

"We were young and foolish back then, and both of us made mistakes. It doesn't mean we can't be friends now," he said, and took a step toward her.

No. That wasn't what she wanted. She needed him to retreat, not come closer.

"That's exactly what it means, Cam. I don't want to be friends with you, I don't want to sit around having idle chitchat, and I sure as hell don't want to reminisce about the past." She mentally dared him to push her further. He thought she'd been blunt? She was just getting warmed up.

"I guess you aren't the same young girl who used to laugh and dream and always reach for the stars?" he replied bleakly.

"That girl has been dead and gone for a long time," she said, her voice firm, her manner stiff. "If she ever existed. You can see yourself out the way you came in." With that, she turned back to the lonely piano. She refused to turn around at the sound of his footsteps descending the old porch.

Grace's shoulders sagged once she knew he was gone. Coming back home hadn't been a good idea—not a good idea at all. Camden Whitman still had far too much pull on her emotions. But hell would freeze over before she ever let him know that.

Camden Whitman raked a hand through his hair once again and let out a long-suffering sigh. "It doesn't matter how many times I go through this file. All arrows point straight to Grace," he snapped before leaning back in his desk chair and pushing the file away, disgusted with all of it.

"We both know she's not capable of doing this, so you have to be missing something," said his father, Martin Whitman, as he sat comfortably across from Camden. He didn't seem worried at all.

"You've looked at it, Dad. You tell me what I'm missing."

"The file turned up on your desk, Cam. I'm not the one who's supposed to help her," he said before pausing and throwing his son a smile. "You are."

"I would love to know who put it on my desk. That's still a big mystery. Somehow I don't think either of her parents would care enough to want to help her. But I certainly do want to. The problem is that every time I approach her about this, we end up in a fight. She doesn't want to have anything to do with me."

"Well, then, you'll just have to make her listen," Martin said, as if there was nothing easier than getting Grace to pay attention to anything Camden had to say.

"Ugh! It's not that simple. We have history together. It's just . . . I don't know, it's complicated. When she came back to town last year, I could see she was bitter, but it's a year later and nothing I do seems to change those feelings. I can only help her if she allows me to."

Camden moved to his window to look out over the small town square. Two kids played tag in the park while their mother sat on the bench watching them. Sterling was a great place to grow up, to work, and to raise a family. It's why Cam had come back.

At one time, he'd imagined settling down with Grace, having children, and living a happy, normal life. But the world had a way of intercepting the ball even in the best of plays.

Grace and Cam had been friends from the time he'd moved to Sterling. She'd been four years younger than he was, but tougher than any boy, and their relationship had begun out of respect and deepened into a genuine friendship. They'd stayed in contact while he was away at college.

The summer he'd come home with a bachelor's degree in hand, before he'd gone on to law school, he began to see Grace in a whole new way. She was eighteen, beautiful, and going into her senior year of high school. Their love blossomed over the summer, and when he left for law school, Cam had been sure their love could last—but he'd been wrong. By the end of his first year, there had been nothing left for him to come home to.

He would never forget what he'd found when he had come home, and because of it he'd made some very poor decisions during the next couple of months. Since then, the odds had seemed forever in their disfavor, and it appeared there was nothing Cam could do about it—nothing but annoy a woman who just might wind up in prison.

"I've been fighting with her for a year on this," Camden said. "It won't be long before the feds get involved, you know."

"Okay, boy. Let's take another look at the file together and see if there's anything we can come up with."

"We may as well," Cam agreed with a sigh. Grabbing the file off his desk, he sat down at the large conference table in his office.

His father joined him and they pulled out the three-inch-thick pile of papers.

Martin flipped through the stack and stopped at

a bank statement. "Right here is where it all began. Why don't you describe to me what you've figured out, start to finish."

"C'mon, Dad. You know everything I know."

"Sometimes putting things into story form helps clarify it," Martin said. "Let me start our little fairy tale off. Five years ago, one Grace Sinclair, the accused, opened a nonprofit by the name of Youthspiration. You pick it up from there."

"This is so lame . . . okay, okay," Cam said when his father gave him a warning look. "To an outsider, an auditor—hell, to the average person, it looks like all is well in paradise. If you look closely, the donation amounts coming in and then going back out all match up perfectly."

Martin broke in. "There's nothing wrong with starting up a nonprofit."

"What are you doing here, Dad?"

"I'm playing devil's advocate, pretending I know nothing."

"This isn't a game. It's serious. What can you possibly be smiling about?"

"I'm not enjoying the fact that Grace is in trouble. It's just a pleasure to see you so focused about work, to see you on a mission," Martin told him. "Right now think of me as just Joe Schmoe, juror, at your service." Martin sat back and ran his fingers across his mouth as if zipping his lips shut.

"All right, I'll play along. About a year ago, somebody made an anonymous tip to the IRS, telling them that they might want to dig a little deeper into this nonprofit. They dug, and found nothing. So then this file pops up on my desk, and me being me, I can't help but do some of my own digging. The nonprofit looks aboveboard. But when you peel away the layers of the onion and get to the heart of it, something's rotten. All the outgoing checks are written and seem to be going to real organizations, but there are duplicates, and those are heading straight into offshore accounts. Whoever's doing this is smart, though, because the money is siphoned off in such a way as to not raise red flags, and to keep the culprit highly protected."

"How so? If you found offshore accounts, can't the feds?"

"Yes, they can, and I don't see how they haven't yet," Cam said. "Anyway, all signs point directly to Grace."

"And what does Grace have to say about it?" Martin asked.

"She says I'm out of my mind. That she never opened up this or any other nonprofit and she certainly didn't take any money."

"Her word is good enough for me," Martin piped in.

"You're Joe Schmoe, juror, remember?" Cam pointed out. "They don't know Grace. Hell, Dad, *we* don't know her anymore, either. She left home for a very long time. Life has a way of changing us."

"That's BS and you know it, son. Little Gracie would never be involved in something like this."

"I don't think she would, either, but then there's also a bank account in her name, where large dollar amounts are randomly deposited and then immediately taken out as cash. The withdrawals coordinate with the times she's in the area of that particular branch of the bank."

"What do you mean?" Martin asked.

"I mean that she goes to Billings, and then there's a withdrawal in Billings."

"So, it looks pretty bad for her, huh?"

"Yeah, it looks pretty bad. And each time I've tried to discuss this with her, she says she has nothing to do with it, that it's not her, and then we get into a fight."

"You have no other choice but to make her listen."

"Easier said than done, Dad. Now we go back to our history together. It isn't exactly a smooth road."

"This could mean the difference between her going to prison and being exonerated from a terrible crime. You have to make her listen."

"It gets worse," Cam said with a sigh, shutting the folder.

"How can it get worse than Gracie going to prison?"

"I think she either knows who is actually involved and she's protecting them, or she's been aware of this scheme the entire time."

"No way!" Martin exclaimed. "Not a chance."

"I don't know. I'm just trying to get to the bottom of it. I can't contact the IRS without her hiring me as her attorney, and I'm really at an impasse until she agrees to do something about this mess."

"Have you thought of option number three?" Martin asked. "Maybe she wasn't aware this was going on, but she has an idea of who it could be, and she's in denial."

"Wouldn't she want to go after the people smearing her name?" Cam asked.

"Not if it's someone she loves and trusts, and she doesn't want to find out they've betrayed her. We tend to bury our heads in the sand when reality is too much for us to take."

Cam didn't know how to respond to that. It was an option he hadn't even considered. There were very few people in Grace's life she truly loved. Maybe her parents, though he doubted it. And then there was her best friend, Sage, who had just married Cam's brother Spence. Grace couldn't be protecting her parents. They were wealthy, far too wealthy to need to embezzle the sums being stolen here. Yes, the total amount added up to a couple of million dollars, but that was chump change to them.

And Cam refused to believe it could be Sage. She was an incredible woman, in training to become a surgeon just like Cam's brother. No. There had to be another explanation.

"I have to go, Dad." He stood up and moved toward the door.

"Where are you off to in such a hurry?" Martin asked as he followed Cam from the office.

"I'm going to see Grace," he said, determination in each stride. "It's time for a showdown."

"What's your plan?" Martin asked before he got in the car.

"I'll think of one on the way."

Her time of fighting him was over. That was all he knew for sure.